Helen Slavin was born in Lancashire in 1966. After the University of Warwick she had a variety of jobs and moved to live in Wiltshire. There, she got married and had a son and a daughter. Her first novel, *The Extra Large Medium*, is published by Pocket, and she has also written for radio and television.

CROSS MY HEART

HELEN SLAVIN

SIMON &
SCHUSTER

London · New York · Sydney · Toronto

A CBS COMPANY

First published in Great Britain by Simon & Schuster UK Ltd, 2009
A CBS COMPANY

Copyright © Helen Slavin, 2009

1 3 5 7 9 10 8 6 4 2

Simon & Schuster UK Ltd
1st floor
222 Gray's Inn Road
London WC1X 8HB

Simon & Schuster Australia
Sydney

A CIP catalogue record for this book
is available from the British Library

ISBN: 978-1-84739-354-8

Typeset by M Rules
Printed in the UK by CPI Cox & Wyman, Reading, RG1 8EX

To Gillian Hush, with love and thanks

THAT WAS THEN

1975

1

THE TRUE LIES

In the afternoon the rooks came, as surely as guardians.

In Mr Pownall's classroom the windows were arranged in a puzzle of rectangles. At first Grace had tipped and arranged them in her head but then, gradually, her gaze had been drawn to the far side of the playground to where the privet crushed itself desperately against the chain-link fence.

A harsh wind whiplashed the plane trees by the prefab garages. Grace watched the rooks ride it and, with a shift of wings, drop into the topmost branches. Yesterday there had been seven. Today there were nine, one for each of her birthdays. She had felt there was some charm in that as if the rooks belonged to her or, better still, she belonged to them. As if, somehow, she might hurtle out through the doors at the home-time bell and instead of having to push and bash her way through the gates, racing Jonathan, she could soar upwards on wings.

She had seen those wings close to only a few weeks ago. The

rook lay dead by a puddle in the dirt lane that ran between school and the large higgledy-piggledy house opposite. Jonathan had picked it up by the gunmetal grey sword of its beak and as the light caught the feathers they were not black at all but purple-green, blueblack, redbronze. These colours, metallic and fabulous, were never to be found among the felt tips in her pencil case. Then, of course, somebody's mother had been disgusted and shooed them on their way.

Yes. Grace could soar if she were purplegreen blueblack. Up, over the railings. She could rise above the flat roofs of the infant block and skim over the middle playground. The rush of air would feel good against her face, like driving with the car window down. Rooks had thin wiry legs that folded neatly whereas her legs might just dangle, heavy and in the way because she couldn't bend them upwards like . . .

'. . . NOT LISTENING TO ONE WORD.' Mr Pownall's fire engine voice crash-landed her into the branches of the trees.

He was as tall as a tower and his shirt hung from his shoulders as if they were as insubstantial as a coat hanger. His trousers flapped too as if there were no legs inside them, and his hands were so fleshless they looked like Halloween skeleton hands wearing skin gloves. A tiny bubbled sphere of spit gathered in the corner of his mouth. Grace's heart lurched and it didn't settle when she realized he was not shouting at her. She knew every-one's heartbeat would be fluttering now, could see how each of her classmates clamped their lips together, their breathing shallow, trying to become invisible, to not be part of this. But Grace's heart stattered more when she saw that the object of fury was Jonathan.

Mr Pownall was standing before Jonathan's desk, the spit in the corner of his mouth launching suddenly to spatter into Alison's hair. The other children, heads bowed, hands clasped, looked for all the world as if in prayer. As Mr Pownall stooped slightly to rage at Jonathan his sawing elbow brushed the back of Dean's head. Dean flinched forward. Mr Pownall was waving a piece of paper like a battle pennant.

'. . . BECAUSE YOU ARE ENGAGED UPON THIS PUERILE CARTOONING.' Mr Pownall didn't always seem to speak English. The paper crackled at Jonathan. 'DO YOU IMAGINE THIS IS AMUSING, BOY? WELL, DO YOU?'

Jonathan's head moved carefully from side to side and a tiny whisper of a 'no' escaped.

'SPEAK UP, BOY!'

Mr Pownall jabbed the paper at Jonathan's face. Everyone knew where this was going. Mr Pownall built steadily from fury to fisticuffs and there was nothing they could do to stop him. They had all watched Dean draw and fold the silly-willy when Mr Pownall had his back to the class. It had passed from reluctant hand to reluctant hand under the desks. But no one could tell on him.

'HOW DARE YOU WASTE MY TIME. HOW DARE YOU WASTE SCHOOL PAPER WITH THIS TRIPERY.' The paper jabbed again, a tiny line of blood appearing on Jonathan's cheek where the edge had cut him. 'STAND UP. STAND UP AT ONCE, YOU STUPID MONKEY BOY. STAND. UP.'

Stand up to be knocked down. Jonathan was shifting upwards in his seat but not fast enough for the infuriated Mr Pownall whose skeletal hand snapped outwards. The fingers clawed into

Jonathan's pale blue jumper, lifting him, and Jonathan, unable, rook-like, to bend his legs back under himself and take off through the rectangled windows, faltered upwards. His body clonked against the edges of his desk, knocking over the exercise books, sending pens and pencils rolling for cover under other, safer desks. With Mr Pownall dragging and tugging him, Jonathan's bones rattled and rearranged themselves under Mr Pownall's grip. Jonathan's chair squealed against the floor.

Higher, Jonathan rose above the lid of the desk, making it snap open and trap shut, like a crocodile hungry beneath him. Mr Pownall's other hand cuffed at his head, making Jonathan blink and flinch.

'MY WORD, I WILL NOT TOLERATE SUCH INSOLENCE.' His hands slapped out each syllable upon Jonathan's head, Jonathan strangling in the twin nooses of Mr Pownall's bony hand and the polo collar of his T-shirt. There was a melted smell of fear in the air, claggy and suffocating, but no one could look up.

Except Grace. As she looked up she saw the headmaster, Mr Montgomery, cross the playground on his way to the infant block, and knew suddenly what she must do.

Purplegreen blueblack, she took off from her seat.

'GOOD MORNING, MR MONTGOMERY . . .' she intoned with the proper droney seriousness. Mr Pownall, still trying to shake the bones out of Jonathan, had not quite taken in what she said, but the other children, drugged with fear and desperate for salvation, stood too, heads bowed, and joined in:

'GOOD MORNING, MR MONTGOMERY . . .'

As they did so a boy from the neighbouring class scooted out through the playground doors on an errand. The wind took its chance and whipped into the corridor, caught their classroom door and slammed it shut. Mr Pownall dropped Jonathan like discarded prey and turned. Guilty.

Standing amidst the forest of small children he looked wildly around for the headteacher. Of course, Mr Montgomery had been nowhere near, had, in fact, been on his way to give unwanted advice to the pretty student teacher helping out in Class One. In the corridor the playground door was battered by the wind.

Mr Pownall skirted through the desks towards the door. He opened it, took himself a few paces down the corridor. The children remained standing. Grace saw then that Mr Montgomery was moving back across the playground towards the hall doors. Mr Pownall saw him too and, uncertain, stepped out into the playground, his words snatched away by the wind. Mr Montgomery, with a serious face, gave a dismissive wave.

They were still standing when Mr Pownall came back into the classroom. He was going to make them sit down again but the bell rang for playtime and as extra torment he made them stand for a few more moments in utter silence. Other children poured like milk from the surrounding classes, the playground door swinging and clattering. Outside the windows primary-coloured primary-school children began to kiss-chase and tag across the tarmac playground and the scrabby football field.

Then he dismissed them.

'Not you,' he barked at Grace. She hung back and was ready for Mr Pownall's wrath. Wrath. A new word, gleaned from Wednesday's assembly.

'You saw Mr Montgomery enter the room?' Mr Pownall asked, his voice in red pen, suspicious and guilty.

'Yes, Mr Pownall.' The lie was tiny and black like a stick of liquorice in her mouth. She didn't like liquorice and she didn't like lying but it was the only way. She turned it over on her tongue: 'He was carrying some paper.'

Mr Pownall considered. 'What did he do?'

For just a moment Grace considered how huge and dark she could make the lie. Could she say, for instance, that he had wrestled a twenty-seven-foot python into the stock cupboard? No. She had to stay on track with the true lies.

'He came in with the paper and then he looked as if he had forgotten something and he turned and went back out again and then the door slammed.'

Grace kept her voice steady and remembered to look thoughtful. That was one of the most difficult parts of the true lies.

'Tell me again.' Mr Pownall's voice was a slicing cold whisper, the ball of spit creamy in the corner of his mouth as he loomed over her. Grace saw all the veins in his eyes as if someone had switched on an eye map and all the roads were marked in red as they made their way round the globe of his eyeball. But it didn't make any difference, she had it within her. She knew the true lie and she believed it. It was what she had wished to happen and she could say it with even more conviction.

'Mr Montgomery came in with some papers. He was looking at them and then he looked as if he had left something behind and he turned and went back out and then the door slammed.'

She did not elaborate. A true lie must be simple and clean. Mr Pownall looked at her face for a long, mean moment.

'Get out of my sight,' he hissed, standing in her way. Grace stepped sideways around the desk and out of the classroom door. She walked carefully to the girls' toilets.

The toilets were cold, as usual, and smelled bitter with the twin ammonias of girl pee and disinfectant. The playground sounds echoed up through the metal-framed windows in the top of the wall. She stayed there until the bell rang for the end of playtime.

Later, when the home-time bell rang she didn't soar, she didn't push or wrestle. She just felt sad that Jonathan turned away from her, would not speak. When his gran looked up at Grace with her usual home-time smile Jonathan hurried her on up the lane.

There was no one waiting for Grace with a hand to hold. So Grace walked towards town and Nan's shop.

It was Nan who had shown her the power she had, that she could tell true lies.

'Don't you lie to me,' she had said that first true lie day. Her varnished nails had clawed off the top of the blue and white ginger jar and found thin air inside. Not even the scent of the five folded pound notes lingered. 'Where are they?' Her thin fingers had closed around Grace's arm until they ground through her skin, bone against bone. 'Where's my fucking money, Grace?'

Grace didn't know where it was. Maybe the jar had magic powers and the money had vanished, swapped places perhaps with a genie in some distant Arabian lamp. But she didn't say that. She said instead, quite truthfully and trying not to let her voice quaver too badly, 'I don't know, Nan.'

Her reward was the fingers clamping tighter around her humerus, a faint creaking sound coming from somewhere in her sleeve as if the bone would snap under the tension.

'Don't you lie to me.'

Grace didn't know what she should reply. She wasn't lying, she was telling the truth and it wasn't working.

'Don't you lie to me.'

There was a bright sparkle of light from outside, the sun catching in the hideous pattern of the net curtaining as if trying to signal to her.

'There were five notes. Where are they?'

Grace couldn't say anything. What was the sun doing? The light behind was blanking out her grandmother's face. All Grace could see was her thin outline, her charcoal cut-out head, the hairpin bend of her elbow on the jut of her hip. The sun spangled on the heavy gold chain that draped around the knot of Nan's wristbone.

'Don't you lie to me.'

Grace had to. The only alternative was to have her arm pinched black. Then she remembered the cherry brandy Mum had bought in the corner shop. She remembered Mum had let her choose a Walnut Whip, an almost unheard-of treat, and she had been distracted by trying to open the tiny little bag without tearing it. Mum had taken the notes, folded, out of her pocket and handed three or four over in exchange for the chocolate and the cherry brandy. Grace remembered the label on the bottle, shiny and red with a picture of cherries just like the ones on the one-armed bandits at Blackpool. If she told she would be caught later between the twin whirlwinds of Mum and Nan.

Lie. Lie now. Spit it out. Just like liquorice.

'I took it. For the trip. The school trip. On a coach.'

Nan's grip released slightly. 'What fucking bloody trip? Where?'

A train chuffed forwards through Grace's imagination. She was standing on the lines, taking off her red knickers and waving them at it.

'To York. To the Railway Museum.'

And that was it. Grace almost believed in the genie exchange, so magically did Nan release her.

'Don't I have to sign a form this time?'

Grace saw the form on the kitchen table, saw Mum signing it.

'Mum did.'

Grace's only hope was that Nan would not ask Mum about it. There was no trip. No form. There was a Railway Museum. Perhaps she could get a bus all the way to York and the lie wouldn't seem so vast and shiny in her head.

But it worked and the endorphin rush of release stayed with her when, a few weeks later, Mum borrowed Nan's Peking Plum lipstick.

Nan had a hard leather vanity case in a soft grey that she called 'French blue', filled with her cosmetics. This miniature suitcase was the forbidden zone. Grace knew better than to tinker amongst the lipsticks and potions however much the gilded cases and vivid colours enticed her. There was more pleasure to be had from standing a little to one side as Nan put her face on in the hall mirror. The first slap of beigey foundation seemed to blank Nan's face out and then the mascara wand made Nan's eyelashes appear, the pencil drew eyebrows along the balded brow bones. She loved the way Nan smushed her lips together after she'd slathered them in lipstick.

'I didn't take it, Nan,' Grace confessed truthfully. She had not taken the gold-cased lipstick. It was Nan's all-time favourite,

Peking Plum, and had cost her an arm and a leg from the beauty counter at Gillard's department store in town.

The truth was that her mother had taken it the night before for her date with that lanky man, Paul, who had stood in the hallway smelling of engines. Mum had taken it and winked at Grace as if they were accomplices.

The truth was choking her, tight in her throat, its fingers scratching at her skin, making her want to cough. Nan smelled dry. A layer of face and body powder varnished into place with a spray of perfume, something sickly and cheap that she bought on holiday.

Grace wasn't lying. She had told the useless and hollow truth.

Then Nan spoke the magic words: 'Don't you lie to me. Where is it?'

Grace had a sudden image of the park in her mind. A spot under the slide.

'Under the slide in the park. I was going to swap it with Karen.'

'For what?'

Grace hadn't anticipated this. She had been expecting retribution not interrogation. What would she swap it for? Sticky fingers splashed into her memory.

'Her sister's nail varnish.'

'Did you swap it?'

Grace nodded. It was unfolding in her mind, an image of herself in the park under the slide, handing over the forbidden lipstick; as she did so the nail-varnish bottle slipped from her hands and smashed, splattering on Karen's shoes, and they used tugged-up grass to wipe them. Which, of course, was the story she told to Nan.

'Hands,' Nan demanded. Grace offered her hands, palms up, to be whacked, but Nan reached instead to give her the swift shock of a smack across the face. The sting of it sparkled and frittered across her cheek, ending with a long fizzing smart. Later, there would just be hotness.

Nan gave out a snort, like a bad-tempered horse that might rear up at any moment, its hooves breaking into your skull as if it were an egg. The mane . . . curlered set on big rollers just like Nan at the hairdresser's, where she sat in the silver and black chair wearing a black plastic cape. In the dream, later, the horse trotted towards Grace wearing three-inch-heeled court shoes in a brown crocodile skin. Nan's shoes, from the shoe rack in the cupboard under the stairs.

In the cupboard under the stairs Grace found an odd refuge amongst the foot fug of Mum's and Nan's shoes. It seemed it didn't matter how much powder Nan fuffed over herself, she still had smelly feet. The shoes looked bent out where Nan's bones had contorted them into shape. The soles and heels had to cart her about the town making that clip-clip sound that was almost like a theme tune. Or a warning. Here she comes.

She wasn't like a grandma. Other people in Grace's class at school had other grandmas who were rounded and had glasses, or were square and sensible with square bobbed hair. They had grandmas who baked cakes for the tea party at half-term, who had watches and grey hair and, oddly, little-girl shoes with straps across their instep. Grandmas in crimplene slacks or shirtwaister dresses as if they had just come fresh from serving teas in a cricket pavilion. Grandmas who were pale and pink and comforting. Grandmas with wellies on and handbags full of hot mints.

Grandmas rolling around town on bikes or trundling in little run-about cars. Other people thought her nan was cool and beautiful and wanted a grandma like her, with gold-painted toenails and highlighted hair. Grace couldn't see why. Grace did not think that anyone else's grandma got down on her knees in the sawdust in the back room by the cold store at the butcher's and sucked Mr Roberts's trouser sausage. Another true lie that day.

'What were you looking at? Get an eyeful?' Nan had barked.

'I saw Karen on her new bike,' Grace lied, her mind veering away from the memory of her accidental view through the plastic ribbons of the fly curtain in the butcher's shop. A slashed view of Mr Roberts, his blue and white striped pinny, smeared with giblets and wipes of liver, flipped over Nan's bobbing head. The undersoles of her shoes, one with the price label still on, scuffed a little with wear, caught the light on the tiny gold numbers that told her Nan's shoe size. Mr Roberts made odd noises. Grace looked away and resolved not to eat sausages any more, to stick to beans and boiled eggs. 'I think she's got a paper round. Can I have a paper round?'

Karen had neither paper round, nor new bike but Grace held very tight to the mental image of her friend pedalling fast, standing up to get a better purchase on the rise of the hill, replaying and replaying it to settle the magic. It worked. Nan was silent and Grace was once more unimportant, an accessory that didn't quite match.

Nan's shop was called Something Special and almost everything on every rack glittered and spangled with colour. No faint-hearted or shrinking violet dared to come through the steel and glass door. The shop was on a spur from the main shopping precinct and looked out on an expanding branch of Marks and Spencer. Sometimes, like this afternoon, there was a faint smell of pee from the stairwell to the multi-storey car park above. In the glum concrete corridor of shops only Something Special and Fran's hairdresser's at the far end, sang out.

Grace pushed through the door. Inside, the shop smelled of perfumes and as Nan sorted along a rack for a particular size there was the crackle and tangle of man-made-fibre. Through the gap in the curtain in one of the changing rooms, Grace could just make out a customer, her tights pulled up over her knickers. At the counter Debbie, Nan's assistant, was fumbling with the keys for the glass-topped display counter.

'Your fringe needs trimming,' Nan commented as she swept past Grace to the changing room with alternative tops. 'Nip down and ask Fran if the trainee can snip it for you. You look like the Dulux dog. Go on.'

Grace took her cue, knew her presence was not required and duly headed to the silver and black leatherette palace of A Cut Above.

The hairdresser's was busy. Fran was tugging a barrel brush through a client's wet hair. There was the rushing wind of dryers and a chemical smell of perm lotion and colourant. A new girl was sweeping up the hair. Fran herself smiled at Grace.

'Gracie. Busy day at school?'

Grace nodded.

'Take a seat, sweetheart. Mel? . . . Mel? . . .'

The new girl with the broom looked up as if from a dull daydream.

Fran commanded, 'Mel, get Gracie a glass of squash.'

Mel wrestled the pillow of chopped hair into a plastic bin liner and moved off towards the tiny back kitchen.

'I'll be with you in two ticks, Gracie.' Fran wrangled the hair as if it was a wild animal. Grace busied herself looking at the sculptured hairstyles in Fran's book until Mel arrived with the squash. She had barely watered it down, it was thick and syrupy, but Grace had had nothing to drink since breakfast. Jonathan had knocked over the water jug at their dinner table in the school hall.

Fran finished tugging the client's hair into shape and was spraying it. Then she was all smiles and approving cooing sounds and the coverall was whipped from round the client like a magic cape. Transformation complete.

Later, Grace's transformation was also complete. Her fringe neatly trimmed, she was offered a lolly and sent on her way. She did not turn back to Something Special. Instead she wandered off towards the indoor market and Baubles, Bangles and Beads to work out how much pocket money, if she ever, indeed, received any pocket money, she might expend on the tray of rings with big jewels as bright and shiny as boiled sweets.

She returned to the shop just as Nan was locking up and together they clacked up the steps in the multi-storey to Nan's car. She made Fran-ish cooing, approving noises about the fringe.

That night, of course, Mum and Nan were going out. They were being taken to the pub by Mr Roberts and his brother from the butcher's shop. The French blue leather vanity case would be opened and Nan would paint herself in. Mum would have a bath and shave her legs and leave the little hairs in a ring round the tub.

'I've made other plans,' Mum informed them, even before Nan

had got her coat off. Mum was already dressed up and finishing her hair.

'What plans?'

'Other ones.'

'They're waiting.'

'Entertain them.'

'Two of them?'

'You've done it before. Thought you'd be glad. Be greedy.'

Nan had said before that a woman hadn't lived unless she had the Roberts brothers sucking both her tits at once. Grace had wondered if they had managed to suck any milk out but had not asked about it. She had been sitting in the living room and Mum and Nan had been in the kitchen, and she was not supposed to be listening but they were talking too loudly and telling too many secrets. She pretended to be watching the television. She had found that the answer to most of her questions over the years had been, 'Nothing for noses. You keep your trap shut.' So by the age of nine, Grace generally had the good sense to keep her trap shut. Grace tried not to think about the butcher's shop, the floor soft with fresh sawdust and the air velvet-thick with cold blood.

'What other plans?'

'Davey's taking me to Chinatown.'

'Davey? Him again? Who is this "Davey" bloke?'

'You met him at the Freemasons. Couple of weeks back. Anyway, he's got some business bloke he's meeting and I'm making up the numbers with this bloke's girlfriend.'

'A threesome. A foursome,' Nan sing-songed.

So Grace was left with a supply of emergency crisps and a bottle of Tizer to see her through until bedtime.

2

NOW YOU SEE HIM

The beer was sour, the sky was dark, the pub was smoky and Alec knew it was time to go home. Instead he remained watching the far corner by the dartboard where the stocky man's cigar burnt slowly down in the ashtray.

Smiley Mike's attention was fixed on the bubbly, red-lipped redhead he had curled his arm around. Alec had not wanted to come out, but, as usual, Mike had dragged him along on the promise of a friend who never materialized. Not that Alec ever wanted the friend to arrive. In fact, he began to think he might have magical abilities, for the more he wished they wouldn't show the more they didn't. Now the evening had worn down and gradually he had faded and thinned and reached his true state of invisibility.

Alec laughed to himself, took a sip of his pint and let it blur him into a sudden flickerbook of memory to the winter he was thirteen and had wanted to be invisible, even more than he had wished for a flying carpet or that new bike with ten gears.

Every Tuesday after tea he would settle down with his father to watch *Now You See Him*. Even now the scent of a freshly opened bottle of beer sent him hurtling back through time and he would see his father sitting on the old sofa, the music for the TV show playing in his head, a lot of drums and tiptoe-twanging bass.

Now You See Him concerned the adventures of Fraser Halls, a caretaker in a secret government laboratory complex who had accidentally been made invisible. In the course of the pilot episode Fraser journeyed from being the caretaker no one cared about to the most hunted man in the limited location landscapes of the south of England. The scientists responsible for the accident wanted him back to see what they had finally got right and spent most of the black and white episodes seated before Christmas tree-lit computer screens and boiling test tubes of what looked like Vimto. In another lab, far better equipped with swively chrome chairs, a rival group of scientists plotted Fraser's capture so that they too could steal the secret of his invisibility. Alec loved to try to work out how Fraser would dodge the scientists each week. Never mind all their degrees, their white coats and half-moon spectacles, Fraser was endlessly resourceful, outwitting them every time with the judicious use of a length of sticky tape or a folding door. Each episode contained one incident where he might be splashed with paint or coated in chocolate, allowing him a roguish wink at some disgruntled scientist. Neither side was ever interested in giving him back his visibility, no one except for junior scientist Dr Grace Storey. To Alec, at thirteen, Dr Grace just stalled time as she gave Fraser a temporary face with a mixture of Copydex glue and Rimmel foundation. During the weekly they-nearly-kiss moment, as Dr Grace coloured in Fraser's hair with oil pastels, Alec would get up and fetch Dad some more beer and himself a glass of Tizer. He would return from the kitchen in time for the moment when Fraser would embark on his good deed, selflessly helping others in a variety of contrived, implausible and utterly entertaining situations.

There was no way of attaining invisibility which didn't require being poisoned or zapped by chemicals and hazardous rays which the teenage Alec didn't anyway have access to. Instead he disguised himself, found ways to behave so that he could be stealthy, blending in and blurring out. The monochrome of school uniform seemed to sing out 'SCHOOLBOY' as he trudged down the street with his mates. On the street, uniform put you on show, you were badged and belonged. Alec was considering this one afternoon when he should have been factoring in the lowest common denominators, and he couldn't seem to melt away when Mrs Wills stood over him requiring the answer to question seven.

He experimented with different ways of walking: shorter steps, smoothing his stride out. In English they read a story about a cat burglar moving smoothly on the balls of his feet. The other lads laughed, 'Who has balls on their feet, Miss?' But Alec was interested. He dodged nimbly through the crowd in the corridor, finding the snickelways and gaps.

After the home-time bell, a turn or two under the arches of the maths block would let him sidestep out in front of Susan Fledge.

'How . . .?' She looked at him, open-mouthed, amazed. His finest moments. Except for the dreams where Susan made him a new face from glue and make-up and coloured in his hair with charcoal.

Susan Fledge. The first person he became invisible to as she moved into the top set for maths and could be seen kissing Dennis Travener at the Christmas dance. Could be seen, if you were invisible in the corner of the school hall, in your new drainpipe trousers and your crisp white shirt.

And the greatest vanishing trick of all, pulled off by Dad.

He had simply walked out of the front door as usual. Alec had been flicking through the *Dandy* and munching jammy toast as Dad had picked his Tupperware lunch box off the worktop, kissed Mum on the lips.

'Home usual time?' she'd asked.

'I'll be late,' Dad had said, buttoning up his jacket. 'Football practice.'

It seemed the longest football match in history three weeks later when he still had not come home.

There was a story, something fairy tale, made up, as Auntie Jean told him, by women like Mrs Walters at number 32. The tale suggested Dad was living in another town far away with another wife and another son, but Alec couldn't be sure, no one told him to his face. All he got from Mum was hugs and kisses and a ruffle of his hair. His information was slotted out through doors that stood slightly ajar, in voices of iron-filing whispers. Splinters, that he couldn't make into a whole.

He became invisible. It settled upon him like a cloak and he was astonished at the ease of it. He adopted his two uniforms, blurring into the corridors and classrooms, melting, army surplus camouflage-style, into the streets. He had thought for a while that if he could patrol the realm of invisibility he might be able to locate his father. That was the answer: Dad had been made accidentally invisible and no one from work could come and own up to it. If Alec could just fold himself into that other dimension they might meet.

After a year, he didn't stop being invisible. He reasoned that should his dad arrive back and be unable to find him, it might teach him a lesson in how it felt.

Now, sitting in the pub instead of on the sofa, he tried to make the thoughts in his head invisible; to deny that what he wanted more than anything was Dr Grace, armed with a felt-tip pen to colour him in.

Alec took a swig of bitter. He wasn't sure if it was to honour the dim memory of his father, or to swill the taste of it from his mouth. Alec felt like Fraser Halls these days, lost and running. He had broken up with Cherry nearly a year ago and he was not interested in looking for anyone else. Smiley Mike did not understand how he could go without sex for so long, but then Smiley Mike had the sexual proclivity of a dog. He would try anything, which is why he had phoned Alec late one evening last November to ask for a lift to A & E to have the vacuum cleaner attachment extricated from his 'gentleman friend'. That was how the middle-aged casualty sister had put it as she snapped on her rubber gloves. Smiley Mike had got off with her too. Clearly Smiley Mike also had some magical power.

The beer was sour, the sky was dark, the pub was smoky; Alec again listed the reasons in his head, knew he should go home. Smiley Mike, arm looped around the redhead's waist, was leaning in to say his farewells with a wink.

'We're off, mate . . .'

Alec nodded, raised his glass in a mock toast.

'Want a lift?'

Alec shook his head, indicated the unfinished pint. Mike grinned at him, glanced over to the table in the corner by the dartboard, the man's back turned against the room, shielding the little blonde woman from their view.

'Forget it, mate, that little blondie is out of your league.'

Alec tipped the glass as if to toast the advice, took a deep gulp. Smiley Mike shrugged and left, a guiding hand on the redhead's bottom.

Alec was compelled to stay because, over in the corner by the dartboard, the thickset gold-ringed man in the brown leather jacket and slacks was making the tiny blonde woman cry.

She was trying not to wipe at the tears. Trying not to let him win. He was leaning down at her, doggish and hard, his arms making a hairy fence to pen her in. One arm was slung across the back of the leather seating, the thumb and forefinger nudging her back if she chanced to try to move away. The other arm stretched powerfully towards the table, the hand a resting fist. His face was against her ear so she had to turn away to the wall, had to cringe.

Alec couldn't look away. He found himself wondering how Cherry could leave him for someone else. How could she walk away from him when he had loved her? When he had been good to her? Look at this scene, this man and this woman. Did people want bullies and brutes? Shaggy dogs like Smiley Mike? He thought that his heart was ruling his head. Even in all its mauled pieces, spat back at him by Cherry, there was still life in there, he could still feel. When the man grabbed the tiny blonde woman around the wrist with his gold-ringed hand and wrangled her towards the door, Alec watched as everyone looked away.

He sat for a moment watching the bubbles float out of the sappy beer and then made his move to the door, opened it. Let the cold night in.

Gold. Blonde. Sour. Dark. Smoky. Tears. They made a list in Alec's head. The most important list of his life.

Alec paused a moment in the vestibule, not wanting to pounce on Gold and Blonde right outside. He didn't want trouble. He was keeping watch, that was all. He had a gut feeling about the way the man's fingerprints might bruise the woman's wrist. It wasn't his business, he knew that, but if something happened he would feel it should have been his business. Bloody hell, Fraser Halls and his invisible do-gooding had marked him for life.

He was jostled as two couples bustled out of the pub behind him. He stepped aside. They didn't seem to pay him the least attention, he was as invisible as the unused coat stand. He waited another moment and then opened the exterior door.

The couples had made off down the road towards the centre of town. The short-haired woman had tried to flag down the bus and was laughing as it pulled away from them. Her laugh echoed back to him as Alec looked round the car park. There was no sign of Gold and Blonde. He had missed them. It bothered him that the man had driven her away, would be in control. Perhaps they had made up after their argument. They could be pulling into the lay-by at the back of the weighbridge on the A road, Gold apologizing with kisses and he and Blonde moving over to the back seat like eager teenagers. They could get pregnant tonight. Their saving grace. 'D'you remember, sweetheart?' they could reminisce, five kids and a big detached house from now.

Alec turned to go back inside and then realized he just needed to go home. So he turned left to cut across the car park, to see if the last bus had waited for him and not mind the walk if it hadn't.

They were at the far edge of the car park between the skips balanced on the ragged tarmac that gave out onto the playing fields behind. It was the hollow knock of skull on metal that made Alec turn. He had often seen a fox by the bins. The only wildlife he saw was the juddered movement of a man kicking a woman.

Alec should have turned towards the street, kept walking. The only thing he should have stopped for was a bag of chips from Mona's Fry-Up, but Fraser Halls gave him an invisible nod and Alec's feet took stealthy steps behind the row of cars towards the skips.

The man had the woman by the hair now and was crushing her against the metal side of the skip. His other hand was slapping at her head. She struggled but made almost no sound, her voice reduced to small, trapped-animal pants.

'Hey,' was all Alec said. Not shouting, not angry, just calm and sure and up close. The man, giving off a sour scent of beer and oranges, wheeled round, unable to see anything of Alec except for his silhouette outlined in street-light yellow.

He threw her down like a paper bag. That's what Alec would remember. How he discarded her.

Alec kept a respectful distance while the little blonde sorted herself. She was pale and bright and dainty before him, like a faerie, not your pink Disney sort of fluff, but someone more eerie. As she sniffled and reached up to her scalp the thick red on her fingertips spooked her, she couldn't seem to catch her breath then, her eyes opened wide and silvered with fear.

'Let me take a look.' She leaned towards him, her hands reaching out, and braced herself against his chest, her hair tangling like cobweb in his jacket zip. Alec could see the red sparkling on his fingers in the moonlight paleness of her hair. The wound was small, a bad graze, that was all.

'Won't need stitches,' he said with a reassuring smile. 'You'll live.'

He noticed her hand was dirtied with mud, bits of tarmac gravel embedded in grazes on her palms. There'd been a scuffle, hadn't there, while he'd wasted time being invisible by the coat stand.

'You should get cleaned up.'

He took a step back into the car park as if to show her the way.

'Gonna puke.' Her voice was racing ahead of the vomit. As she bent her head Alec's hand moved quickly to catch her hair. He twisted it delicately around his fingers, a knot of safety as she gagged into the darkness.

He had done this for Cherry that last New Year's, after Donny's birthday party, when she thought she was pregnant but it was just food poisoning.

He handed the woman his handkerchief to wipe at her mouth. To dab at the cut on her head.

'You got a car?' he asked. She shook her head. Alec put his hands in his jacket pockets. 'Right. We'd better phone for a cab, then.' He made to go back inside the pub, she didn't follow. She was shaking her head, tearful.

'Can't go back in there. I'll walk to the rank.'

She turned to walk and lost her footing. Alec darted to catch her. He could feel how she was trembling all over. Fraser Halls's face hovered into his mind. He knew exactly what Fraser would say, so he said it.

'I can walk you there. It isn't far.'

Alec kept himself between the woman and the kerb as they walked along in silence.

The taxi rank was outside the town hall, less than a five-minute walk away. Once there, however, there were no taxis to be seen. It was cold, she was shivering and starting to look a bit green. Alec took off his jacket and draped it round her shoulders. It was padded, warm, and her eyes teared up, her skin taking on an even more definite hint of greenishness.

So he walked her across town to the Three Horses Estate and the fifteen-storey block that towered above the network of council housing. The sign read 'Bigby-Weathers Tower', named after a councillor who'd been in charge of the development of the estate in the sixties. 'After the war . . .' was his favourite phrase, his own participation an excuse for all his tyrannies as a councillor.

Alec stood outside the lobby after she moved inside. She was edgy as she waited for the lift, turned twice, three times, to reassure herself he was still there, watchful. The lift was out of order Alec realized, and besides, she was still wearing his jacket.

They walked up to the seventh floor in silence. At her door she was shaking too much to turn the key. She wanted Alec to check inside. She waited in the open doorway as he looked in the kitchen and noticed something home-cooked in a casserole dish sitting on the hob and the untidy but clean intimacy of her things strewn around the bathroom and small bedroom. The scents of her made him think of Cherry and what she had taken from his life.

The woman was still panicked, even after he made her a hot drink. As he took his leave he told her to deadbolt the door behind him if she was anxious. He waited, as she asked, for her to do so. Heard the bolt slide, the key turn, the lock tumble.

'All right?' he called, a response, muffled, coming from within. 'Bye.'

He might as well walk home and he thought about Mona's Fry-Up, but when he reached the bright shop front not even the savoury vinegariness of the smell convinced him. He didn't feel like it, hadn't washed his hands from holding the woman's blood-ied hair, thought of her vomit spattering on tarmac. Mona waved from behind the range. Alec waved back.

Waved goodbye was how he would think of it later.

3

EMERGENCY CRISPS

The house had seemed so bright and shiny as Mum and Nan got themselves ready, clomping up and down the stairs in their high and higher heels, snacking in the kitchen, as brash and tinny as any of the pots and pans. The white spotlight of the fridge, the shine of eyeballs, the sparkle of heavily applied eye make-up in a tinsellated purple. Their noise, the television noise, even the outside noise came in louder, the door open as the window cleaner leaned against it and Nan rummaged in her handbag for some cash. His brash gold bracelet and his Steve McQueen hair seemed to bounce the hall light off itself. He might see them later and he'd get a round in, he joked as he flashed their cash.

With a chankle of anklets, a snap of handbags and a warning to be in bed by the time they got back, they were gone. Bang. Door shut. And, to Grace, it seemed all at once as if the house had eaten her.

Even armed with the emergency crisps Grace found the house frightening. The stairs were the worst. They creaked and stretched as if a mob clambered up and down them. Something pinged metallically in the kitchen as the toaster cooled, but to Grace and her bag of crisps it sounded like pirates twanging their scimitars to test them for sharpness.

She switched the lights out because she didn't like to draw the curtains. She had tried before to sit in the lighted house and watch the television but she heard outside sounds and couldn't see what was going on. She knew that with the light on inside and darkness lurking outside, people could see in and would know she was alone, so she had learned to switch off all the lights and look out of the window.

It was a changing landscape and the lights from the passing cars were pretty and golden. The noise of the engines gunning as they passed kept her company; she knew then that other people were out and about in the world. She would watch the neighbours, Tony Craddock on his bike, Mr Bennet across the road putting his bin out, leaning to pick the weeds from the cracks in his decorative boundary wall. Sometimes his son would work on his car late into the evening, a bright white light plugged into the garage, the yellow cable trailing like a long thin snake. A snake that could reach all the way around Grace in tight coils. The plug looking like fangs as it bit into the socket. Grace found she had to watch the snake, the way it switchbacked as Anthony Bennet moved under the car. Only Anthony could tame it, grasping it behind its orange plug head.

His snake light switched off, Grace would be aware suddenly that behind her back the sky had darkened deeper, twilight had been chased off by the night and the house would groan as it digested her.

Nan always warned her to be in bed before their return but Grace hadn't the courage to be upstairs alone. She knew that if you hid under the blankets the hungry monster wouldn't get you but he just might if, having already trawled Nan's and Mum's rooms, he'd come up empty-handed. Grace needed to be sitting, her back pinned against the corner, not lying down trying not to breathe under her blankets. Her habit was to sit in the dark until the dark was too scary. Then she would move to the hall and, dodging the carpet wolves, she would scoot into the cupboard under the stairs. She had a big rubber torch in there that she had found in the shed and she would use it to read books. Crooked into the angle of the stairs she listened out for the taxi. In the moments between hearing the engine tick outside and the sound of the taxi door slamming she would rush upstairs and into bed and be pretending to be asleep before her nan and Mum had filled the kettle and lit their goodnight cigarettes.

The carpet wolves. They had not been in the old beigey-coloured carpet with its flat pile and the worn patch where it turned left from the front door towards the kitchen. Then one afternoon Grace had come home from school to find a man fitting a new dark brown carpet that trailed itself all the way up the stairs onto the landing. Mum was in the kitchen brewing tea and tweaking her hair.

'Shoes off on the new carpet,' she barked and Grace took her shoes off. The brown wool was soft and comforting underfoot and she thought, in daylight hours at least, that she liked this new carpet.

But then daylight hours stretched and darkened.

She needed the toilet in the night and she switched on her

torch. Its little beam seemed sucked into the rich peat brown of the carpet and the toilet door now seemed a hundred miles away across bare plain. It seemed to shudder like fur. But she was nearly peeing and she could not pee on the new carpet. A tentative skip took her onto the landing. Hop. Skip. Hop. But behind her the carpet seemed to lift and stretch and from the corner of her eye she saw the first of the carpet wolves as he slunk behind her. She stopped dead, her heart drumming, her breath held as she swept the beam across the place the wolf had walked. She saw nothing, until, out of the corner of her other eye now, another wolf, loping into the bathroom.

Grace darted into the toilet and shut the door. She did not turn on the light and she angled herself on the seat so that her pee would hit the slope of the bowl and not make too much noise. Her ears strained beyond her own watery sounds to hear the wolves on the landing. A creak of floorboard under paw reached her.

She was ready to go back to bed now. But for a few moments she could only stand with her ear pressed to the toilet door listening to the landing. She opened the door carefully, her torch beam dimming as the battery wore down.

'What the hell are you playing at?' Nan snapped at her. Grace felt her body flash with fright, rising out of her nightdress and falling back into it. Nan flipped on the light. 'You frightened the life out of me. Get back in bed.'

Grace, scuttling back to her room, decided to sleep the opposite way around, her head nearest the door. She burrowed under the covers and hitched them over her head until just a sliver of bedroom could be seen, illuminated by the bright warm stripe of landing light coming through her door. Nan headed back to her room and the light blinked off. Grace watched, unblinking, and fell asleep waiting for the carpet wolves' long noses to poke into her room.

In the morning Nan stood in the kitchen by the sink, spitting smoke towards the window. The kitchen was at the front of the house and looked out across the handkerchief lawn of the front garden to the street. Already other children were off to school and Larry the milkman was riding shotgun on the float, scooting with his little basket of milk bottles, his blue coverall pockets filled with tubs of cream. His son, Maurice, was driving. Maurice was tall and gangly with a thin moustache that made Grace think a harvestman spider was coming out of his nose. Nan stood sentinel, her right hip knocking against the blue melamine of the cupboard door.

Grace reached for her cereal in silence. There was barely a spoonful left in the box but Grace knew this was not the moment to mention it. Instead she tipped out the inner packet and all its dust and dampened it with a dribble of milk. She was trying to remember if there were any bananas. She could take one and eat it on the way to school, if Nan would just keep her back turned.

Better yet, Nan made a sudden pounce into the hallway to click the front door open. As she did so Grace nabbed her banana from the basket beside the fridge. It was a big one, bright yellow and greenish around the stalk just the way she liked. Nan always left them too long, too speckled brown and floury tasting.

'Get you a flap fitted,' Nan growled as she moved back into the kitchen followed by Mum, panda-eyed with last night's make-up and still in her glad rags although a ladder was running up her black tights.

'Tea brewed? I'm parched.' Mum's hand reached to feel the side of the teapot. It was cold. She turned to busy herself filling the kettle, fishing wet tea bags out of the sink.

'Good night, then? With Davey?' Nan quizzed.

'It was a good night. He's a good bloke.'

'Do I know him?'

'I told you, you met him at the Freemasons, few weeks back. The Pool Night?'

Nan hissed out cigarette smoke and seemed to stare into it deeply as if she would find the memory there. 'Stocky. Brownish hair, shaved down? That the one?'

Mum gave her a look. 'You don't have to make him sound like an identikit picture.'

'Didn't think about me waiting with the taxi, then?'

The kettle was steaming, the water rolling inside the metal as if it knew what was coming, panicking.

'Waiting? For who? Me?'

'In the square. Ten to, with the taxi, like we agreed.'

'Yeah, but you were with the Robertses. I thought you were all set to go home with them.'

'I'm left there like a fucking lemon.'

'We agreed, same as always, don't wait more than five minutes.'

'We agreed to share the taxi.' Nan stubbed out her cigarette on the steel draining board.

Mum raised a hand to her hip, shifted her weight, defiant. 'You're a grown-up. I'm not your mother.' As the kettle clicked off

Mum turned to Grace with a stone face. 'You're going to be late for school.'

And, thankful, Grace took the banana and her escape route.

They had not finished when Grace returned home after school. Nan had had a slow day in the shop to think about it all.

'No. I think this is about you getting dumped by the Robertses.'

Nan was shaking her head steadily from side to side, a pendulum, serious and in the right. 'This is about courtesy, Lorraine, it's about you thinking about someone else for a change.'

Nan must not be getting her own way if she was calling Mum by her full name.

'Thinking about you, you mean. The world just bloody spins in your direction, Mother.'

Grace was one step through the front door. Her key seemed to have jammed in the lock as if it was holding her back but Grace fiddled it free.

'Piss off out of it, you.' Nan was striding out of the kitchen towards Grace, grabbing her shoulder and pushing her backwards, away from the argument. Grace was unbalanced, caught the corner of her eye on the butt of the Yale lock. Mum now snatched her back.

'Don't take it out on her.'

'I'm not taking anything out on her. Stop using her as a shield.'

Nan yanked at Grace's sleeve. Mum tugged at her hand. Grace pinballed between them until Mum opened the door and shoved her outside, shoved money into her hand.

'Nip up the shop, get yourself some—'

But Nan slammed the door nearly on Mum's hand. Grace

could see them distorted through the tulip glass panels in the front door.

In the shop she spent ages bent by the boxes of crisps wondering which flavour to choose, something she knew she'd enjoy or something new she wasn't sure of: pickled onion, prawn cocktail. In the end, after Mrs Hirst had huffed and puffed enough from behind the counter, she chose cheese and onion and a Fry's chocolate cream.

Later, in the park, the crisps were sickly and the chocolate seemed filled with melted toothpaste. The evening darkness at the edge of the playground started to bleed across to the swings. Grace had stopped swinging ages ago and was lolling now, her stomach on the seat, the toes of her shoes pushing against the tarmac. She pretended that she was a diver, flicking each foot as if it wore flippers. Looking down at the swaying ground, the gravelly bits became coral.

She wondered if it was safe to go home yet. Then she looked up and saw Mum at the street gate, signalling to her. Grace jumped off the swing, ran across the damp grass.

'Your tea's ready.' Mum smiled, her arms folded against the evening cold. 'Come on.' She winked, so it was all right again. They huddled up the road together.

The phone rang later and Grace would remember this was the first time Davey had been in the house, that very first moment of the bell, the voice on the other end of the line talking to Mum. Grace could see the eyes at the back of Nan's head were alert, watching Mum twizzle the phone cord, scratch at her hair, even as the eyes at the front of Nan's head flittered over the pages of a magazine.

Purposely, Mum said nothing after she put the phone down, sat back at the table and picked up her coffee. Grace could see the question marks rising from the top of Nan's head. They popped like bubbles. But Nan said nothing, reached instead for her bag and her smokes.

'You off out tonight?' Mum spoke after half a mug of coffee.

Nan puffed at her cigarette, shook her head.

'Want to meet Davey?' Mum offered it, face full on to Nan, her eyes glittering with challenge.

Nan shrugged. 'Is he worth the bus fare?'

Since Grace had guzzled the cheese and onion crisps in the park earlier she did not bother when offered crisps by Mum as she pulled on her coat.

'Get them crisps from the cupboard. . .and there's some biscuits in the carrier on the worktop. I've opened the pop bottle, just don't spill it this time. I don't want another sticky mess all over the floor again, lady.' Grace looked up in time to see Mum's pouting kissy lips on their heat-seeking way to her face, Mum glowering playfully at her through smokily painted eyes. Grace thought she looked masked, like a robber.

'Bed before we get back,' Nan cautioned, as if to break the curfew would mean instant transformation into a pumpkin or a frog. And then it seemed as if their taxi headlights might be the last light Grace would ever see.

It was not bin day in the morning and a determined drizzle had started up so the street outside was empty. A pack of three dogs, a lanky black and tan, a white and black sheepdog cross and a woolly-looking terrier patrolled, stopping to sniff at gateposts,

tracking friends and enemies. Mrs Nickolds next door had complained about them. They were living on a rough patch of land
between the back of the houses and the council estate. Other dogs,
left to roam at will, joined them occasionally and fights broke out.
Now Grace felt uneasy. The little woollen-haired terrier was at
their gate, turning and sniffing and making agitated snuffles at his
confederates. He was investigating the gatepost and then he
sniffed along the edge of the path. The lanky black and tan and
the sheepdog cross joined him, making pawprints on the front
lawn. As they did so Grace scrunched herself down into the back
of the chair. There was movement on the periphery of her vision,
something had risen to its feet in the hall. The carpet wolves were
on the move.

It would be dark soon. She needed to get to the cupboard.
Outside, one of the dogs gave a short conversational bark and
then cocked his leg against Nan's miniature flower barrel and
peed on the draggled nasturtiums. The carpet wolves moved as
one towards the tulip glass door. Grace took her chance, crept
from the chair and made the leap through the living-room door.
As she hop-skipped across the peat-brown pelt of carpet she saw
how the wolves gathered by the front door, watchful of the street
dogs, whose jumping shadows were twisted by the glass. Grace
shut the cupboard door very quietly and wedged herself into the
furthest corner under the staircase. It was then she remembered
she had left her rubber torch in her bedroom.

She sat in the dark, her knees hugged up tight. As her eyes
adjusted she saw the thin peel of light at the edge of the door, soft
and orangey and flecked with the passing lightning of white as
cars sloshed by in the rain. She could hear it now, patting against

the front door, against the long thin window at the top of the landing.

She did not know how long she sat and listened in the dark. She couldn't see the little red-strapped Timex watch Mum had given her last Christmas. She only knew it seemed like for ever and her stomach was griping about having had nothing to eat. It gurgled at first and then started to stab at her so she had to unfold herself and stretch.

The small silvered face of the watch showed ten past nine in the dim glimmer of the street light through the jamb of the under-stairs-cupboard door. Grace pressed her eye to the slender gap, felt her eyelashes brush against the woodwork. She could see almost nothing, no sign of the carpet wolves. Perhaps if she was very quiet and trod very carefully she wouldn't disturb them. Her stomach gurgled in agreement and the door creaked slightly as she opened it, as if it whispered 'Coast is clear.'

She was three steps from the safe haven of the cupboard when she felt the hairs on the back of her neck prickle. The carpet wolf rose out of the floor behind her; she could hear it breathing. Grace turned to see the amber coals of its eyes and knew at once the other wolves were rising from the stretch of carpet that lay between her and the kitchen door. One stretched its jaws, yawning, teeth glinting, the other wolf shook out its shoulders, the street light showing sparks of copper and gold hidden deep in its fur. It turned, its wide paws steady against the floor, its head raised. Its low, resonant growl rumbled through her like the sound of a passing lorry, making it seem as if her ribs clattered together. And then her stomach answered, giving out a snickering snarl all its own. Grace gasped at the sound. The tallest carpet wolf settled back on its haunches, the one nearest the kitchen door seemed to shift a little, making a way for her. She took an uncertain step forward. The carpet wolf behind her did not attack. As she moved onto the lino of the kitchen they settled into a watchful triangle, as if they guarded the door.

The light from the fridge seemed as powerful and far-reaching as a lighthouse. Grace reached for the cheese. It had been left unwrapped and had grown cracked and gnarly so she grated it up, taking care not to shave anything off her fingers. She dolloped some salad cream onto it and slathered the mixture onto some bread. Cheese thus sandwiched she poured herself some of the cherryade. The bottle was unwieldy and she spilled some. Before she could find a tea towel to mop up, one of the carpet wolves reached out a hessian tongue and lapped at the sugary puddle.

Grace sat then in the kitchen doorway with folded knees, her back against the jamb and the carpet wolves closed in, soft and comforting, keeping her warm.

Three glasses of cherryade later, when she needed the loo, the carpet wolves tracked with her upstairs, one behind, one in front, the scout, and one at her side, so her hand could reach out into its soft fur and stop herself shaking.

She retrieved the torch from her room but instead of heading back into the cupboard Grace sat on the landing, her back against the bathroom wall. Around her the carpet wolves patrolled, the tallest padding down the stairs to once more take up its watch at the front door. It was past eleven by her silver-faced watch when the carpet wolf at her side nudged her awake in time to hear the taxi ticking over outside the house.

It was past three when she woke from a dream and saw the carpet wolves ranged across her rug, muzzles twitching in sleep on outstretched paws, except for the tallest who sat by the door, ever watchful.

The next afternoon after school she did not bother going to find Nan at the shop. Instead she walked beyond the precinct to the library.

They had been once before on a school trip last year. The librarian lady had shown them how to use the Dewey catalogue to find what they wanted. Grace riffled through a few drawers and made notes of the titles in the back of her roughwork book. The library had three books about wolves. They were heavy and Grace wondered how she would carry them home, but as she opened the first a neat printed label on the flyleaf declared: 'FOR REFERENCE USE ONLY. NOT TO BE REMOVED FROM THE LIBRARY.' Grace looked at the number on the last page, over a hundred; she had better start reading.

So it was that two hours later, Grace, on being asked to leave the library because it was closing time, found herself asking the librarian, the frothy-haired blonde lady from the school trip, if she could take the books home. The lady shook her head but promised to keep them for her until next time.

'Come this way.' The librarian smiled and took Grace to a little desk under an arch and Grace filled out a card in her best handwriting in exchange for three library tickets.

A man with overalls on and a huge ring clanging with keys let her out through the heavy wooden library doors. Outside, the sky was darkening and the street lights were winking on.

*

You might have thought they had never existed without him, so swiftly did Davey's name punctuate their every sentence.

Not that Grace ever saw him. Her first encounter with his presence was a night filled with odd dreams of laughter. She had awoken several times and as she sat up in bed, trying to scramble out of sleep, the air seemed to be made of smoke. There were none of the usual home smells: Nan's cigarettes and perfume, the background greasy deliciousness of egg and chips. The carpet wolves kept close by her, their muzzles twitching at the exotic perfumed fug. Grace made herself into a smooth pebble of girl beneath her blankets, falling back asleep to the drone of chat from downstairs, a masculine sound. Davey.

In the morning he was gone but the smell of his cigars lingered. Grace found the two or three stubs, like cat turds, in Nan's best ashtray.

Another morning he had left his jacket draped on the end of the banisters. It was leather, a deep chocolate brown, creased like a face. It smelled powerfully of cold car, cigars (they were in a special case in the inside pocket) and aftershave, something orangey that reminded Grace of Christmas and PE.

'Get your paws off that,' Nan snapped, catching Grace trying her arm in the dangling sleeve. Nan snatched the jacket up, pulled a wire coat hanger from the cupboard under the stairs and hung it on the hook inside. She shut the door with an officious click and glared at Grace. 'Nothing there for noseys.'

It didn't seem to matter to them how late Grace was from school. There seemed more welcome in the natural history section – 'Corvus Frugilegus (Rook), the most sociable of the corvidae,

is chiefly a resident of temperate, boreal, paleoarctic regions . . .' –
than on her own doorstep, so Grace didn't hurry home.

She liked it if it rained on the way home and the headlights
made the rain into silver slashes. Grace would arrive home hungry
and bedraggled and they didn't turn a hair. Grace would hum to
herself as she towelled her hair in the bathroom, and when she
finally arrived in the kitchen they'd be eager to show off the new
present from Davey. A box of plastic-packed Edam cheeses or a
Party Seven keg of beer. Davey was a businessman, a man with a
card for the cash and carry, a man who could get them anything.

He bought Grace a tub of white chocolate mice. They were
waiting for her one Thursday morning. Mum was jigging around
the kitchen, clacking her heels in time to some tune on the radio.
Grace was reaching for a bowl, reaching for the box of cereal, a full
box, one of ten boxes that Davey had recently supplied them with.
As she turned to the table Mum had placed the catering-sized
white tub in the centre. She winked, fussed Grace's hair for a
second.

'What d'you reckon to that, then?' she asked with a nod to the
tub. As Mum fetched the milk from the fridge Grace took up a
seat at the table. The tub was packed with tiny white mice
moulded from chocolate. They were tumbled in every which way
and Grace thought they looked trapped, as if someone, possibly a
giant ginger cat, had lured them into the tub on a promise of
Swiss cheese. The ones who were right side up seemed desperate,
clamouring to push out beneath the others who were upside
down. Dead-looking.

'Pressie for you,' Mum said, sitting down with her mug of tea,
'from Davey.'

It was a new sensation. None of Mum's boyfriends had ever bought her a pressie before.

The mice tasted chemical and sickly.

Davey took on the guise of Father Christmas, someone who only visited at night while she slept and who left presents in his wake. Grace did not have much contact with Mum's boyfriends, most of her memories of the men were scowling faces glimpsed through a smokescreen of cigarette, the backs of heads of figures seated at the kitchen table, back to the door, leg folded across knee, feet in big shoes or boots tapping impatiently to the radio or to some inner tune Grace couldn't hear. Gold rings seemed to glint through most of the memories too, heavy chunks of gold decorated with sovereign coins or black onyx, silver rings that seemed to be fashioned from tiny skulls. All the memories were associated with the words 'Why don't you go and play in your room?'

Nan's husband, Grace's grandfather, was, as Nan put it, 'long gone', which Grace assumed meant he was dead. Her own father did not figure in their lives at all having been 'long gone' before she was born. However, Grace wasn't sure that this time Nan meant he was dead. Her dad was simply a blank of space, as if someone had taken scissors and snipped around him. He had never featured, there were no photos and until she was four Grace assumed that everyone lived with their nan and their mum. Most of the people who had collected her friends from playgroup and school had been nans and mums. It was only in Class One that someone asked about her dad.

If Grace asked questions she did not get answers.

'Have I got a dad?'

'Nope. Do you want this boiled egg?'

There was nothing to go on. Most of the time she completely forgot she was supposed to have a dad, remembering in odd brief flashes, the kind of moment you have when you realize you've left your umbrella on the bus, but nothing more.

The only other man in her life was Mr Pownall.

It seemed to Grace that ever since her true lie to rescue Jonathan, Mr Pownall had been colouring in her exercise books in red felt-tip pen. No matter if she had tried hard and there were ticks, there was no 'Good!' or 'Sound effort' at the bottom like there was on Jonathan's book. Even Thick Thimon got a neatly printed 'Well tried'. His Samson portrait had a starring role in the 'Temple Tableau' on the display board behind her. The pillars Samson was bound to were cut out of sugar paper and painted in with thick black powder paint. Everyone had been allowed to make figures for the temple crowd scene. Grace had made a figure of a fine lady wearing a red tissue-paper toga with bright orange wool spiralled on for hair. There had been a big plastic ice-cream tub of sweet papers and Grace had crafted a golden crown for her fine lady and a silver girdle. A girdle. A kind of belt from ancient times. She had read about them in the library last week in a book of Greek myths. Grace lost herself in the manufacture of her sugar-paper goddess.

They had gone out for lunchtime and on their return Mr Pownall and some of the boys had begun putting up the display. The temple pillars were stuck up. All except Grace's pillar. She had felt-tipped curlicued carving at the top of hers, had tried to make it look like a lion's head and mane. It was nowhere to be seen. Grace watched as Mr Pownall and his helpers worked their way through the pile of pillars. The children started to stick their temple figures up and a small scrap broke out over the rubber glue. Mr Pownall shouted, someone knocked into the tables and sent two jars of paint-daubed water sprawling across the floor. Mr Pownall shouted again and then sent Grace with Thick Thimon to fetch the mop and bucket from the caretaker's room.

It was locked and Mr Kent was elsewhere so Grace and Thick Thimon had to wait around in the entrance hall. The huge coir doormat sat like a hairy island on the polished parquet floor.

'Grathe? . . . Grathe? . . . Reckon we could thkid it?' Simon asked, his foot scuffing at the edges of the mat, watching it shift and slide. Shaking her head, Grace turned away to look at the fish in the big tank by Mr Montgomery's office.

Mr Kent in his crisp blue coveralls came in through the door to the infants with his toolbox and let them into his stockroom, which smelled powerfully of floor wax. They waited for him to fill the bucket with hot soapy water and then wheeled it back through the assembly hall towards their classroom.

Grace was allowed to mop the floor, neatly wiping up the mess of paint water and glue.

'That's enough. Don't need to see your face in it,' Mr Pownall remarked. As he did so Grace looked at the display. She could not see her fine lady's face with the felt-tip Cleopatra-style eyes anywhere. Simon grabbed the mop and was slopping water.

'ENOUGH.' Everyone froze. Mr Pownall made a feint as if he was going to lash Simon with the mop handle. Simon flinched and Mr Pownall jabbed the mop handle towards Grace.

'Take it back,' Mr Pownall commanded. Grace took possession of the mop. Simon began to wheel the bucket.

'No. It doesn't take TWO of you,' he stated and handed Simon a stack of *Maths at Work* workbooks to give out.

But it did take two of them. On her own Grace found the bucket veered and was unruly. Her arms ached from trying to hold the mop and steer the bucket. She knew better than to leave a trail of mucky water along the corridor and through the hall.

By the time she returned the Samson display was finished and the class were working their way through page six of the workbooks. Grace sat down quickly to begin. She wasn't finished by the time the afternoon playtime bell rang. Everyone was sitting up straight ready to go outside, packing up pencils, closing workbooks.

'Not you.' Mr Pownall's voice was a full stop and his finger speared towards the workbook page. Grace felt a rush of panic. It was as if she couldn't think straight when Mr Pownall was near. She felt her eyes sting with tears and blinked them back. Couldn't see the page if she cried and, besides, she didn't want Mr Pownall to see she was a crybaby. Everyone knew how he treated crybabies. She was nearly at the last question on page six. Nearly. Nearly.

After a moment of scratching at the board in his spider-writing Mr Pownall turned. 'You may go outside when you have completed page seven.' He put his chalk down, wiped his hands on the dusty cloth he kept in his pocket. 'I will return momentarily.' And he headed off to the staff room for his cup of tea.

Grace felt the panic rush out of her, following him like a flood tide through the door. Gone. She took a breath. No one else had done page seven, she knew. It was quiet, no one could see, she would do page seven. Then, tomorrow, when they were all asked to do page seven she would be able to go straight to page eight. Her pencil needed sharpening.

As the wood curls fluttered down she saw her temple goddess lying at the bottom of Mr Pownall's metal bin, beneath a couple of snotted tissues and some sugar-paper offcuts.

Back in her seat, the numbers on page seven tangled. She looked up. As she did so she saw that the rooks had come. Five again today, one perched on the gable of the nearest pre-fab garage. As she watched two more flapped into view, dodging their way into the topmost branches. The rooks shifted and sorted positions until they were perched, could see clear across the playground. Grace understood suddenly why they had come.

One. Two, three. Four. Five, six, seven.

She folded the goddess into the pocket of her pinafore. Secret. Golden. Girdled. Then she sat back at her desk and began to untangle page seven.

When the bell rang and Mr Pownall returned, Grace, page seven completed, was sitting up straight at her desk, arms folded.

Mum and Nan didn't realize what was happening. Grace did not tell them that she had had no playtimes since the Samson day. Each day she arrived at school to find that her answers to page seven had been rubbed out and each playtime she redid them. For variety, and probably because he was wearing out all the school erasers, Mr Pownall also kept her indoors on a variety of cleaning and tidying tasks. No pencil sat unsharpened in the pencil pots, no stack of craft paper remained unshuffled, no glue pot sticky.

But home-time was the worst. Mr Pownall dismissed everyone according to a regimented system of orderliness. Eagerness to leave would get you nowhere, but sitting rigidly to attention with your shoelaces neatly tied would. Grace sat each afternoon with her anorak zipped to her chin, arms folded, spine achingly straightened, as each child dismissed around her upended their chair onto the desk. Inner Side were neat and quiet, they could go. Back Top Row may go, but no, wait, Grace, not you. She sat alone, the upturned chair legs kicking out around her.

'Stand up,' he would say after he had spent two minutes wiping the blackboard, straightening chairs. Grace stood.

'Five times table.' He would request it, like someone ordering tea at Montefiori's. Grace rattled off the table, all the way to twelve times five.

'Eight times table. Backwards. From twelve.'

When it became clear to him that Grace knew all her times tables backwards he threw down a new challenge.

Hands on your head.

Stand on your chair.

Stand on your desk.

Mr Pownall says hop on one leg. Wrong leg. Begin again.

Mr Pownall says sing your six times table. Odd numbers first.

Mr Pownall says. Mr Pownall says. Mr Pownall says.

But Mr Pownall did not see the rooks gathering. Each afternoon as he read a chapter of their story book aloud, Grace looked out towards the trees. There were two rooks at first, standing watch by the highest nest. As Mr Pownall finished the story and everyone readied themselves to go home Grace, returning from the cloakroom, would see five rooks in readiness for the five times table. A crack of wings brought seven for the seven times table.

The class had had PE and Mr Pownall had used Grace for target practice during the wet-weather game of Benchball in the assembly hall. Now everyone was outside because the rain had cleared and Grace found herself at her desk with the freshly blanked page seven. She knew all the answers off by heart. Outside, the rooks had gathered on the banking at the edge of the playing field and were picking out worms like spaghetti. Grace knew suddenly what she would do.

Page seven took her no time to complete and pages eight and nine were not a problem. She had brought the pen from home. It was a Parker pen with a tiny silver arrow for the clip. It had a green and silver casing and was another present from Davey. It had been waiting on the table at breakfast in a neat plastic box.

She completed page ten just as the bell rang and the children began hurtling across the playground. She could hear the door banging open, footsteps cantering in and Mr Pownall's voice.

'OUTSIDE. WAIT IN AN ORDERLY LINE OUTSIDE.'

In the distance she could hear Mrs Lucas's voice as her class monitors fetched the instruments trolley – 'Tambourines, Gillian' – and the chinkle of triangles being taken out of their box.

Mr Pownall did not open the workbook until much later in the afternoon. They had had their spelling test and now it was quiet reading time. Grace's heart was thundering and she felt sick. The book before her didn't seem to be written in English, it was written in small black sticks all at odd angles.

He opened the workbook, reaching as he did so for a new packet of stubby rectangled erasers. As the page fell open he didn't look up, he seemed to turn to stone. The workbook page almost turned by itself. Backwards. Again. And again. Grace wondered if time was spinning backwards, if there was the faintest possibility it could rewind itself to the true lie moment and she would do it differently, would sit as ashen-faced and tight-lipped as everyone else.

As Mr Pownall began to dismiss the class – 'Simon. Very smart. You may go' – so the men from the council unlocked the gate at the far end of the playing field and unloaded the mowers.

'Alison. Ramrod straight. You may go.'

He sent them out one by one on this afternoon. The mowers started up in a cloud of black diesel that furled into the stand of trees. Where there had been three rooks waiting for Grace, now there were none.

Mr Pownall folded the workbook back on itself, the spine cracking. He put it down in front of Grace.

'Who gave you pen permission?' he asked. Only the neatest handwriters were given pen permission. Grace had beautiful joined-up writing, far more graceful and tidy even than Mr Pownall's, but he had denied her pen permission. Grace was silent. No true lie sprang to her mind. All she could see were the stick markings she'd made, the plus and minus and equals.

'Did you go into the pen cupboard and take a pen without permission?'

Grace shook her head.

'Show me the pen.' His voice made the words into slices. Grace didn't move, she knew what would happen to the pen; it would be taken to The Drawer and she'd never see it again.

'Give me the pen.' He took a step closer so that his thigh, whipping forward, could jar the desk, make the jaw of the lid snap at her, its rounded edge catching Grace in the ribs.

'Now.'

Grace was immobile, did not even flinch as his arm came soaring out of the sky and the palm of his hand lashed across her cheek with a sound like splitting timber.

She could feel every fingermark on her skin. It was burning, but that might have been the heat given off by Mr Pownall's face as hot white flecks of spit fizzed at the corners of his white-lipped mouth.

'Get-out-get-out.' He yanked her out of her seat by her shoulder socket. Grace heard her bone creak, the soft material of her anorak stretched taut beneath his fingers.

'Get-out-get-out.'

He was half-chasing, half-carrying her towards the door now, her feet tippy-toed under her.

Then the door shut and she was in the cloakroom and the cold spring draught through the doors revived her, icy against the scorch-marked handprint on her face.

Grace found she could not walk as far as the library. Her legs were jelly and she couldn't breathe. She had not cried, did not want to cry, but her lungs felt dry and scoured out. There was a horrid squeaking noise and as Grace walked through the shopping precinct she realized it was her own breath making it.

She could not go to Nan's shop. Nan would be cross. Instead she walked the long way round past the indoor market to bring her out in front of A Cut Above.

Inside, she was glad it was busy, Fran twirling hair madly, all the washbasins soapy. It would be safe inside. No one would notice her.

Grace pushed the heavy glass door open a little and slithered in. There was pop music playing on the radio and someone laughed. The noises softened Grace's edges as if she had travelled out of the real world and now she'd landed back. She took the seat in the far corner of the window by the big Swiss cheese plant. She thought she could hide under the almost umbrella-sized leaves and watch their cut-out shadows cast onto the floor. But now she was there she just felt glad to feel the chair holding her up. It felt as if all her blood was running too fast and she was still making that horrid squeaking noise. Her left eye was blurry where Mr Pownall's thumbnail had grazed across it. Just thinking about that made her breath squeak even more.

And worse, far worse, Fran spotted her instantly. The hairdryer ceased, Fran's lady turned with half-done hair as Fran's mules clacked across the shop.

'Gracie?' Her voice was soft and anxious. She reached up to touch Grace's hair gently, to smooth a soft and cooling hand across the handprint scar. 'Gracie, who did this?'

Grace had more squeak than breath and funny little splashing black puddles in front of her eyes. Fran reached around her and held her tight.

'Gracie . . . Gracie . . . you're safe now . . . safe now . . .'

Grace melted into Fran's soft, black jumper, felt her lips kiss her hair, the mingled scents of vanilla skin and hairspray soothing her. She could feel the vibration in Fran's chest as she turned to the salon.

'Mel, get some of that squash and a couple of chocolate biscuits now. Sandra, nip and fetch Yvonne.'

Later, nipped and fetched summed up Nan's mood as, Grace now at her side, she locked up the shop. The keys made a harsh sound as she dashed them into her handbag.

'And don't be late in the morning, we've got that German delivery coming in,' Nan barked at Debbie as she stepped away.

Grace felt to blame for Debbie's whipped-dog expression as Nan's hand clawed at her sleeve.

'Come on, you.' She glanced down at Grace's face, her eye barely glancing over the slapped cheek. 'What you were thinking of I don't know,' she began as they walked towards the car park steps. 'Showing me up like that. God's sake, Grace.'

But at home, the handprint a more faded crimson now, Mum thought very differently. Nan had stood before Grace pointing a painted fingernail at her and saying what a thoughtless brat she was. Mum took one look at the handprint then her fingers chucked Grace lightly under the chin. 'Who did it Grace?'

'God, the FUSS that has to be made over a junior school scrap.' Nan's lighter tutted in disgust as she lit her cigarette.

'Why don't you give your gums a rest, eh, Mam?' Mum snapped at Nan and then stroked Grace's handprinted cheek.

'Oh yeah. Why don't I? Being bloody fetched from the shop as if it was a national disaster. Making a right drama out of it all, showing me up in front of—'

Mum turned, pointing now, their two outstretched fingers like duelling pistols aimed at each other.

'This is not about showing you up. Christ, Mam, look at her.' Mum's fingers pinched Grace's chin, jerked her cheek around towards Nan.

'So? She's not bleeding, is she? She's not cracked her skull open, has she? What's the fucking fuss about?'

Nan pushed Grace's head this way, that way, riffled sharp nails through her hair. 'She need stitches anywhere? I don't think so. Go and wash your face. Now.' And she gave Grace a mean shove. It had no real force behind it but jelly-legged Grace lost her balance, toppled and the slightly splayed legs of the kitchen chair finished the job. It seemed, as she landed with a crack on the lino, that she broke like a vase.

After the tears had scalded the rest of her skin Mum took her upstairs and they washed her face with a fresh flannel and changed her clothes. Then Grace was deposited in front of the telly with some cherryade and the cure-all of a Curly-Wurly.

Mum had shut the kitchen door and the television interrupted the rest, so Grace caught only snippets of raised voices and could make no real sense of them.

'If you hadn't been prick-teasing Dougie Pownall . . .'

What Grace could not know, did not ever find out, was how Dougie Pownall, released from his classroom into the pub, had lusted over his beer one Friday at Nan, a woman with the emotional sensibility of the neatly cut pork chops she blow-jobbed from Roberts Brothers Butchers. Dougie Pownall filled an empty corner of her Friday night while she waited for those very same brothers. It was no great leap for Dougie to begin a vendetta against Grace. Dougie thought he had become a teacher to impart knowledge to the next generation but really his only vocation was venting his bitter spleen on a handy supply of powerless nine-year-olds.

The kitchen door was whipped open and Mum stamped out into the hall. Grace heard her pick up the phone.

'Oh I'll sort it. She's MY daughter. You've done e-fucking-nough.'

Then she looked up and hooked her foot around the living-room door to tug it shut.

*

The next day Grace breathed more easily in what seemed to be a pocket of invisibility. Mr Pownall did not see her. His eyes glanced across her as he searched for an answer to question nine. Anybody? Anybody except that invisible girl in the back row.

Outside, the rooks had gathered in the treetops having picked the playing field clean. Grace did not need to count them, to know there were nine. Mr Pownall walked home that way, cut down past the garages to his little house. She saw them clawing out his hair, knitting it into the fabric of their nests, feeding his eyeballs and the soft bits of his tongue to their dagger-beaked chicks.

'Back Top Row, you may go,' he said as the bell rang for home time. Grace scuffled out and headed home. It was Wednesday and the library was closed.

On Thursday Mr Montgomery introduced the class to a new teacher, Miss Addecott. He did not mention Mr Pownall. Grace found her eyes wandering to the door, waiting for him to enter. When Mr Pownall did not come her gaze slithered towards the garages and the rooks snagged in the treetops, looking fine-feathered and fed.

They were going to have a music lesson. Someone had to go and fetch the instruments trolley.

'Alison, would you like to go? And Grace?'

Grace and Alison walked down to Class Two to collect the trolley. As they moved through the entrance hall Grace noticed there was another smell weaving its way to her under cover of the floor wax and the wet coconut whiff of the coir doormat. It was strange and yet familiar. As they wheeled the instrument's trolley back through the hall Grace suddenly knew what the mysterious scent was.

The combination of Christmas and PE that made up Davey.

4

THE LOCK TUMBLES

Alec looked at the pile of invoices and court forms on his desk and thought of them travelling to the typing pool where Gina or one of the others would make carbon-paper sandwiches of them. Then they would be 'enveloped', as Mrs Fea, the supervisor, put it. Gina would lick the envelopes and they would be sent in a canvas bag to the franking room.

That was the difference between Gina and Mrs Fea, Alec reasoned. Gina licked the envelopes she sent. She'd hold them to her lips with those painted nails, nails that looked like car enamel, a filed and glossy perfection. Then the lips, also glossy, would part and the tongue lick across the gummed edge.

Mrs Fea, on the other hand, had a hideous Bakelite dish on her desk containing a mouldering sponge that had done service since 1952. She damped it each morning and her nicotine-yellow fingers wiped envelopes across it at Formula One speed.

A couple of mates had suggested that Alec ask Gina out. Smiley Mike had even gone so far as to drop his name into a few idle chats by the tea trolley and this one-man survey suggested that Gina would say yes.

Alec liked the look of Gina, that was true. Different from Cherry in every way. Darker colouring. More womanly hips with a deeper parabola to her arse as she bent by the filing cabinets. The varnished nails and perfect make-up interested him in as much as he'd like to wipe it all off and see what the real Gina was like. He suddenly imagined her in a bubble bath and saw his hands, gloved in bubbles, unable to hold all of each breast. They were spilling and tipping over his fingers, smothering his palms, where Cherry's had fit exactly, which made him think of her nipples and the bumps and runnels of them under his tongue.

Gina was too plastic for him. It was nothing to do with Cherry having hijacked his confidence. Nope. Nothing to do with that. He couldn't concentrate now, he needed to stretch his legs.

The company rarely caught up with the debtors they pursued. Alec had worked there for three years and was no longer shocked at how people absconded and vanished. They paid a private detective agency a retainer to search out their most costly debtors but even they simply sat on the money and filed monthly reports of how many hours they'd staked out the bingo club car park and come up with nothing. They had a team of bailiffs who fared better. They were led by a lean, grey Scot, Alistair, who was in competition with the detectives and was racking up a record. He was tenacious and single-minded and there was nothing he enjoyed more than an early morning swoop on rented accommodation. Alec didn't like him. He made his back itch because he thought of Corporal Drew.

*

When he was seventeen Alec had joined the army. When he broke the news his mother couldn't speak without crying for two days. He was part of a team and although the drill sergeants shouted and some nights he fell into bed with every bone aching in his body from the punishments and assaults he'd put it through, he felt he was not wasting time, that he was fulfilling a purpose, to protect, to be a guardian.

He muscled up. He was fitted out. He liked the angles his face made now he was shorn of hair, felt he was transforming, becoming his true self, a man of sinew. He threw himself into everything, honing his skills of observing people. He wanted to be a jump ahead. He was eighteen. He hadn't known any better.

Eventually Alec was posted to Northern Ireland and began duty at a vehicle checkpoint on the Fermanagh border. They were out in a cold and damp portakabin on a country road where they were to keep a weather eye on traffic in red diesel as well as the terrorists.

He didn't mind partnering Keith Robertson. Keith was all right, a fair-minded man with a wife and a little kiddie who might sit and play cards with one eye out for owls. Keith was into the wildlife and interesting to talk to on the long dark nights. On the other nights Corporal Warren Drew was the wildlife, a man as mad as a bear.

One Friday it was late and having cheered up his evening harassing old ladies coming back from a knitting bee in a cross-border village hall, Corporal Drew was delighted to spot the Hillman Imp. With dark, ivy-green bodywork and a funny little beige plastic roof it was a vehicle Alec recognized. The girls inside were sisters who played folk music in local pubs and clubs. They had seen them several times before and each time Corporal Drew had tried out his charms on them all. His eye roved always to the eldest, a tall slim girl named Audra with long chestnut hair that, to Alec, looked as if it contained moonlight. Audra lit up Corporal Drew's night sky.

She had smiled and been polite the first time they stopped them. She spoke in a soft voice when Corporal Drew asked her questions. He made them up, stood with a clipboard as if they were all written down and he had to be official and tick every box when in fact there was nothing written on the clipboard. Audra answered every question.

'You're all sisters?'

'Yes.'

'Names?'

'I'm Audra . . .'

'The eldest?'

'Yes. Next is Anne . . .'

Anne held up her hand from the back seat and gave a nervous but polite smile.

'I'm Ellen,' said the dark-haired girl beside her. Corporal Drew leaned into the open window, ostensibly to get a better look at the two sisters but in reality he was inhaling the scent of Audra.

'Good. You there, who are you?'

The girl in the passenger seat struggled not to flinch.

'She's Aoife. She's our youngest.'

Audra gave her a warm and reassuring smile of safety. As her head turned to her sister her sheaf of chestnut hair fell gracefully from behind her shoulder. It seemed to sigh, Alec thought.

Corporal Drew tried to take a telephone number but Audra

was diplomatic and called on the protection of her dad who did not allow them to give out their phone number.

'It's official. It's on my form.' Corporal Drew insisted.

Alec could see the women tense, as if their little car shrank smaller and their shoulders knitted closer together. Audra's polite brightness sparkled, brittle as frost.

'Don't want to get me into trouble, do you?' Corporal Drew insisted.

Drew tried the number next evening. It was a fake. No such number, came the dial tone.

A week later the Hillman Imp was pulled up again at the checkpoint. Once more it was late, after midnight. In the back Aoife had been asleep, leaning against her sister's shoulder. She had awoken now and was wide-eyed as Corporal Drew made them all get out of the vehicle.

There was no need to get them out. Alec moved near to Corporal Drew, tried to speak privately.

'We don't need to do this, Drew. Just leave it.'

'Shut it.'

Corporal Drew turned to the sisters, huddled into their coats in the winter cold. He waved the muzzle of his gun at them, swinging it from its shoulder strap as if it was his third arm.

'Coats off and over there.' He motioned to Alec. 'Search the pockets.'

Alec hesitated. Corporal Drew barked at him, making the sisters jump out of their skin at the sudden outburst of sound as if he had shot at them with his voice. Alec searched the pockets and found the usual debris of sweet wrappers and tissues.

'Nothing here.'

'Empty your bags, then.'

He pointed with the gun again. The sisters looked confused, looked towards Audra. Corporal Drew took a step, hooked the muzzle of his machine gun into the strap of Audra's bag and lifted it from her shoulder. He tipped the contents onto the roadway, kicked through them with his boot.

'Didn't get paid tonight, then?' he asked. 'Gig didn't go too well, did it not?'

'It went well enough, so.' She reached into her skirt pocket, took out a small envelope. Corporal Drew motioned for her to hand it over but when she did he wouldn't reach for it, made her step nearer, nearer until they could have been dancing. He took the envelope, counted the money. Alec handed the coats back to the sisters and they received them with nods of thanks.

'That phone number you gave me before . . .' he folded the notes over his fingers as if he was going to put them back into the envelope, but instead he held her to ransom, '. . . can't get through. Dial tone says no such number.'

'Must have misdialled it. Only takes one number out of its place, doesn't it?' Audra's smile shone forth, Alec felt it had the power of a protective forcefield. He thought for a minute that they were princesses, some magic brood that had been out dancing, and that Corporal Drew was tugging at something dark he would never understand.

'I might have misremembered it. Write it here. On the back of my hand.'

He took a pen from his pocket. Did not relinquish his hold on the fold of notes.

'You know, it might be better if you give me your number. I've already told you about my father. He's very strict about who I see. Very paternal, so he is.'

Corporal Drew said nothing, offered the pen like a dagger. Which Audra did not take.

'I'm sorry. I don't mean anything by it. It's just the way my dad is. I don't want to cause you trouble, Corporal Drew.'

Alec could hear what she was trying to do but all she achieved was to bind herself more closely to Corporal Drew.

'You won't cause me trouble. You don't know me yet, Audra. That's all. You'll come to know me.'

Alec thought that Corporal Drew was so determined to extract phone numbers and promises that a van load of the Irish Republican Army pulling grenade pins out with their teeth would be waved through. Audra wrote out the number and was allowed back in the car. Alec saw Audra shaking and knew it wasn't the cold.

That number was the right number but, somehow, Audra was never in.

Alec dreaded the next guard shift at the checkpoint. Corporal Drew was on again and his mood was charged as he lay in wait. Alec thought he looked taller, stretched with tension. He was full of jokes and stories and each time an engine could be heard his eyes were like darts through the window. It was a quiet watch. Rain saved them that night. Gush. Splatter. Wash. Through the guttering on the guard hut.

'I can't hold it any longer, I have to have a wazz. Hold the fort.' Corporal Drew moved the two steps to the cramped room with the chemical toilet inside. As he shut the door Alec heard the engine. He stepped out to see the Hillman Imp approaching over the brow of the hill. Corporal Drew was whistling 'The Wild Colonial Boy' through his teeth now and Alec could hear, above the rushing of the gutter, the pissing-horse torrent flowing from Corporal Drew.

The Imp slowed but Alec knew what he must do. It was very late and Corporal Drew was worked up. Alec stepped forward three paces and waved them on with an urgent gesture. Audra, driving, changed up a gear and drove on through. Alec saw their white faces ranged through the car, Audra's white fingers on the steering wheel. Their brake lights tipped over the next hill just as Corporal Drew stopped whistling.

Back in barracks Corporal Drew talked about her. The girl who did not know what was good for her. Him. Life was that simple.

Whenever he dreamed about the following watch Alec saw the stars wink out and night spread itself like ink. Audra had come over the brow of the hill and Corporal Drew had let her drive closer, closer, closer, until it seemed he would have sense enough to wave her through. He stepped out at the last moment, making her stamp on the brakes, the wheels skidding so that she didn't hit him. The car skewed just slightly. Audra was about to wind down the window but Corporal Drew was reaching for the door, opening it.

'If you would please step out of the vehicle, miss,' he requested with aristocratic politeness. Audra did not hesitate. Left the keys in the ignition, her handbag on the seat beside her, her coat slung across the back seat. She had no smile that evening, did not blink.

'If you would please step into the guardhouse, miss.' Corporal Drew ushered her with a sweep of his arm to the step of the portakabin. Alec felt his heart lurch against his ribs. Audra did not step forward. Drew jerked his head towards the open door. 'That's an order.'

Audra held his gaze steady. 'You can't give me an order. I'm not a soldier. I'm a civilian.'

'I can do what I like, I'm the one with a gun.'

Alec took a step towards Drew. 'Let her go.'

Drew gave a scornful laugh. Alec took a couple of steps to put himself between them. At the second step Corporal Drew launched his elbow backwards, and as Alec folded Corporal Drew punched upwards into his face and he tumbled, his cheek grazing against the road surface, aware of Corporal Drew picking Audra off the ground and carrying her into the portakabin. Alec lunged at his ankles trying to pull him down but Corporal Drew kicked at him as if he were a bothersome dog.

The door locked as Alec, nose bent out of shape and bleeding down into his uniform, grabbed for the handle. Inside, Audra gave a roar of anger and fear. Alec shouldered the door and it gave slightly. He battered himself at it until it fell forward and he stumbled in. The main room was empty and Audra's grunts of resistance could be heard from behind the lavatory door. Bump. Thud. Clatter. Scuffle. Alec pushed at the door. Corporal Drew had her on the floor behind it so Alec could not get in.

Through the window. The square of it just large enough to admit him, lifting himself into it by the guttering, feeling the slimed leaves and crud of the gutter under his fingers. He dropped down inside. Corporal Drew had Audra pinned and was unfastening his belt as Alec leapt on him from behind.

Later, Alec drove her home in her own car. Her parents were at the door as the car rolled up. Her brothers were piling out of another car that had pulled up in the road before him. Alec did not wait around for explanations. He ran the five miles all the way back to the guard hut.

Corporal Drew reported an incident at the checkpoint, made up a gang of terrorists and a fictitious car to explain their bruises, which Alec did not correct.

'You're a good lad,' Corporal Drew had congratulated him, with a wrestler hug and a slap on the back. 'You'll go far if you stick with your mates,' he assured him. Alec did not feel like a good lad as he choked on the truth.

Alec was relieved when Audra's brothers mistook him for Drew and shot him. As he lay in the road watching the car's head-lights supernova into the night he wanted to laugh but his lungs seemed to be full of liquid. Corporal Drew had not been on duty that night. Audra's brothers recognized only that this bastard was the bastard who had dropped her home, battered and distressed, and run off into the night.

Alec was invalided out shortly afterwards. Corporal Drew had a brother in the motor trade who needed a good mechanic, would give on-the-job training as a favour.

'Hoi. That string I pulled. My brother says you won't take it.' Corporal Drew had Alec cornered in the corridor. 'What you play-ing at?'

Alec could remember the electrical shock of fear he had felt as Corporal Drew's square hand landed, avuncularly threatening, on his shoulder.

'It's a good spot. He'll see you right.'

Alec had only one thing to say. 'You don't owe me anything.'
Corporal Drew had shrugged it off.

Alec was twenty-four now. He didn't want to be with the debt-collection company but he didn't know where else to go.

Alec did not watch much television these days, not since the end of *Now You See Him*. He had never been in the habit of it. He read sci-fi and thrillers and he cooked, and sometimes played five-a-side with the lads from work.

That last evening, he had come home late but he'd still made the casserole. It was an old favourite, chicken, leeks and mushrooms, served up with buttery mash, just the way his mum had taught him all those years ago. She had begun to teach him to bake when he was small. After his dad left she took a job. The insurance office where she worked was on the eastern side of the city, a good bus ride away, and it meant she might not always be home in time. Alec liked to cook. It relaxed him. He worked with men who didn't even heat a tin of beans in a pan; there was Lee who lived on pies from the local baker's and Paul who ate from the chippy every night except Sunday when he was forced to fall back on his own resources and eat jam sandwiches. That was as far as they went, the spreading of jam on bread. Alec didn't get it: food was a fundamental, you need to eat so learn to cook. They ribbed him a bit about being poncey but Alec didn't care. He cited Michael Caine in that Harry Palmer film, seducing a blonde with a scrambling of eggs.

He'd been out of the office for a couple of days that week. Terry, his boss, had asked him to drive out to the coast for a meeting with one of their more diligent detectives in Morecambe on the Monday. He had a good lead on one of their debtors so Terry asked Alec to nip out there with Alistair and the paperwork. Alistair liked this detective, Mr Brewer. Mr Brewer had been a teacher and had what Alistair called 'instinct'.

They spent two days sitting in a car parked near Happy Mount Park as Alistair and Mr Brewer swapped divorce stories until Mr Brewer's 'instinct' told them the debtor had got wind something was up and done a further flit. It had been a change of scene, one Alec had not realized he needed. He had spent the time looking out of the car window at the distant view of the Lake District that it afforded. He had walked, in his head, along the zigzag of ridges. The sea air got into his head and he wondered about making changes, he wondered about running away to the seaside himself. But then he got back into the car and drove home and made the casserole, and the sea air was breathed out of him.

When Gina approached his desk on the Thursday and said, 'There are two policemen here to see you. In Terry's office, right now,' Alec's mind was preoccupied with case 127/E our ref: AH/GW. He assumed that Mr Brewer had had another attack of instinct and landed them someone.

Alec didn't see the look on Gina's face, or rather he did see it but he didn't interpret it. There wasn't any need in that moment as he rose from his chair.

He would dream later of staying in the chair, of turning away from Gina, clicking and re-clicking his plastic company pen and proofreading his report 127/E our ref: AH/GW.

Terry was standing behind his desk.

'Shut the door, Alec,' he said in a tight, quiet voice. One of the officers stood up and the other, riding shotgun beside him in a beige raincoat, stood too.

'Alec Holm?'

'Yes.'

'I'm Detective Sergeant Hayes, this is my colleague Detective Constable Strachan . . .'

Alec gave a nod to the constable who, hands in the pockets of his beige raincoat, did not nod in return. Now, looking back, Alec saw that here was another red flag he had not seen, a bright crimson pennant fluttering over the detective constable's unswerving head.

'We'd like to ask you a few questions about your relationship with Deborah Winstanley.'

Alec faltered, trying to dredge up the name, she must be one of his old cases because the name wasn't ringing any bells. He looked blankly at the detective constable who produced a photograph.

At first, Alec didn't recognize her. Her make-up had not been rubbed off in the photo and she looked bright and shining, her smile wide and genuine. Only at last did he see the faerie woman from the seventh floor.

Alec explained he didn't have a relationship with this woman, had not, until now, known her name. They asked questions. Alec gave truthful answers. How he had helped her at the pub. Walked her home. They listened.

Within half an hour he found himself in the back of a police car, heading towards the police station, ready to help with their enquiries.

A neighbour had found her on the balcony on Monday evening. She had come out after work to water her geraniums and had seen Deborah Winstanley's hand poking under the gap between their balcony rails. At first, she had told the police, she had seen the curled fingers and thought it was a mouse.

They asked Alec why he had not come forward earlier and he answered truthfully. He had been away, had not, in any case, seen the news or listened to the radio. He told them about the days away in Morecambe and about Alistair and Mr Brewer's instincts.

They asked about events on Sunday night and Alec told them everything he could remember, from sitting in the pub with Smiley Mike and his latest squeeze to the moment he waited on the landing until Deborah Winstanley locked the door to her flat. Then he also remembered waving to Mona outside the chip shop. Notes were taken and he made a statement.

But they didn't let him go.

There were no windows in the interview room. Alec's watch seemed to stop dead and then, on a whim, scurry forward three hours.

'Do you remember what time you left the pub with Deborah Winstanley on Sunday evening?' the sergeant asked. Alec shook his head, then thought about the question, shook his head again, wanted to make everything clear.

'I didn't leave with her.'

'You said earlier that you walked her home.'

'Yes. I did. Later. But she left the pub with the other bloke. The one with the gold ring. The bully. I saw them leave and I—' Alec was blinded by the knowledge of how what he was going to say would come out as 'I followed her.'

'You saw her leave. What did you do?'

'I followed. I had a gut feeling about him. That was all. He was rough with her.'

Alec could remember it. He saw clearly the grip the man had on her. The way he had wrangled her out of the pub. The way everyone had looked away.

'But you didn't have a relationship with Deborah Winstanley? You didn't know her until Sunday evening?'

'That's right.'

'So why did you follow her out of the pub?'

'I followed them. I thought . . . I thought he looked like trouble.'

They nodded. As if agreeing. As if now a policewoman would enter with a cup of tea and a couple of biscuits and ask him to describe the bully with the gold ring to an Identikit artist. Alec could head home as the picture was circulated. He would be found. They should ask Alistair and Mr Brewer for assistance in the search.

Instead they brought in his handkerchief, stained with Deborah Winstanley's blood. It was in a neat plastic bag, like a sort of museum exhibit. Which it was, as reality, for Alec, became history.

Alec wondered how they knew about it. It was a year ago and nothing to do with this. Then it struck him like a slap that they had questioned Cherry. He remembered the moment, or he thought he did until they began to remember it for him.

He had not wanted to fight that evening. He had wanted to make up and as they walked to the restaurant he had a realization that this was it, the end was here and they would not make it up. Cherry had been curt, giving single-word answers, and several times he'd looked up to find her giving him an odd look, as if he was a boring stranger to her. But Alec had wanted to try.

He had been trying enough for her to slap down the menu before they'd even ordered.

'Could you give us another minute?' he had asked the eager waitress and in turning away he had lost sight of Cherry. He had looked back and she was gone, the menu tilted at an awkward angle across the place setting. She was at the door, walking out. Alec had felt embarrassed and terrified in equal measures. She was like sand now, filtering away from him.

He had not so much walked her home as followed her. He would give them that much. She had tried to get a cab but no one would stop and he had stuck doggedly to her, and when she strutted off on those mad stork-leg high heels he had kept a few paces behind her. Keeping an eye on her. Protective still, even as he understood she was no longer his to protect.

'Will you pack it in, following me?' she had whined wearily at him at the crossing. Her shoulders curved in on themselves with exasperation at him. She couldn't keep her face towards him. He remembered her little boxy handbag, shiny black. Her sigh of deep frustration, the little catch of sadness as she spoke.

'Give it up, Alec. Will you? Please?'

He had to see her to her door, to make it a goodbye. If he just saw the door close on him, he would be able to accept things. He hadn't said this, he had simply followed. Looking back he could see how she might have seen that as menacing. He wasn't a laugh-riot at the best of times, he accepted he was serious, that that had been a deciding factor for Cherry. He could not make her see what was in his heart. He didn't have the mechanism. If she had loved him, had known him at all, she would have seen anyway, it would have been revealed to her. There was something positive to be had from this, then; he could realize his loss wasn't as vast as he'd thought. She was the wrong one. That was all.

But he could see how she could say now that on that last night he had followed her home and looked menacing.

He drew a mental line. He made it thick and dark because the next part needed separate space, clear ground.

They asserted that he had tried to attack her.

They sat in the interview room, the ginger-haired inspector and the detective sergeant in his smooth suit. They read the information to him from what seemed to be a shopping list they had drawn up about him.

Followed. Menaced. Attacked.

Think back. He had an imagined image of the attack now, in his mind. He could see himself slapping Cherry as they stood at the crossing. Saw himself grabbing her to him, holding her tight, making her let him kiss her. He saw it like a film they had edited into his head.

He hadn't done that. He had only stood in the cold night, hands in his jacket pockets, thinking how he wanted her to look at him, how he wanted to kiss her even if it was goodbye.

Think clearly. Slice away the emotion; the way his heart had punched in his throat so he could barely breathe.

They had walked up her path and she had said, 'You're not coming in. I've nothing to talk about.'

'I want to say goodbye,' he had replied, letting her know he knew it was the end. Cherry had opened the door, let it swing into the hallway. Alec saw it was the last moment. She would shut the door and it would be finished.

'Goodbye.' Her voice had been as harsh as the slamming door. It had taken his breath away. He'd wanted more, a leave-taking.

He had rung the bell.

'Go away,' she'd shouted from inside, as if he was a Halloween prankster. And he had battered on the door. Hammered his fist against the glass, kicked out at the wooden panels beneath until the paint flaked like dandruff.

The neighbour had come out then: 'I'm calling the police.'

But there had been no need. He had turned away, not wanting to hurt her. The only person hurt that night was him: his heart, hanging inside his ribcage by its last elastic sinew, his toes, bruised inside his paint-scuffed shoes, his fingers, aching.

He had to concentrate. Remembering back he thought that if they were being accurate then he had, in point of fact, attacked the door, but they weren't here for humorous asides. He was not here for a parking offence.

Once more, carefully, he described the man, the ring, the brown leather jacket.

'What am I wearing, Mr Holm?' The detective inspector moved and his leather jacket creaked around his shoulders, he crossed his hands, angling the left one so that the thick gold wedding band caught the harsh overhead light.

'No. His jacket was more worn. Creased up. Lighter brown.' But Alec could hear in his own voice that he could be describing anybody, making this up.

The detective sergeant cleared his throat. It was obvious now that they had fashioned ideas about him, sat across the table from him, serious-faced, making judgements. It felt like some grotesque version of *Guess Who?* and their guesses were haywire, they didn't know him. They were making him up.

Here were two people, professional men, trained detectives, who had decided he was more than likely to have stabbed and strangled the woman, left her body on the balcony of her seventh-floor flat at Bigby-Weathers Tower. If they had known him at all they would have understood the truth but he was a stranger to them, a man with blood on his jacket, with faerie-blonde hairs tangled into the zip, a man who had left a range of fingerprints in a seventh-floor flat.

He sat very still and cold, as if his blood had stopped running because it knew what darkness lay ahead and hadn't the courage to go there.

5

THE END OF THE JETTY

If she could draw a map of everything and stick in a coloured pin where it began Grace would choose the moment Miss Addecott asked to see Nan.

It had been a long three weeks for Grace since the strap split on her school shoe. She tied it up with an elastic band, looping it round through the little hole and the buckle but almost as soon as she did that the sole began to lift. As she walked it flapped so that her left foot looked as if it was talking to her as they walked. It was glued and flapped itself free five times before Mum found the used-up tube and the dried-up glue on the kitchen floor.

'How many times do I have to tell you, Grace? If it's finished put it in the bin and clean up the mess,' she had shouted. But she had not said anything about the shoe.

At last the back seam split just as the tight squeeze of the toe across her growing feet began to blacken her nail. Miss Addecott, for there was still neither sight nor sound of Mr Pownall, had asked Nan if she could come in to see her after school.

Miss Addecott had shown Nan the shoe, a shabby, exhausted remnant and its slapper of a sidekick. Where the left shoe was rent and torn and smirched with old glue, the right shoe was worn into assymetric wedges, the leather as thin as skin over the far edge where her little toe always wore through.

'. . . so you can see why I have had to send Grace home in her plimsolls today.' Grace's plimsolls were the same ones she had had since Class Three. She was thinking that the little mermaid in the story must have been wearing similar plimsolls and that was why she felt she was walking with nails in her feet. Miss Addecott smiled across a background face of patience and goodwill. Nan seemed to flinch a little.

'Plimsolls?' she snorted derisively, a superior smirk over her face.

Miss Addecott's expression batted away Nan's scorn with a flash of good-hearted threat. 'If she doesn't have any other shoes –' here she glanced down at Nan's pink-painted toenails sprawling from the open toes of some bronze leather strapped sandals – 'then she could wear her plimsolls for another day. After that I think the headmaster would ask you to keep her at home. Mr Montgomery is very hot to trot on school footwear.'

An arch of plucked eyebrow from Nan. 'Is he?'

'All that's required is a suitable shoe. Mr Montgomery prefers them all to wear black but as long as the footwear is sound . . .'

Hence their after-school trawl of the shoe shops of town. Whilst Nan was not ashamed of Grace's footwear, she was horrified at the thought that Grace might be kept out of school and, God forbid, need looking after all day.

For Grace's one pair of hard-wearing clumpy black school

shoes, Nan purchased three pairs of high heels with strappy straps for peeping painted toes. Grace's shoes were made of army surplus leather and felt as if they had reinforced concrete in their soles. They were too big but Nan had insisted in the shop that was 'growing room'. Grace sat at their usual burgundy leatherette booth in Montefiori's coffee shop feeling the shoes trying to break her off at the ankles.

'Sit up,' Nan barked. She was sitting opposite Grace, flicking through a magazine and turning her spoon endlessly in the liquid smoke of her coffee. Grace watched the whirl of steam from the cup and sipped quietly at her coke float. 'Keep Grace Quiet' should have been a section on the menu, filled with vanilla milkshakes, coke floats, egg mayonnaise sandwiches and Genoese fancies.

The black-haired woman approached. She was petite, wearing a shiny black plastic raincoat and pointy black boots on thin legs. Bird legs. With her pale face Grace thought she seemed like a rook. Her eyes were smokily done; she was monochrome where Nan was ruby and ochre.

It happened in such an instant that it seemed it hadn't happened at all. The woman's arm whiplashed out, a small square box of a handbag at the end. The bag clipped Nan across the face. Her left cheekbone took the brunt of bag versus face, and her head torqued sideways like a boxer's before she slewed in the seat. Grace watched as Nan's right hand swiped at Grace's coke float as she fought to stop her slithery leather skirt slipping her under the table.

The shining monochrome woman aimed a pointy boot and kicked. The table lurched again and again and the coffee leapt and splathered but the rook woman had gone before it dripped down onto Nan.

The owner and the waitress moved to help, their hands tugging the table out to reveal Nan twisted beneath it, her skirt rucked up around her waist and showing off the stockings she was wearing.

She was stunned enough to be helped up and the waitress was sent to call a taxi. Grace was kept quiet with a replenished coke float, which she drank because she was supposed to and threw up fifteen minutes later in the taxi. Over her new shoes.

'It has been a bitch of a day' was how Nan greeted Mum on her return from work, and in the morning Grace was greeted with a packed bag and the news that they were taking a break and going to the Lakes. As Nan put it, Debbie could take care of the shop and, after the Archangel Addecott's shoe lecture, who gave a toss about school. They piled into Mum's car and belted up the M6 in a drone of wrong gears and fug of cigarette smoke.

It was Davey's caravan. All the caravans belonged to him, slotted in between the woodland of Scots Pine and Douglas Fir, each with its own little tarmac driveway spurred off the main drag. Mum's battered Renault Four clackered at the left turn into the parking space and they all piled out. They were like lightly smoked herring after their hour or more in the tobacco-chogged car.

'Can't get the door open.' Nan's long fingers snaggled at the key and twisted the handle as if the door could be Chinese-burned into opening. 'He's given us the wrong key.'

Mum chacked up the concrete steps, elbowed her mother out of the way. A twist. A click. The screel of metal on metal as the door opened outwards.

'Get that oiled, for a kick-off,' Nan growled as she pushed inside. Grace was dragging the suitcases and as she pulled the last one over the threshold Nan snatched her French blue vanity case. 'Give that here.'

Davey owned not only all the caravans in the park but also the land they stood on. The sign at the gates read 'Fell Fir Holiday Park'. This particular unit was his alone and in the summer he would sometimes come here and spend six weeks supervising his paying holidaymakers. It didn't involve greeting holidaymakers, he left that to Maureen in reception, and it didn't involve cleaning toilets or mowing the neat rectangles of grass between pitches. It involved opening the tills and taking care of the money. It involved ticking off the maintenance team for a skew-whiff fence and teasing the girl at the till in the camp supermarket. It involved taking his slim cigar out of his mouth long enough to bark an instruction and point. Sausage fingers, Grace thought when she imagined Davey, squared-off sausage fingers, a chunky gold ring on the third finger of his right hand, the light catching off the steel tines of his sunglasses. Not that Grace had ever met Davey. She had answered the phone once and he had said, 'Put your mum on.' No, any image in her head of what Davey looked like came from the scent of his leather jacket and cigars and the pieces she had coloured in for herself from her mother's comments.

Davey was mythic to Grace now. Not only was he a leaver of gifts, he also could get them out of an emergency situation. He was handy in a knock-down, drag-out-of-the-coffee-shop fight. He was handy if Mum was stuck at the supermarket overloaded with bags (with the booze for his party – in their household the fridge was a polar wasteland). He was handy when organizing a visit from one of his mates who owed a favour that could be paid in plumbing.

That first evening the black clouds kept their rain and the wind whispered through the trees as Mum clacked along the tarmac towards the chippy.

'Bloody creepy trees,' Mum muttered and pulled her cardigan tighter around her.

Grace didn't listen to her mother, the trees didn't seem creepy at all. She liked the silhouettes they made against the open sky, the far distant outlines of the mountains, the glimpses of the lake below. And the wind seemed to be saying, *Grace Grace Grace*.

Nan had packed nail varnish and hairspray but not vinegar, salt or coffee, so Grace and her mother were also to call in at the camp shop, where Davey had arranged a tab for them. Mum tried not to look surprised as the girl at the till told her this, pretended, instead, that she'd forgotten 'a few bits' and sent Grace back around the shelves for a loaf of bread, some butter and jam. Then they waited in the chippy, Mum's eyes focused on something out of the window, her eyes glazed.

'Sorry, love, I was miles away,' she confessed when the girl behind the counter called their order.

When they had trudged, chip and grocery laden, back to the caravan, Nan was already dressed up for an evening at the club and had put plates out on the small caravan table. As the newspaper unfolded and let out the hot savoury steam of the meal so Nan eased up and joked about the emergency holiday. 'Who cares about school? Knows too much anyway, that one,' she said with a sideways look at Grace.

This mood seemed very dangerous to Grace. Nan's winking

good humour could tip into sourness without warning. She was like a firework you shouldn't have gone back to.

After they locked the door on her, Grace watched from the front window of the caravan as they tottertapped down the tarmac towards the clubhouse. A car, lights just on in the twilight, slowed and they stuttered out of its way onto the grass verge, their heels sinking in where it was wet after rain. A few more steps and the curve of the road vanished them.

Grace had had no chance to explore other than the expedition to the shop. Nan and Mum had been keen to have a quick tea and doll themselves up for the evening and so Grace had moved from being wedged into the back of Mum's car to being wedged behind the Formica-topped table in the kitchen corner of the caravan. Now she looked round. Her room was tiny, the bed long and thin. Nan had taken the room that was filled with a double bed and Mum had taken the other room, even thinner than Grace's, and piled high with a bunk bed. It seemed to Grace that wherever you went in the caravan you had to squeeze past.

Grace did not watch television much. There was one in the caravan and Nan had switched it on for her before they left. Grace turned it off, just as an audience began a huge rolling wave of laughter. Silence. Footsteps pitter-pattered over the roof of the caravan. Grace listened and then watched as a gull took off with a yell.

There were not many people at the caravan park. It was, after all, out of season. Grace saw it was mostly older couples, a few families with smaller children. She watched two girls, much younger than herself, as they switched on pocket torches and stood shining the light through their hands. They conferred, these sisters, their heads joined together as if they weren't simply talking, as if their mouths moved, their brains communicated through the connecting wires of their hair. Maybe it worked like that with sisters, Grace didn't know. Tired of seeing the red glow of their blood the sisters darted off down a small path into the trees, their parents sauntered after them, chatting, the dad carrying cardigans.

She could see them still, moving through the trees, the shooting stars of torch beams and their outlines, like charcoal people rubbed into the landscape. It was the family who led her to the lake. As the light fell and the view began to change she noticed that the trees were thick and the hill rose behind but something they were running down towards glinted like steel.

Grace watched as the father lifted binoculars to his face. She peered hard, trying to find a line through the trees so she could see what he was looking at. A bird flapped into view, a flying smudge through the treescape, giving a flourished skid to send up a white frill of water. The lakes. That's what they called it.

Grace knelt up on the hard cushions of the built-in seating. She wished she had binoculars to bring the outside closer. She would lift them to her eyes and the cramped rectangles of the caravan would go away, and with a tilt of her head she could be in the treetops.

Later she went to bed without changing into pyjamas. She hid herself under the thin blankets that smelled of old smoke. It was cold, even with her jumper on.

Next morning, they were grumpy. 'Hungover or shagged-out, or both,' Nan considered through a cigarette. Mum's hair was a tangle, dry and knotted with last night's hairspray.

'Where'd you get to?' Nan quizzed.

Grace ate her cereal quickly, seeing that it was time to try to escape. She was too late. Mum plopped herself and her mug of tea beside Grace. If she wanted to leave now she'd have to slide under and out.

'Taking a survey?' Mum snapped and slurped at her tea.

'You got off with the one with the gold tooth, then?' Nan pushed, standing over the table, resting a mug of tea against her folded arm as the smoke furled from the cigarette between her fingers.

'Smelly armpits.' Mum gave a grimace. 'He was like cheap chocolate. Scoff the lot and wonder why you bothered.' She looked at Nan who gave a wry grin and they both laughed. 'But his friend . . . he was the full monty.'

Nan sucked the last dregs of life out of her cigarette before stubbing it out in a saucer. 'Go there again tonight?'

'Might as well. The clubhouse is shit.'

Mum suddenly seemed aware of Grace, turned on her as if scalded.

'What you still doing here? Go on, then, it's the great outdoors. Go and hunt owl pellets or something. It's educational.'

She shifted to let Grace out. Grace catapulted through the door. As she ran across the grass she looked back, saw them sitting across from each other, fresh cigarettes in hand, puffing smoke like dragons.

She had an overwhelming desire to take the path through the woods but it had to be like the last chocolate, she would save it up in case the whole place turned out to be a giant coffee cream. First she would wander around the caravan park, along the tarmacked roadway to the shop.

A woman was sitting reading a magazine in the tiny launderette. Hot damp air smelling powerfully of soap powder fugged across the path. More caravans. Most empty. A bin area and a maintenance shed. A lawn mower parked up outside, beside a wheelbarrow.

And always, at the edge of her vision, water glinted through trees.

At last, she saw a way. It was as if the path opened by magic. It was at the far end of the caravan park, when she had exhausted all the tarmacked dead ends.

The dirt track, trodden by summer season's visitors, wound its way through the trees. Grace picked her way along, careful of roots. There was a heavy scent, rich and delicious, and the synthetic noises of cars and people at the park, the radio at the shop, the thrum-drum of the launderette all faded under the trees.

She walked towards the glint of water, the trees and earth giving way to a shingled shoreline. Grace began choosing pebbles like jewels: speckles or slate, some ochre, some wetted to a slithering green, some scarred and pitted, others smooth as sealskin. Sometimes heaving up a large stone just to feel its coolness in her hand, to see the insects scattering in the gap it had made. She put those stones back, too heavy to carry. As she picked her way across the shore she was aware of water, licking at the edges of her sight.

She took her shoes and socks off. Here, the cumbersome, ugly school shoes Nan had bought kept her feet safe, made her nimble across the shoreline. Now the stones that had seemed so rounded and smooth felt sharp beneath her sock-sweated skin. She balanced and tottered her way to the water.

Grace was not a swimmer and was not tempted much further than ankle deep. Her warm skin was no barrier to the ice-age coldness of the water, but she withstood it, distracted by the world beneath its surface. She could see clearly, only the odd flurry of mud thrown up by her slithering feet. Small fish with a twitch of tail darted suddenly from nowhere and melted instantly away again among the dank green turtles of rocks. The sunlight lay molten across the surface of the lake as if it couldn't sink in. Further, just a few steps, lank serpents of weed. She looked up. It seemed as if she was surrounded, the water stretched and expanded everywhere. Where was the land? Where was it? Panicked, she turned and slipped, her face slapped by the cold water, her feet unable to find a footing. Water up her nose, down her throat, the clank of rock against elbow as she pushed down, pushed up, her arm thrusting against the bottom of the lake. Upright at last, the lake behind her, she fled to the shore and her shoes.

She was wet to the skin. Only one shoulder of her dress had managed to avoid the dunking. A speedboat thrummed past and in its wake the water lapped hungrily at her feet, the ankle-deep waves tipping, seeming huge, as though the lake crashed over and clutched at her. Grace pulled her socks on over her wet skin, jammed her feet back into the dry land of her shoes, looked up.

And was lost.

It was late afternoon. Her little red wristwatch said four o'clock, which would account for how hungry she felt. As she looked around nothing seemed familiar. In collecting pebbles she had lost her way, her time, her direction. Trees huddled together and hid the land. A tour boat, its scallop-edged canopy flapping in the breeze, chugged away from her now as if that too was leaving her behind. She felt the panic as if someone had kicked her in the back. The lake was in her, it was beginning to pour out of her eyes. She sat herself on the tussocked edge where the land gave way to the shore, her knees pulled up tight. Just as she felt she couldn't breathe, that she was going to drown on dry land, she saw them, in a stack of swaying treetops a few hundred yards ahead of her. Five of them. Come to find her. Surely as guardians. *Comecomecome*, the rooks seemed to crow at her, unhurried.

It seemed obvious that she had to walk back the way she had come, but as she had stooped for pebbles she'd turned and spun and not kept track of what was where. Then it came to her, and as she laughed the rooks seemed to laugh, *Comecomecomecomecome*. She had not crossed the lake. The lake had been on her right as she came through the trees from the caravan park. To return she simply had to keep the lake to her left.

So she used the stretch of water like a guide rope, stepping at the edge of the shore now and pausing every few yards to peer into the trees to see if there was anything she recognized. As she moved the rooks kept watch.

It was half an hour before she found a path through the trees. As she moved nearer she could suddenly see the back of a caravan, its window blank. She saw she was not going to appear magically beside their caravan; however something was familiar, the back of a wooden building nearby. She walked towards it. The maintenance shed. The wheelbarrow was still there but the lawnmower was gone. She could hear it buzzing in the distance.

The caravan was locked. Mum and Nan were nowhere to be seen. The clubhouse was closed until six. Grace, cold, wet and hungry, wondered how many years she might have to starve on this concrete step. Her stomach rumbled like thunder and she felt herself grow shaky. She couldn't remember what she'd had for breakfast. The breeze caught the bedroom window, flapped at it carelessly. If she could find something to stand on, maybe . . .

She used the bin, dragging it from round the back of the caravan. Once inside she changed her clothes, hanging the wet dress on a wire hanger in the long thin cupboard. Then she made herself a jam sandwich which she folded into her pocket with some Dairylea cheese triangles. She was locked in now. As she helped herself to a glass of Tizer she considered. She might get into trouble. It would be better to wait outside on the step than have to tell a true lie about how she had climbed in. If they didn't know they might leave the window open again. The only alternative would be to be dragged out and possibly spend the night in some pub car park, sitting in the back of some smelly car with yet more crisps. That had happened once before when they had gone to Scarborough. No. It was better to keep silent, and tomorrow, if she was locked out, she could climb onto the bin once more.

Nan was pleased to see her on the step, waiting.

'Got bored, did you?' she sneered as she almost stepped on Grace. The key ground in the lock as if it didn't care to let Nan in. 'Bastard bloody thing.' The magic words; the key turned. Nan put the kettle on, lit a fresh cigarette as Mum clattered in from the shop with sausages and instant mashed potato.

Grace watched the family once again that evening as they made their way on their after-tea walk. Mum and Nan had clip-clopped off, not to the clubhouse this time but on, further, to the village and the pub, arguing as they left about a taxi home because, as Nan grumbled, it would be 'fucking dark by then'.

Grace took her rubber torch from the bottom of her bag. She had saved the chocolate biscuit she'd been offered at tea. Now, she flicked the catch on the window of her own room. The bin was not below her, it seemed a long way down, and she didn't think she could do it. She rested her head on the plasticky window ledge, could just make out the figures of the family at the lakeshore. The girls were throwing pebbles into the water. The mum stood at the jetty's edge, her arm raised to shield her eyes against the evening sun as she looked out over the water.

Grace felt the harsh metal edge of the frame bite into her bottom as she balanced half-in, half-out of the window. Then she was plunging and just as she felt she might drop for ever, the ground caught her. She stumbled slightly, retrieved her torch from where it had rolled under the caravan and she was off.

This time the woods felt more familiar and as she staggered beyond the trees she noticed the rise of land opposite, a house; she turned right, she could see an island in the distance. Landmarks, pathfinders. She felt like Tarzan. The rubber torch jammed into the waistband of her trousers was now a hunting knife and she dodged and skulked between the trees. The family, just beyond her, were a herd of gazelle and she, Tarzan, must watch for the lions.

The family had walked to the end of the wooden jetty. The two girls were squabbling now and the mother in her white sleeveless dress looked harassed. The dad stood at the very tip of the jetty staring through his binoculars. He commented on what he saw, pointed an authoritative finger into the landscape but the mum was bored and tired of refereeing the children.

After they had gone Grace stood at the end of the jetty for a long time, the lake lions with their manes of choppy lake water drifting langorously towards her. The jetty seemed more wobbly than she'd imagined. She looked out into the darkening landscape and longed to see what the dad had seen, to fly across the lake with her eyes. Grace fizzed inside, her eyes wide open as she tried to make them stretch to the corners of everything.

It would be useful to have a horse. A tall white horse. She saw herself, hands twisted into its mane, lifting herself onto its back. With a shudder and snort and muffled heartbeat steps it could carry Grace away under the cover of the trees across the soft forest floor. Something white skirted the furthest edge of her eyeline. She took in a tight breath. What was it? Down, further into the woodland, it moved beyond the caravans. A noise of twigs breaking underfoot. There. Again. A white sliver through the trees and a pattering noise. Like heartbeats. Hoofbeats. The horse moved through the trees towards her, halting beside her to snaffle at some leaves. She could smell it, powerful and dungish; its hide jittered under a pinch of flies, the tail coarse and strong switched forward, back. She held her breath in case by breathing out she might blow the horse away. It lifted its head, snuffled at her face, her shoulder, before it moved beyond her, clomping down to the waterside. She tried to follow, picking her way easily through the roots and branches.

At the waterside the horse had vanished. The light was almost gone now. Grace's eyes scanned the shoreline. The horse was not to be seen. How had she done that? Could she do it again? But then the night seemed to turn the lights down even darker.

Grace tripped and hopped and dashed up the pathway towards the thrum-drum golden electrical light of the launderette.

She climbed back in through the window, not caring that she kicked the bin over in her haste to scrabble into the caravan. Pulling the latch on the window, snatching the red patterned curtains closed, she dived into bed. She did not even take off her shoes.

Next morning the kettle whistled Grace awake. At the worktop Nan was stabbing out a cigarette as if it was a poisoned dart. 'Who tipped that bloody bin over? Was it you?'

'Badgers.' Grace's liquorice-flavoured tongue soured the cereal.

'Nip down the shop and fetch some milk.' Nan's fingers scratched in her purse, handed Grace the coins. Grace scuttled down the steps and ran to the shop, enjoyed the rush of air around her, imagined how it would feel to ride the white horse.

She walked back, careful of the chilled bottle of milk. As she reached the steps Nan leaned out of the doorway and gestured for the bottle.

'What did you do, wait to milk the bloody cow?' she grumbled as she moved back inside. Grace stepped up. There was a large paper bag on the table. Mum, combing her wet hair, winked at Grace.

'Morning.' She pushed the bag towards Grace. 'Something for you.'

Grace was confused. It wasn't anywhere near her birthday.

'From Davey,' Mum said, with a broad smile, another wink. Behind Grace, Nan scraped the burnt bits off the toast into the sink.

Grace reached, opened the bag. Binoculars stared back at her.

With the binoculars she could take off with a lift of her arms and wander at will among the treetops. The nests were a complicated tangle. The rooks always had something to crow about, flapped, fretted and foraged together.

Her arms ached from holding the binoculars to her eyes. They grew prickly with pins and needles after she rested them. She could still feel the imprint of the binoculars on her face.

She wanted to climb the trees, look down at the jetty from where the rooks were but it meant crossing Coniston Water. Grace had seen the little ferry boats chugging backwards and forwards from Water Head Pier but she didn't have any money. They might let her work on the boat. She could be like the girl who tied up at the mooring. Grace had watched her yesterday darting between land and lake, tugging at the ropes. She had a leather belt with a money pocket, took fares and handed out tickets. Grace could do that. She might never have to go back to school. She could stay here and work on the water. Nan and Mum could go home without her. They would never have to buy another packet of emergency crisps. They could sign a permission slip before they left.

Her arms had stopped aching. She put the binoculars to her eyes again and leapt into the treetops.

Eventually she had to go back to the caravan. She had eaten the emergency crisps and the chocolate biscuit she'd saved from last night's tea. She'd drunk the can of pop. The fizz and the sun made her feel thirsty and weathered as she wandered back through the trees.

She had her own paths now, ways she had picked through the woods to bring her back into the copse of trees behind their caravan. This way she could step in and they would not see she had come from the lake.

'Stay away from that bloody lake,' Mum had shouted after her

a day or so before. 'You'll drown.' Grace heard her, the tone of irritation at how untidy and inconvenient that would be.

Now she was passing the kitchen window as Mum opened it,
flapped a damp tea towel out onto the drying rack that looped off
the frame. She left it draggled there. Grace could hear their voices.
Nan's hard as flint.

'I'm just wondering what the fuck I'm supposed to be doing
while you're off with him.'

A clash of dishes.

'I don't know, Mam, you're a grown-up. Entertain yourself.
You did all right last night with that bald bloke.'

A snort from Nan. 'What do you know? He was a right escapol-
ogist.'

'What?'

'A talk merchant. Didn't get a drink out of him all night, then
he thinks I'll walk to Water Head with him.'

A wry laugh from Mum. 'We're only here because you had to
mess with Colin Hadfield. You couldn't keep your knickers on, so
don't blame me.'

'Colin. Forget fucking Colin.'

'You should have.'

'You think you're so fucking clever.'

'Don't start.'

'He gives her presents to keep you sweet, Loll.'

'You don't know him.'

'Neither do you. Why hasn't he met her, then? If he cares so
much, Loll, why isn't he pulling up in the car right now taking
you both out to Grasmere for a boat ride, eh? Buy the kid some
gingerbread?'

A silence. Grace leaned her forehead against the side of the caravan. A percussion of cutlery being tossed into the little metal sink.

'I'm still going.'

'Fuck off, then.'

'I will. I fucking will.'

A hollow slap as Mum slammed the plywood bedroom door, followed by a ripping strike of match and Nan stepping out onto the doorstep. Under the cover of smoke Grace ducked under the caravan, scuttled on all fours, silently, past the cables and gas pipes and toilet sink pipe. Scooted out on the other side. Thought she might go and look at the postcards of the different lakes on the carousel in the shop.

But the shop was shut so she had to go back.

That evening Nan was home before ten. Grace, sneaking her way back through the caravan park with the guiding light of her rubber torch, did not see her sitting on the step in the dark, puffing at her cigarette.

'Where the fuck have you been?' Nan snarled from the darkness. And then, not wanting an answer, 'Get to bed. And give me that.'

Her long purple-painted fingernails snatched the torch, lobbing it into the darkness before Grace could think. They heard it clomp against a caravan somewhere as Nan shoved her in through the door.

She hid the binoculars, wrapped them in her smelliest T-shirt and stashed them behind the little boxed-in cupboard, knowing that Nan had thrown the torch away not because she was angry that Grace had been out in the woods in the dark, but rather because she thought the torch was one of the presents from Davey. Grace got into bed fully clothed and pulled the blankets over her.

She lay under cover, her breath steaming back against her face. They had been here nearly three weeks now and the sheets smelled damp and sleepy. She thought about Davey and the presents, not just the binoculars and the mice, but the fact that he had taken away Mr Pownall.

She had never met Davey. She didn't care whether she ever did. This way he was as comforting as a carpet wolf. If she saw him he would probably be like all the others, hairy and intimidating. As it was she didn't care why he gave her the presents, she just cared that they were interesting.

The next morning Mum had not come back to the caravan. Nan had filled the space with smoke, sitting angled into the sofa watching the caravan park. Watching the maintenance man and his barrow of tools. She watched him for a long while, long enough for Grace to change her clothes and find there were no cornflakes left.

'There's bread.'

The bread was damp and speckled with green mould. There was no butter. Nan dragged on her cigarette as she fiddled the money out of her purse. She gave Grace the coins as she shoved her out through the door.

'We need milk an' all and a box of tea bags, and get some beans or something for your tea.'

As Grace returned from the shop laden with provisions she saw Nan talking to the maintenance man by his wheelbarrow. He was stepping now towards their caravan and examining the lock on the door. He oiled it with a little can of 3-in-1 and Nan offered him the key to try. Grace noticed that Nan had done her hair, changed her jumper, put her heels on. He stayed for a cup of tea, standing with ceremony to drink it on the concrete step.

'I've got mucky boots on.' He winked at Nan.

He was gone before Mum came back. She had a bag of sausage rolls from the baker's in town and a fold-out white card box of cream-filled chocolate eclairs.

'Get your glad rags on, we're off out,' she announced breezily. She was tugging a blanket off her bed, folding it into a shopper.

'Out where?' Nan's eyes narrowed behind her smoky breath.

'Tarn Hows. Not stopping in here another day. Get out, see the Lakes.'

'Why d'we have to drive all the way to Tarn bloody Hows? There's a lake, there.' She jabbed a purple-nailed finger towards the trees, the slivered views of Coniston Water.

'Grace, put your jumper on, it's a bit chilly.' Mum ignored Nan, changing her shoes to flats, fluffing her hair as she stood at the mirror, taking out a new lipstick. Nan clocked the fancy casing.

'Present? What did you have to do for that?'

Mum turned then. 'Are you coming or not?'

'I've got plans.' And Nan stabbed out her cigarette, counter-fluffed at her own hair. They were elbow to elbow in the mirror now, Mum being nudged out at last by Nan's much sharper elbows.

'Just as well. Davey's meeting us there after. Might drive over to Keswick for a meal.'

'Might,' Nan said, her gaze holding Mum's for one triumphant second before shifting to the contents of her handbag. A box of smokes, her purse.

They parked Mum's little runabout up the hill and walked down the wind of the road towards the tarn.

It was not a hot day. Grace felt cool in her T-shirt and jumper but other families, more hardy than her own, sat about in swimming trunks on the grass and pebble shoreline. A couple of boys, barefoot, white-skinned as ghosts, picked their way across the stones. Grace watched them jump into the cold black water with a bellowing yell, then she took out her binoculars and lifted herself into the trees.

There was a vast rookery in the distance ranged in the tops of a swathe of tall trees. Something inside Grace that had been raw-edged and nervous settled. He would not come, she would not have to meet him. Now that she was no longer thinking about Davey, her eyes skimmed out over the water through the twin tunnels of the binoculars.

She saw the boy swimming. He had started with a wild crawl, hooting and laughing as the cold water splashed him. Now he was cutting through the water with a clean, strong breaststroke. Grace envied him. She could not swim, had never been to a swimming pool. She watched each Friday morning after assembly as the children from Class Seven climbed aboard the coach with their shiny plastic swimming bags to be taken to the local pool for lessons. Grace longed to stow away, to find out what the water felt like. The boy was so sure of himself, turning to yell at his brother, his body resting on the surface, his toes lifting in a wave. His shouts echoed from the hillside close around them.

At the shoreline the family from the caravan park had arrived, the girls in chocolate-brown trousers and blue anoraks already collecting pebbles as the mum poured tea from a flask, unwrapped a Battenberg cake. The mum glanced across to where Grace's mother sat with a magazine, one hand flicking cigarette ash, the other idly scratching at her leg. The look on the mother's face was picked up on the father's as they exchanged a word. Grace turned her gaze back across the black and silver water.

The boy was as stilled and effortless as a grebe, pushing further across the water. And was gone. Grace blinked, looked with her real eyes instead of the lenses. Nothing. Black. Silver. Water. She peered into the binoculars again and as she did so a hand reached, grasping air as if it sought Excalibur. Grace felt a sharp breath plug her throat; she stood as if someone had put electricity through her but she couldn't speak. The binoculars fell. Across the surface she saw the hand rise again and clutch at nothing. The dad from the caravan-park family was already waist deep in water, striding out and now lengthening his body, stretching his arms above him, an arrowhead shooting into the water. For a second everyone on the shore drank their tea and looked out blankly at the landscape and then all was movement and shouting. The brother, the boy's father now clattering into the water, the mother, grey-faced, clutching a towel.

Grace saw where the family dad had dived and been covered slickly by the black water. Another man now in a rubber dinghy, paddling out. As he did so the caravan-park dad surfaced and in his hands he held the boy's head. He was gasping, his face a stone as the other man tugged the lifeless boy into the flabby yellow dinghy.

For moments they breathed into him. Finally the water spurted out through his nose and mouth, the small puddle being the water's last hold on him before he juddered back to them, his mother cradling him in the towel. Grace would remember the caravan-park dad spearing himself into the water as though the boy were a fish he had to catch, how the weed had tangled into the boy's hair as if, in those moments under the surface, he had been transforming.

She would remember that Davey had not come.

Nan ate egg and chips in silent triumph at the fold-down table. Then, after a coat of make-up, she headed out for the evening.

'Don't wait up,' she crowed.

Mum washed up and watched the telly. It was dark outside. Grace sat on her knees, her face squashed against the window, feeling the cold of it on her tongue. She had been out earlier to find the torch but there was no sign of it. Mum had told her to go and ask at the shop but Nan had stopped her.

'Give over,' she'd hissed through a lungful of smoke. 'Get Davey Dickhead to buy you another.'

Now as Grace watched, the car's headlights didn't stop. They seemed to track across the grass towards her. She pulled back from the glass. The lights flashed on-off-on, the horn peeped. Mum looked up, leaned towards the window. The lights flashed again. Mum moved to the door, stepped out in stocking feet.

Grace watched as Mum approached the car, saw her sliced into the night, patches of her face illuminated by the light reflected off the window. Grace could not see the driver, just a vague head shape, a shoulder turned towards her mother.

As Mum stepped back across the grass, the car was reversing, moving off. But no, Mum was pulling her jacket on, fiddling in her bag for her lipstick.

'Listen, Grace, I've got to go out. You know where the biscuits are and there's some pop left.' She didn't look at Grace, instead she spoke to her own reflection in the mirror as she sprayed at her hair. 'You'll have to leave the door unlocked, love, I don't think your nan has a key. Bed by ten, right?' Pointing her finger, the nail purple-painted just like Nan's, and then a parting wink.

The car had turned around, the lights flashed brighter again as Mum skittered across the tarmac towards it. It was pulling away even before she'd got the door shut.

In the morning no one had come home so Grace helped herself to cornflakes and half a loaf's worth of toast. She planned to scour the caravan park for her torch.

As she stepped out of the door, pockets filled with chocolate biscuits, Nan was coming up the steps. Her eyes were black-smeared with mascara and she had no shoes on. One was hanging out over the side of her handbag as if it wanted to escape and Grace noticed the heel had snapped off.

'Where you off to?' Nan grumbled.

'Exploring.'

'Long as you're out of my sight.' And she pulled the door shut behind her.

Grace used the binoculars to hunt for the torch. The grass blurred and focused as she moved across it, her back stooped. There was no sign of the torch and she began to look in places it was impossible for Nan to have thrown it. Grace moved through the park, searching behind and under every caravan until she reached the gates that led onto the road. She walked along the road for a while, one eye on the ditch. There were frogs, a few scuttling rats. No torch. But Grace did not give up on it; while it hadn't been found there still seemed to Grace some chance it could be found.

She cut back into the caravan park through a service gate off the road. It was five-barred and locked with a big padlock and a chain so Grace climbed over it. For a few moments she straddled the top of it, her feet twisted round the lower bars to steady herself. She was a rook. Perched.

She slipped down to the soft woodland floor and followed the service road back towards the caravans. There were a couple of vans parked beside a long low building made of wood with a corrugated roof. In an office at the far end there were bulldog-clipped papers pinned to a noticeboard.

'Because I'm at fucking work . . .' a man's voice jarred into the birdsong.

Grace darted quickly into the trees and was orientating herself to get back to the caravan when she heard Nan.

'Take a tea break. Christ, if last night's anything to go by you won't need more than five minutes.'

There was a thumping sound, like books being thrown down.

'I don't remember inviting you round here, love. I remember a good time was had by all and we called it a night.' He was angry.

There was the sound of a toolbox clanking, the lid being slapped shut, and the maintenance man emerged from the door. Grace watched from within the undergrowth. Nan teetered behind him on heels. She'd done her make-up, faffed at her hair. She looked bored and cross.

'What about tonight?'

'No. Look . . .'

'You on for another?'

He clonked the toolbox into the back of the little black van, slammed the door. He was chankling keys in his hand, edgy and impatient. 'I'm busy.'

Grace could not see the man's face but she could see Nan's expression. It was the face she pulled when she'd tried very hard to sell something very expensive and hard to shift and the customer just wouldn't let her have her way. The kind of thing Nan chose on a buying trip that ended up in the 70 per cent off sale. He got into the van and almost ran over her, reversing out towards the service gate. He didn't even look back, simply turned the van onto the road and drove off.

Grace sat in the undergrowth for a long time. The lions came to sit with her, the lionesses keeping watch through the woods. It would be warm sitting in a lion's mane and it would smell of heat and catness. Then it began to rain and Grace started back.

The rain pounded them. The caravan rattled under it and the sky began to darken as if night were hurrying in. Grace was sitting at the far edge of the fold-down table. Mum was frying eggs. The fat was spitting and Grace could already see the edges of the egg fraying like gold lace. They would taste chewy and metallic but she could say nothing because they were fighting.

'Keep your bloody voice down – the whole fucking park can hear you.'

'I don't bloody care. Let them hear. It'll be a fucking education.'

They had been scrapping for nearly an hour. Grace was wired and twisted with the tension of sitting as still as possible and keeping her trap shut. She knew if she moved she would be snared in it. She wanted, more than anything, to lift her binoculars to her face and fly up to the trees. There was a window behind her, perhaps she should just lift it and dive out. She saw herself running and running through the trees to the stones at the edge of the lake where she would be purplegreen, blueblack. The end of the jetty would fall away beneath her as flap-flap-flap she skimmed out above the water and the rooks would rise to meet her.

There was the slam of a door that brought her tumbling back onto the surface of the fold-down table. More slams and bangs. The sound of something glass breaking. The frying pan was smoking now, prickling and bitter. Mum chucked the eggs away and reached for her purse. She handed Grace some money.

'Get yourself down the chippy,' she said. She leaned down and smoothing Grace's hair she kissed her on the forehead. She looked tired. Grace could see where her hair had outgrown its dye.

She sat in the launderette to eat her chips. A while later a car drove past. Davey, a hand at the wheel, his face obscured by Mum leaning forward in the passenger seat.

'You'll do as you're told.' Nan pushed Grace towards the car door. Grace didn't get in. She felt panicked. They couldn't go home without Mum, could they? Was Mum staying here with Davey? Was that it? Was that what the argument had been about before? Mum was leaving them? Grace wanted to stay too. She wanted to work on the boats from Water Head Pier.

'Get in the car. Now.' Nan's voice was low and cold. She had loaded her cases into the boot and was slinging Grace's things on top of them with a last forgotten pair of shoes. She grabbed the scruff of Grace's neck and thrust her towards the car, pulling the door open too fast so that Grace's forehead collided with the edge. The pain was like a bell sounding in her head. Nan shoved her too hard so she tripped and fell into the seat well. Nan tugged her up by her waistband, flung her into the seat.

'Don't mess me around, Grace. I'm not in the mood. Get in the fucking car.'

They drove then. Too fast. Nan lurched round corners and over hills. Sometimes the road was so narrow that the sides of the car scraped against the hedgerow, the wing mirror on Grace's side was bashed and bent.

She had no idea what was happening. They were going home. They were leaving Mum. Why couldn't she stay here with Mum?

Later they stopped at the roadside so she could be sick. Thrumming back along the motorway in the dark, Grace fell asleep and dreamed of the carpet wolves howling for her in the hallway.

6

ALL DOORS, NO WINDOWS

Alec had never thought of a window as a necessity until now. He had taken them for granted, even the ones at his flat with the rotting frames and the black mould. He wished now he had taken more time to stand with his toast at the kitchen window and look out over the garden below.

The garden maisonette took up the two stories below him and the couple who owned it kept a washing machine and some old bikes in the garden and they let the plants and shrubs go to seed. Everything was wild and matted. In summer there was a rose bush so tangled into a forsythia that only Alec, viewing from above, could see the blushed pink roses. They were a vast and fragrant canopy that lasted for about a week and a half. Alec had often looked out, just for a moment, a quick glance to check the weather, and there they would be in the periphery of his vision. Or else he would be in the middle of a swift reach to push the window open and wedge the sash with an offcut of wood. That's how bad the window was, it had to be wedged open or it slid like an overweight guillotine. But all those times he'd only glanced. Now he wished he'd pulled up a chair, sat in the window and watched the world outside. The flats were in a long terrace of Georgian houses that backed onto rack after rack of smaller Victorian and Edwardian terraces. There were people wherever you looked. If he had only looked.

His lawyer brought word that the couple from the ground-floor maisonette were interested in buying his flat. Until that moment Alec had kept the flame of hope stoked: he would go to trial and everyone would see the truth. It would be that simple. Although the police interrogation and the run-up to the case had tried to piss on that flame, Alec had lain awake at nights blowing on it, feeding it with the scraps from his list. His lawyer, Blair Austen-McNeil, had come in with the news about the flat and did not laugh it off or at any point in their meeting say, 'Forget it, you'll need a home to go to in a few months.' Instead he said, 'They're asking if you'd like to have it valued. I can set that up if you like, my brother-in-law is an estate agent.'

Alec felt as if Blair Austen-McNeil had licked his fingers and squished out the flame of hope. If he let his neighbours have his house valued, if he took their offer and moved his things out and their life in, wasn't that admitting that he was guilty? That he was going to prison? He had plans to go home after this, to sit on the hard kitchen chair with a mug of tea and one of those pies from the baker's that bloody Lee was so fond of. He planned to sit there for about a week, let his beard grow, watch the neighbourhood. Perhaps that's what they should ask at the preliminary hearing, never mind 'Guilty or Not Guilty' but rather 'For Sale or Not For Sale'. *Why are you planning on getting off, Mr Holm? Because we all believe you did this.*

Blair Austen-McNeil reminded him of Tarzan. Each time they met Alec imagined that the lawyer would travel home on an array of vines, looping through the town with an operatic war cry. His suits were smart and expensive and made for him, but underneath he looked solid, as if he were all meat and no bones.

He was not like the lawyers Alec had seen on television or in the films. He didn't seem to care much. He had a jolly smile and a blinding optimism that bore no relation to Alec's situation. From Alec's viewpoint there was nothing to be blindingly optimistic about. After Austen-McNeil's brother-in-law had valued his flat he saw very clearly that Blair Austen-McNeil believed he had done it. He had even tried to persuade him to plead guilty, mentioning, schoolmarmishly that 'owning up now will go better for you later'. But Alec had told him, 'I didn't do it.'

At least, that's what Alec thought he had said. He was becoming uncertain about a lot of things just lately. For instance no one could find the man with the gold ring and although Alec was locked in a cell and had no means of checking, he felt no one was really looking for him. Alec knew instinctively that this man was the stabber, the strangler. He replayed in his head the moment Gold Ring had wrangled Deborah out of the pub. He could feel the way his gut had twisted, the same feeling he had had at the checkpoint as the little green Hillman Imp breasted the hill.

Which they also knew about. Except in Blair Austen-McNeil's version of events it was Alec who attempted to rape Audra, it was Alec who was chased off by her brothers and eventually shot. He remembered the story Corporal Drew had made up about a gang of terrorists. The lie that had protected Audra's brothers squatted on his own life, and the incident with Audra now reflected badly on Alec. He had been shot. Questions were being asked. There was nothing on record about Warren Drew, about Alec squeezing himself in through that tiny window to save Audra. There, another window to look through for all eternity. Alec sifted it around in his head constantly. Her brothers had shot him, that was true, but for the wrong reasons. He had never really blamed them, never complained about it or gone round to the house after he was patched up, for he understood why, he saw the misunderstanding and lived with it. It hadn't mattered. The only thing that mattered was Audra, that she was only a bit scuffed and nothing more. What was important was that Audra had got away, unharmed.

He had dreamed about Warren Drew a couple of times. He dreamed he was sitting on the bunk in his cell and he was going over his shopping list of facts: *gold, blonde, sour, dark, smoky, tears.* And Drew stepped into the cell and offered his hand, just the way he had offered it to Audra all those nights ago: 'I might have mis-remembered it. Write it here. On the back of my hand.' On the back of his hand, the words *followed, menaced, attacked.*

Thing was, he should have kept with his 'mates', he should have taken Drew's offer of a job with his brother. He should have stayed in that crowd. Warren Drew would know how to stop this, would talk and lie his way out. Alec had no ideas. He only had the truth, flimsy and paperish against the bold black strokes of police notions.

He felt foolish for doing so, but each time he spoke with Blair Austen-McNeil he mentioned the man with the gold ring and asked about the search. Finally Blair Austen-McNeil said they were not looking because to the police the case was almost closed. They had their man.

'But he's their man. He was with her.'

'No one else remembers him.'

Blair's usually illuminatory smile was dimming. Alec remembered how everyone had looked away.

'There were other people in the pub. They must have asked them.'

Blair's smile switched off. 'They have a witness who remembers you with Deborah Winstanley. Remembers you and can place you in the lobby of the pub and in the car park by the skips.'

'I don't understand.'

And Alec didn't understand. Why did they believe someone else's misremembered lie and turn their faces away from his truth? It didn't seem reasonable. It blurred and bewildered him so much that Blair had to explain three times in increasingly simplified ways that pleading guilty and getting on with it was better than pleading not guilty and going to trial and then being found guilty. He made it sound, finally, that if Alec simply held up his hands in shame he'd be ticked off and told not to do anything so naughty again.

'But I can't do that. I didn't kill her.'

Blair's optimism faltered and he looked weary for the first time.

Later, of course, very much later, Alec found out that Blair had a holiday planned, a few weeks at his house in the south of France, and the prospect of a longish trial with no hope of success for his client was rather getting in the way of that.

'With good behaviour you'll be paroled, you don't have a history of violence or wrongdoing, Alec. That will count in the end. At worst you'll do twelve years.' Blair Austen-McNeil discarded a decade of Alec's life as if it was a jiffy, a few hours whiled away in an airport lounge.

It was, in the end, an open and shut case. They opened the door, made him step inside, then they shut the door.

The sweat box in the prison van was a cocoon. He was being metamorphosed. At the prison they took his clothes off and they searched every part of him. He thought they might look up his arsehole and see some vital piece of evidence, something that would show them what a mistake this was, what a nightmare. The doctor checked him out on the medical wing, peering with a light into his eyes. Alec hoped that he might see that night's events unfold on the screen of his retina. He imagined the doctor taking in a shocked gasp. *You're right. You didn't do it. I see how it happened.*

But the doctor didn't gasp, he simply ticked boxes on a government form. Then they put him into a cell and shut the door. The warder moved off, accompanied by the musical tringle of his set of keys. Later, at lights-out, men shouted out from the tiny windows, an opera of obscenity that kept Alec from his nightmares.

The food was bad, his appetite worse. One afternoon he realized that soon there would be more belt than waist, that his prison trousers bagged about him, and he felt a flash of terror. If he vanished, if he became the Invisible Man once and for all, the only thing anyone would remember about him was a lie. Determined to act, at lunchtime he headed down to the hotplate and took the gristly casserole, grey pulverized mash, carrots. The meat was inedible, like offcuts of carpet, but he drank down the gravy, soaked it into the potato, the twin horrors demolished in a few mouthfuls. He crunched through the carrots, stickish, cold and hard, and when two of his tablemates didn't eat theirs he scrounged them.

Within three weeks they were calling him Dustbin.

They had consigned him to a box and now he had to use that box to save his old self. If he sat and looked at what had happened he would not make it. Instead he parcelled Alec Holm, with a last click of his office pen, into that box. A keepsake.

Outside the box, he signed up for a scientific research programme thinly disguised as an 'inmate fitness scheme'. He ran for miles each day on a treadmill wired up to a heart monitor, breathed in and out through a flexible plastic tube, a clip on his nose. He escaped then, found his brain travelled him backwards to Bournemouth, with Mum.

It was Mr Shearwater, from the insurance office where she worked, who had taken them there. Alec's mum was one of only two women in the office, sharing administrative duties with a small mousy girl named Tabitha, who worked on the reception desk. He hadn't liked Tabitha. On the few occasions when he was allowed to visit the offices Tabitha seemed twitchy and ill at ease. Her face narrowed into a vanishing point of perspective somewhere under her nose. Her hair was a sandy blonde colour and scraped into a thin rat tail at the back of her head. She had long fingers like claws, a mouse in girl's clothing sniffing behind the counter as Alec waited for his mum.

What usually happened was that once a term, instead of heading straight home, he was allowed to take the bus from school and travel across the city to the insurance office. Then he and his mum would go to the Kardomah for a special tea. He liked the Kardomah. He would never be finished trying all the cakes in the shiny twirling display.

Except, of course, one day he was finished because he came out to meet Mum at the office and instead of just Mum there was a man, a tall mousy man who might have been from the same litter as Tabitha. He offered his hand for Alec to shake and introduced himself as Mr Shearwater. That afternoon they did not go to the Kardomah, instead they had tea at Parkers in St Anne's Square. They never went to the Kardomah again. When he had grown up and travelled into the city one afternoon to look around the record shop he remembered those teas and thought he would go back, only he couldn't, it wasn't there any more. By then, of course, neither was Mr Shearwater.

It had been an odd time, that year of Mr Shearwater. He had come to the house for roast Sunday dinners on several occasions and once a fortnight he 'accompanied your mother to the theatre' while Alec stayed at home with Auntie Jean who wasn't his auntie at all. Mr Shearwater tried to fit into their house but Alec saw straight away that he didn't; even when he took his jacket off and tried to lounge in the chairs with a Sunday paper he was as stiff and folded as an uncooperative deckchair. Alec felt as if he was holding his breath until Mr Shearwater left.

That summer they journeyed to Bournemouth. Mr Shearwater had his own car, a Rover, and they travelled in that. Alec noticed that Mr Shearwater didn't fit into his own car. It was very clean and smelled of polish. They were going to stay in a hotel, something they had not done even when Dad was around. Alec had never been on a holiday when you had to sleep away from home.

They stayed at the Whitehall Hotel beside the Gardens. As Mr Shearwater and Alec's mother spent their afternoons strolling, taking in a band concert and lingering over scones in tea rooms, Alec took himself off and explored the Chines.

He'd got too hot mauling up and down the beach, finding his throat getting sticky at the thought of some other kid's ice cream. One bright Tuesday afternoon it was like a mirage, every screaming brat on the beach as boiled red as a lobster, breadcrumbed with sand, holding a molten ice cream. He could have won a prize that day, the only kid in Bournemouth without an ice cream. In the evening his head pulsed and he felt both blistered and chilled. He couldn't face the meal set before them on the white tablecloth. He was sent to bed early feeling very sick.

In the morning, revived, Mr Shearwater cornered him in the lobby after breakfast and offered him a canvas hat.

He fished in the Coy Pond, finding it by chance one afternoon as he followed the water from Westover Gardens. He scoured the rockery for spiders and beetles and resolved to bring a stick and some string and one of the paperclips from the hotel reception to make a hook. Then the old man in the tweed hat wheeled up with his barrow,

'What the devil d'you think you're doing? Clambering over everywhere.'

Alec felt the injustice. He had been very careful of all the plants, had even put the spiders back. He let himself be chased away with a swashbuckling of trowel.

Next afternoon he brought his makeshift fishing kit and kept a weather eye out for Tweedy.

'You'll catch nothing like that,' said Tweedy's voice behind him. Alec shot up, startled, his exit blocked by the cotoneaster he was hiding in. His foot caught underneath itself and he tumbled. Tweedy helped him up, Alec steeling himself for a slap. Instead Tweedy sat and puffed at a pipe and gave a lengthy critique of his fishing tackle and technique.

Tweedy had emerged from a tall gate that gave onto Coy Pond. Alec had glimpsed the garden beyond it, just a gated view, a long slice of mature shrubbed green, a bank of dahlias in full bloom, technicolour pinks and yellows, oranges and reds. Others scarlet, tall, almost black stems. Alec dreamed now that he walked through the gate and Tweedy caught him.

Tweedy brought out a beaker of tea and a jam sandwich, the bread cut thickly. They sat in companionable silence, Alec on the edge of the pond, Tweedy perched on a bench nearby. Never caught a fish.

The following day Mr Shearwater took them to Poole on the ferry, and to Brownsea Island the next. On the Saturday they were heading home.

His mother was ill shortly afterwards, had woken him in the mornings as he heard her vomiting in the bathroom. She'd been pale, eyes wide and somehow black instead of green.

Mr Shearwater came for his usual Sunday roast but, after a brief chat in the kitchen, behind a closed door, he did not stay to eat it. He left, driving off in his Rover. Alec's mother did not come out of the kitchen.

A weekend or so later Alec was sent to stay at Auntie Jean's. He slept in her little box room for two nights and on Monday Auntie Jean ran him to school in her little car.

He knew now what had gone on that weekend and he knew why Mr Shearwater had had no appetite for Sunday dinner. His mother was never the same. It was as if Mr Shearwater had crumpled her up like chip paper, licked the salt off his fingers, given his usual polite burp and was gone.

Sometimes, on the treadmill, Alec chased Mr Shearwater, sweating and formal in his worsted suit, from Sandbanks to Hengistbury Head.

His mother came to visit him in prison only once. She was unable to speak and her eyes took on that Shearwater blackness. Then they moved him to another prison, put miles more between himself and his mother.

He was allowed out just once, in a last-minute handcuffed dash to his mother's funeral. He stood at the graveside, manacled to Mr Woodruff.

It seemed that the dirt that tipped over her coffin, the gape of grave, the crowd of headstones in the cemetery, were all part of the ceremony of his own final separation from the real world. There was no one to care now, no one to give a damn.

As soon as the ceremony was over he was whisked back to prison, like the president.

Alec wondered what Fraser Halls might do and he did not have to wonder hard. He would vanish himself into the walls, he would outwit them, he simply wouldn't be there.

*

They called it the Dogs' Home, his new home now he was offi-cially signed and sealed as a convicted murderer. He realized the first of his prisons had been only a bad dream, a prelude to the true dark of his nightmare. His neighbours were murderers and rapists and thieves and robbers and batterers. The only way he could manage it was to think of it as the army. They were all in it together, this out-of-the-way posting.

His appeal failed, as he knew it would. No one had looked for the man with the gold ring and the bullying fists. Having too much time on his hands in his cell, Alec went over in his head what might happen if Gold Ring's temper got the better of him again with some other faerie blonde, someone else he could knock about by a pub skip, someone else he could leave for dead on a balcony. If that happened, they would come for him. He didn't want apologies, the cracking of a regretful smile, the offer of a con-ciliatory handshake; he just wanted a key and an open door.

He could remember the particular Tuesday when these thoughts almost broke him. He had woken from a nightmare in which Gold Ring was butchering Audra in that checkpoint toilet. He'd woken in a sweat that the showers couldn't seem to rinse off, a persistent sprinkling of cold diamonds making his skin prickle. They would come for him, that was what the nightmare was about. He spent the day edgy and distracted, every door that opened made him get to his feet. At association he couldn't sit down.

'Easy, soldier,' Mr Woolverton said as Alec leapt at the carillon of keys. This was it. This was why Mr Woolverton was looking at him, concerned. Mr Woolverton knew. But then Mr Woolverton looked away, nodded to Rhino, in for GBH and in the middle of his O level revision, that he was wanted in the governor's office.

Alec saw that Mr Woolverton watched him for the rest of the day with a look of concern. Was Alec about to start a riot, about to escape?

He was about to snap. He could feel it now in the late of that Tuesday afternoon, how his seams stretched and began to come away.

Back in his cell he sat on the top bunk and tried to control it, to pull his seams tighter. As he took deep breaths, his heart racing, he heard Dr Grace Storey in his head: 'It's an isotope.' He remembered the episode with a sudden grainy black and white rush. Fraser Halls perched, tense, on Dr Grace Storey's lab desk. Sweating. Heart racing. He had been injected with a tracking isotope, something noxious that was intended to make him glow in the dark so that the evil scientists could find him and take him. As he looked up he was Fraser Halls, the cell became Dr Storey's lab and in the corner Dr Grace Storey herself, white-coated, with her back to him, worked at the table. What had she been doing? Isolating the isotope and then finding some substance to neutralize it.

He steadied himself. He imagined Dr Grace very clearly, the desk cluttered with phials and test tubes. As he sat gripping the edge of his bunk Dr Grace outlined him in black to hold him in place and now she boiled some of his blood, put it into a centrifuge to separate out his component parts.

Gold. Blonde. Sour. Dark. Smoky. Tears. The elements of the isotope that poisoned him.

He looked up, saw through the hardly-worth-it-window the cross-hatching of bars and razor wire beyond. The horizontal of wall and field and the vertical of trees. In the topmost branches rooks had settled. There was an illusion created, as if they were tiny and perched on the cross-hatchings and striations of the prison. He remembered a holiday, after Mr Shearwater. They had gone to stay with Auntie Jean's brother and his wife on their farm where rooks were building nests on the edge of the far field. His mother had told him that rooks brought luck with them. 'They foretell death,' Auntie Jean's brother had intoned, digging a box of bullets out of the dresser drawer. 'Only if they leave,' his mother had whispered and eaten her breakfast. Later Alec looked over the corpses the farmer and his son had strung up in the yard and was sorry.

Here they were, come to remind him he wasn't quite dead. He watched them flap and settle and shift at his eye level and they were allies.

The list shifted in his head. He was working in the kitchens, preparing old carrots, hard and frosty or else with skins so soft they ruffled instead of peeled. Picking the eyes out of potatoes, he thought of Mona and that last wave.

Stair. Night. Star. Bright. Light. Car.

A navy-blue Ford Cortina. He had paused at the roadside to let it pass. He had walked the diagonal across to the pavement and nicked around the corner garden and down the ginnel that cut through to the main road. There was one light there, clean and white like a star. A dog turd beside the lamp base. A discarded chip wrapper fluttered against the chain-link fencing. The leaves in the hedge. Not a privet hedge. Beech. It turned brown in the autumn but the leaves stayed on. Was that when he had come to her? When Alec's back was turned towards home? Look away now. And the rumble of the machine as he loaded the buckets of potatoes into it thundered away the thoughts.

He dreamed of her door, shut against him. The image would stay for what seemed like hours, his hand on the badly painted matt grey of the council-flat door. The white plastic numbers wedging themselves into his forehead as he leaned forward. It did not matter how often he dreamed it, he could not see the numbers on the door. He had not looked at that moment. They had not been important. He was never going to see this woman again after all. Now, of course, she was in his head each day. But seventh floor was all he knew. He saw her finger in the lift, pointing at the button and then a golden burst of light as she turned her pale faerie face towards him, asked him if he'd come in and check the flat was secure.

After the kitchen work he decided to sign up for the mechanics course and learn a trade.

Keep walking, he thought, every footstep takes you nearer. Although nearer to what, he had no idea.

7

LIKE A STORY

Grace felt she had been kidnapped. Nan stood at the kitchen window, billows of smoke snorting through her nostrils. Mum was still not back and there was nothing to eat in the house. Grace had found a wrinkled apple in the salad drawer of the fridge and had pinched the mouldy patches off the last few slices of bread before she jammed them in the toaster. Even toasted, the bread tasted old and fusty.

Nan had been out their first night back. She had togged herself up and shut the door on Grace. Grace was uncertain what to do. She looked out into the street with trepidation, the cars that passed and the dogged-stepped people on their way with somewhere in mind frightened her more than the woods at Coniston Water. Here everyone had a plan and the bus fare, there were boundaries and limits. She knew she could not go to the pub and see what Nan did. She had been there only once before, remembered a high room full of brownness, old men staring at her as if she were a monkey. There had been a sharp metallic sparkle of the optics above the bar and the mirrored wall behind it.

'She Loll's kid?' The man at the bar had handed Nan a wad of bank notes. Some debt paid.

'Well, she's not mine,' Nan scorned, not losing count of the notes in her hand. The man at the bar had offered Nan a cigarette.

'Who she look like, then?' the man had joked. 'She got "Made in Britain" stamped on her arse or what?'

'Whoever she looks like, he ran the four-minute fucking mile before she got here.' Nan had bustled her out amid bronchial laughter.

Grace sat by the window waiting, she knew Nan wasn't coming back any time soon and found that each time a car pulled by she was watching to see if Mum was inside it. Maybe she would take a taxi.

As darkness fell the carpet wolves rose around her. She needed to move away from the window, hunker herself down into the safety of the pack, drift off to sleep comforted by the wolves, the scent of shoes and the Hoover.

She could not know that she would open her eyes in the morning and the world would have tilted, just a degree, enough to throw it off its proper axis and begin its spiral downwards. A tilt that began with Nan's hand shoving at Bill Roberts's back as he turned it to her, got back to his pint. A shove because she saw the look pass between Bill and his brother, a contemptuous amusement. She shoved hard, her arms all bone and spite, and his beer splattered forwards. Now he turned but where she expected a playful wink, a wrestle of arms ending with his around her, he showed eyes like pebbles, a man annoyed, looking at something which was tiresome to him. He couldn't slap her, not in front of everyone, but his arm flinched upwards. There was a moment, a laugh and a bristled pal nearby growling low encouragement.

'G'on, lamp her one.'

Yvonne picked up her glass thinking to dash it in his face but at the last moment she knew better, knocked it back and walked out, strode out on those killer heels. Yes, the bastards were all watching and they'd all see how great her legs were, lean and muscled and desirable to be between. Not like that frump bitch he was with, looking like she'd made her own dress, fucking chiffon sleeves.

Yvonne waited outside for too long, getting through a smoke in the doorway of the insurance firm. She thought she'd watch them, see where he took her; but when they came out, Bill Roberts, offering up the frump bitch's raincoat, saw Yvonne in the doorway and pointed her out to his brother who looked, laughed. The frump bitch didn't turn to look. She slid herself into that raincoat, got a compact out of her bag, was carefree and cared for.

The next morning they were ready for work and school, Nan breakfasting on Lambert & Butler, Grace melting the grated remains of a cracked knob of cheese onto bread that was more fur than crumb. Nan was scrabbling in her purse, handing over a whole pound note.

'Here. Take it. Get some milk and bread on your way home. And I don't want you hanging round the shop. Or Fran's either. You piss off back here. No messing.'

For a moment Grace wondered if a pound was enough to get her to Coniston. Even if it wouldn't buy a train fare perhaps she could walk there and the money would keep her supplied until she had her rightful job being shown the ropes on the ferry boats at Water Head Pier. And then the door opened and let Mum in.

She was wearing her raincoat, dark blue, belted at the waist, and her black calf-length suede boots.

'You took your fucking time.'

Mum said nothing, did not even blink, and then she looked away, towards the window. 'I might not be stopping.'

Nan lunged forward gawking through the window, mock puzzled. 'Oh? Why? Where's shitface, then?'

'Mam.'

'They seek him here . . .' gawk, gawk through the window, her neck jerking, speckles of spit landing on the drainer, 'they seek him there . . .'

'He wants to take me away. Just a couple of weeks in Spain, go and see his brother out there.'

Nan hedged, unsure where this was going. Grace thought of slipping away now, wondered if anyone would be here when she got back from school. She had a pound, she could just go. She felt the fabric paperiness of the note in her hand. Jonathan could fold it into a bird for her, he was good at origami and its sharp creases. He could make her a pocket rook to protect her.

'She's missing more school?' Nan queried. 'And I've only just got back, I can't leave the shop.'

Mum unblinked again, her eyes steady on Nan's face, like someone sighting a rifle, taking in a breath before firing.

'No. Just me. Take me away.'

Nan gave a snorting laugh, stubbed out one cigarette on the drainer and yanked her bag across the worktop to reach inside for another. She flipped the box with one hand. 'What have I said?

What have I said, Lorraine? Why buy presents for a kid that isn't his? I warned you. I fucking warned you.'

The other hand dredged up the lighter, the sparklick-sparklick of her thumb against the mechanism.

'It's more than a holiday.'

A long contrail of smoke from Nan's mouth.

'It'd be more . . . a honeymoon.'

Nothing breathed in the kitchen except the cigarette in Nan's hand.

'You fall for it. Don't mind me. I'll still be here when you're back. So will she.' A finger jabbed towards Grace.

'Grace, upstairs and get your clothes in a bag. You're going to stay at Aunt Sylvie's for a bit . . .' Mum spoke quietly from the doorway, opened the kitchen drawer to pull out an old string shopper.

Nan's arm whiplashed it shut on her fingers. 'Get out of my drawer.'

There was a blank moment, Mum staring at Nan then reaching for Grace's shoulder. 'Upstairs, love . . . use my little case, the one under the bed . . . now . . .'

'What the fuck are you doing?'

Grace, rising, felt herself fall downward against the chair as Nan lashed out at her, pushing her out of her way as she stepped towards Mum.

'You think it's that easy? You think you can just piss off?'

Mum tried to step towards Grace. 'Come on, Grace.'

Nan wedged herself between them.

Grace didn't try to get up, she concentrated on not slipping off the chair.

'You're a stupid bitch, I'll tell you that.'

'Grace?' Mum reached a hand, Nan slapped it down hard.

'And when it all goes tits up this time . . .?'

'It isn't like that . . . He's . . .'

But Nan wedged the words between them.

'You going to come scuttling back from Spain when he realizes he doesn't want you and her, just you? Or will you just send us a fucking postcard? Our Sylvia won't keep her, I tell you that . . . So you just going to fucking shunt her back to me?'

Mum seemed to snap upright suddenly, all her attention away from Grace. 'He wants us. A ready-made family. Wife and kiddie.'

'He's never even met her.'

'For Christ's sake, Mam, he went into school for her, sorted out that mess with Dougie Pownall. Your mess . . .' The word seemed to hiss around the room. 'So what, she's not his, but he'll take us both on. He will do it. I know him. I want him.'

'That right?'

Nan's cigaretted hand shoved at Mum's shoulder, the gesture as light as a feather, as hard and immovable as iron, blocking her.

'You can't stop me.'

'That right?'

There was a flapping tussle, Mum pushing against Nan, Nan laughing, her arms like swords.

' I don't need to be living here with you.'

'Fucking do.'

'I'm not going to end up . . .'

'Fuck off.'

'. . . being you . . .'

'Fuck off.'

'. . . shagged-out and sour . . .'

'Fuck off.'

'I'm thirty-two. He might be the last man that wants me as a family and not just a Friday night fu—'

Nan took a sudden, deft step backwards, pulling free of the fight, but standing tall and triumphant.

'I'll tell him. About all of them.'

'Christ, Mam, I'm thirty-two and I've got a kiddie. He always knew I wasn't the Virgin Mary.'

'The Lakes? Shall I tell him about the ones you did there?'

Mum was silent suddenly, her face marble-white and cold.

Nan leaned in, snarling, 'Who took you in?'

'Mam . . .'

Mum tried to push past to reach Grace, Nan's finger a barrier stabbing at her shoulder, springing her back.

'No home and knocked-up, Lorraine. Who did you come crying back to?'

'Grace, get going . . . upstairs . . . now . . .'

Mum tried to move around the wall of Nan, feet shuffling in a horrid stunted dance.

'Grace . . .'

'I've fucking FORKED out for you and for THAT!' An arrowed finger caught Grace on the temple.

'Grace . . . now . . .'

Grace, struggling on her chair, snaggled at the edges of the Mam/Nan shuffle, her every move blocked by the jut of Nan's hip, the dagger of her elbow.

'You fuck off now, Lorraine, you're NEVER coming back.'

'Grace . . . Grace . . .'

Mum's face, eyebrows lifting encouragement, a pleading

smile, viewed through the triangled frame of Nan's hand on her hip.

'I'm fucking warning you.'

Mum grabbed at Grace then, her fingers a cuff around her wrist. Grace's legs knotted as the chair legs tripped and tumbled her. Mum catching her, Nan catching her and the two would rend her apart.

'Fucking BITCH.'

Nan winning, yanking Grace free of her mother, twirled her outwards as if they were jiving until Grace's head clonked against the edge of the stainless-steel sink.

'Look what you've done,' they yelled in perfect unison and then they flew at each other. Grace fell, feeling Nan's shoes kick her, her mother's feet stumbling over her so all her bones felt knocked out of joint. A cacophony of grunts and swearing. Nan's claw fingers in Mum's hair were bending her, angling her, Mum stumbling against Nan's frame.

'Let me fucking GO.'

Mum's arm lashed out, clonking against Nan's cheekbone, Mum's fingers tangling and yanking at Nan's hair. Grace saw the knife dart from the open drawer like a silver fish between them, Nan's knuckles white around it like someone trying to catch it. The thick triangle of blade that had sliced chips, had nicked into Mum's fingers a hundred times because she was careless. The blade vanished all the way inside her, Mum's breath hissing like a snake, Nan pushing against Mum, an odd rippling sound coming from her, Mum falling against Nan, leaden. Grace watched her feet fold, the heels of her boots angled and uncomfortable as she pushed back against Nan.

'Grace . . .' The sound gurgled out of her.

Nan struggled against the weight, her shoes skidding on the shining red of the floor, the heels too pinpoint to find a purchase. Nan's legs stretched, bending beneath her as Mum's weight pushed her over. Nan sprawled on her back, the shining red now blackening at the edges. Nan grunted, gasping, rolling herself out from under Mum, shoving the weight of her towards Grace, coughing, unable to breathe. Mum's arm folded between them, hard. Mum's face, her eyes so close Grace could see herself reflected in the green irises.

'Grace,' like a long sigh of wind through the trees, Mum's last breath on her face.

Then Nan pulled Mum away, tugging Grace from under.

She could see Nan's face now, saw her lips moving over and over but she couldn't hear anything. Only the word 'story' and then 'tell a story'. Nan's hands in the sink washing the pots there, red.

Then Nan hunched over her, squatting on her haunches. Grace could see up under her skirt where her thighs folded, to the white nylon triangle of her knickers.

'Grace . . .' Her name was sharp in her ears, Nan shaking her, once, twice '. . . a story, Grace. We have to tell it like a story. *Are you listening to me?*' Everything about Nan was like a knife. 'Are you listening?'

Grace's eyes moved to her mother lying on the floor, her arm twisted strangely behind her back. Nan's cold hand clamped Grace's jaw, wrenched her face forward; she leaned in close so Grace's breath was tainted with cigarettes and lipstick.

'Understand? Me, you and a story . . . We have to tell it like a story. Or they'll take me away . . . to prison. Prison.' She was shaking Grace hard, making sure the facts mixed in. '. . . And you. You'll go an' all . . . only the prison for kids is called the orphanage 'cause you haven't got anyone but me and I haven't got anyone but you . . .' shaking her, jolting foolish ideas out, jabbing sense in, '. . . not fucking Auntie Sylvie. No Dad. No Davey. No no one.'

Then the police and the ambulance had come and Grace moved through the forest of people, branches of arms sweeping her forward to the dark inner of the police car. Outside, everyone watching like at the Whit Parade. Grace could hear the drum.

Nan was holding her hand tightly, a reminder of her warning about what would happen to them both if Grace told the wrong story. They had studied Victorian orphanages at school, coloured in bricks and black windows to make a collage, and drawn thin dirty children in brown ragged clothing, children who ate gruel and worked up chimneys. Grace saw she was only words away from that. It was Nan who had shown her the power of the true lies. She needed the power now, all of it. But Grace couldn't think of the true lie that was required, could only see the red water and the silver fish and her reflection in her mother's eye.

Detective Inspector Fry had requested the WPC with the best smile and, looking at WPC Craigie, he wondered which idiot thought that was a good smile. She'd got all the facial expression of a blow-up sex doll. He'd requested someone soft and Craigie was harsh and blonde and pointed in every way from her nails to her bra-sculpted breasts. He sent her off on a fool's errand and called Smethurst back in.

Detective Inspector Derek Fry was fifty and retiring in a month.

He was going to run a B & B in the Lakes, just by Coniston Water. He had always been a career copper – how else had he clambered all the way to Detective Inspector? – but in the last twelve months it had all fallen away, like climbing Snowdon and finding fog at the top.

First his wife had left him, after twenty-odd years.

'See, you don't even know how long.' She had shaken her head, then stooped to that funny little overnight bag and trotted out on those funny clogs of hers to the waiting taxi. She'd met someone new and bearded at a pottery class.

'What pottery class?' he'd wondered aloud and Beverley had not laughed, only looked sad.

Yes, he missed her. Christ alive, he loved her. But he felt a relief, somehow, a pressure lifting, the burden of having made her so unhappy. So he let her go.

And his police work failed him. He didn't know whether it was a breakdown or he was tired and losing his touch, but he couldn't seem to catch the criminals. Fair enough, the failure rate on the local burglaries; for that sort of nonsense you worked your way through your list of prominent nominals finding out who was in or out of clink and made housecalls until you caught him watching the racing on the stolen telly or clipping the stolen necklace round his girlfriend's neck. No, there had been a shooting, an unusual occurrence on his turf. He was too far out of the city for all that. He marvelled at the way the community turned on the Italians at the Trattoria on the main road, everyone deciding they were the Mafia. DI Fry could still be sideswiped by the rank stupidity of his fellow man. He knew the shooting was nothing to do with this hard-working man, or his capable wife and bright kids.

DI Fry had a sense of smell about crime. Perpetrators had always given off a scent of almonds to him. He had never been wrong. It seemed no other officer had this gift. At the scene of the shooting he had been accompanied by a detective constable who hadn't been on the team very long. Tall, pepper-haired, in his early thirties. He had come into the office that morning and Fry had instantly picked up the scent and been perplexed that it was here, in his workplace. He couldn't seem to peg it at first and then later, when they had been called out to the alleyway, it had grown stronger, almost overpowering. A cloying fug around the detective constable. Fry was finding it hard lately. They had picked up no leads on the shooting, had tried to link it into the small fringes of organized crime that sometimes spilled out their way, an infrequent gangsters-on-a-day-trip scenario. The detective constable still stank of almonds. When he had a week's leave and headed off to Ilfracombe with his fiancée, Fry couldn't smell almonds any more. But there was nowhere to take it. He'd had a colleague years ago, Bernard Prior, whose skin always prickled in the presence of a perpetrator, but neither of them had talked about it much. No one else seemed to share their experiences. Fry wished he could get in contact with Bernard, drag him down here to stand beside the detective constable. If he asked, they'd all think he was barking.

Beverley had always believed in it.

To the others, the death of the woman was tragic but simple, a horrible and freakish domestic accident, a lesson to us all not to be careless with knives. Smethurst had spoken to the neighbours.

'She brought the kiddie back alone a few days ago . . .' They pondered this. To Fry it was like a jigsaw with two sides, either the grandmother had taken charge of the granddaughter to give the happy couple some time alone, some time to propose or . . . Fry knew which side of the jigsaw his instincts favoured. There had been a set-to at the caravan park and the grandmother had come home in a huff. The wedding would upset their little family group. Motive and opportunity.

Enquiries had been made at the caravan park but no one had noticed anything out of order.

Fry knew straight away that the grandmother was lying. He struggled hard, just about able to smell the almonds beneath the fumes of heavy perfume, cigarettes and sweaty nylon knickers. But it was impossible for him to be certain. She sat in the room and told him it was an accident. They had been in the kitchen talking about Loll's engagement, the little kiddie had got hold of the knife from the drawer when they hadn't been paying attention. 'She didn't mean it,' Yvonne insisted. 'It was just an accident . . .' Lorraine had tripped on the chair leg and fallen against the kiddie and the knife and it had all been and gone in a moment. They'd just come back from a lovely holiday in the Lakes together. Everything was about their future. At that point the woman's face had emptied of all colour and Fry found himself leaping out of his chair to catch her as she toppled from hers.

Engagement. The word had chinked in his head as she said it, like the unintentional dropping of a coin. He watched her eyes, saw the diffraction of light, the shift of a moment.

When she'd recovered and been plied with restorative tea he asked her again.

'Davey,' she told him. 'We were in the Lakes staying in his caravan. The three of us.'

Her face bleached again and she asked if she could light up a cigarette.

They should talk to this Davey character although Yvonne didn't have many details. There was a brother in Spain who couldn't be found, who officially owned the Lake District caravan place. Other than that, this Davey bloke was the invisible man.

It was a struggle to hold on to the faintest breeze of almonds that drifted to Fry above the musks the woman gave off. What he should do was strip her naked, shower her off and have a bloody good sniff. Still, that would only cause its own problems. Fry decided it was time to talk to the granddaughter.

'Did you go somewhere nice on your holiday, Grace? Where did you go? Do you remember?'

Grace nodded.

'Do you think you can tell us? What was the name of the place you went to?'

Grace decided that was safe to say because that was before and it would not touch the lie. 'Coniston Water.' Her voice came out tiny in the high room.

'Did you have a lovely time? With your mum and your nan?' The police lady smiled at her.

Grace saw herself at the end of the jetty, saw pebbles and water so clearly that she wondered if she stilled the pictures in her head to hold them safe she might be ripped out of this room in an instant and dropped there. She held her breath.

'What did you do?'

Grace's head filled with sharp voices, with the clonk of torch against caravan, with the harsh sizzling of over-fried eggs. She emptied it. Thought only of binoculars.

'Davey gave me binoculars.'

Grace's voice had shrunk down to the size of a mouse scuttling the edges of the room, trying to escape.

The room felt like the understairs cupboard only she couldn't get out and the carpet wolves were not here on the slippy lino of the floor. She wanted to hear the taxi roll up outside, the engine ticking over, Mum's and Nan's heels clicking up the path.

Grace wondered if her teeth would leak black, the taste of liquorice was so thick in her mouth. She saw the kitchen, clean and sparkly, and Mum in her blue raincoat and the boots, and they were holding hands and whirling around, Nan clapping, cigarette dangling from her lips, ash falling. They were singing that song from the playground, 'Here comes the bride . . .' Grace held tight to this vision of her mother as they whirled faster and faster, the liquorice taste seeping around her mouth as she imagined it.

Sitting in the interview room with this little girl (what was she? Nine? Almost ten?), DI Fry was confused. He couldn't smell almonds at all, instead there was a waft of liquorice, just a faint tang as if his colleague might have a quarter of Pontefract cakes on him or a couple of loops of liquorice bootlaces doing up his shoes.

He turned to Constable Porter, on guard by the door, when the girl headed out with WPC Smethurst for a toilet break. 'You haven't got any liquorice on you, have you?'

Porter looked up at him as if it was a brainwave. 'Not a bad idea, guv, get some sweets in, get the kid at her ease.' And he sent someone over to the market hall for a quarter of dolly mixtures.

But the sweets didn't put her at her ease and who could blame her? He'd been to the house, seen the mess before it was mopped. Hence his request for a smiley WPC because Smethurst was serious and brusque. Miss Whiplash the lads called her, though not to her stony face. Personally he liked Smethurst's stony face, it had a sculpted perfection to it that she didn't daub with cosmetics, and she smelled of clean woman, not the usual disguise of powder and Coty. She smelled naked. He felt his face blush at the thought and sent her off to dredge him up another cup of tea.

The girl, Grace, did not eat the sweets. Told not to take sweets from strangers no doubt, alongside being told to look right, look left and look right again from the safety of the kerb. She didn't drink the squash either.

'Would you like some tea?' WPC Smethurst offered Fry's own, freshly brewed mug, a bellied-out china thing Beverley had bought at the market. Grace gave a small nod and her hand hooked itself around the handle. She took thirsty little sips. Fry thought she looked thin and underfed.

'I could run and fetch some biscuits,' offered WPC Smethurst but Grace looked wide-eyed, stark. As if they had offered her a poisoned apple or a deadly comb.

They had talked to her and talked to her until she felt as flimsy as paper, as if her dress was held to her with folded tabs.

'What happened, Grace?'

The small chunk of liquorice began to dissolve itself, make her mouth water.

'I didn't mean it,' she began. 'I didn't mean it . . .' Tears came and blurred the room away. She could be safe now, under the stairs.

'What didn't you mean, Grace? It's all right, you know, you can tell us . . .' The police lady's voice was almost as quiet as her own. Grace saw the place where the true lie would go. She wiped at her face. The police lady handed her a handkerchief, but Grace was afraid to use it, to turn its whiteness sticky and black.

Grace saw the truth and turned it, shaped it into the true lie. She told them how the knife was like a fish. Like the ones they'd seen in the aquarium at the zoo on the school trip. It was their big knife, the one she wasn't allowed. She shouldn't have been playing with it because Mum and Nan always said not to touch the knives. But it looked like a fish. And they were talking about Mum going on a holiday, on a honeymoon. They didn't see her. She didn't mean it.

'I didn't mean it.'

Grace saw it happen, saw her mother slip on something red, a lake the size of Coniston Water. She saw Mum dancing about, catching her heel on the splayed metal chair leg, like the time she had caught it before and she fell and sprained her wrist. Grace saw the scuffed and bending high heel. Truth knitted into lie.

'She tripped . . . on the chair leg . . .'

She saw Nan tottering into the kitchen on her heels and snagging her tights on the screws that held the seats on. 'Those fucking chairs,' she'd barked, except Grace did not say that.

She said, again, softer still, 'I didn't mean to.' Her voice sounded odd to her, fainter, like a pen running out. 'But . . . she fell . . .' The truth of the lie.

Detective Inspector Fry did not mention the overpowering aroma of liquorice during the last interview with the girl. He'd looked hard, there was nothing in her mouth. Clearly something did not sit right and his instincts, in a very backhanded way, were trying to help him. But he'd be buggered if he could work it out.

In the end, after the inquest returned a verdict of accidental death and the paperwork was filed, the grandmother had pleaded a desperate case for keeping custody of Grace. In fact DI Fry had been astonished that this brittle middle-aged woman disguised as a dolly bird was capable of any emotion. In the end, the fact that she never shed a tear swayed him. It made her seem genuine. A real pro would have pulled out all the stops and sobbed to sink a battleship. This Yvonne woman didn't push it. She stood a tall, dignified, shop-owning pillar of the business community and made the case that life should be made as normal as possible for her granddaughter after the tragedy. The grandmother, it struck him, had a plan.

Of course they drafted in Rachel Windrush, arriving like the saviour of the universe the way she always did. And, as he always did, he left off her correct title of 'Doctor'.

He felt for Grace. DI Fry never wanted to talk to Dr Windrush, not because she was a psychologist and he was intimidated, no such luck. It was worse. He felt she didn't listen. Even if you were just chatting in a corridor with her she bore an expression on her face as if she was thinking about how shiny her hair looked. She'd sat in meetings with one of those elegant giraffish legs of hers cocked over the other and it always struck him that she did so in order to get a better look at her expensive new shoes. He'd seen her once through the window of Russell Wantage in the precinct. He'd been with Beverley on a rare shopping trip, a day off to catch his breath after the Briden Edge murder had gone to court. Beverley had been waxing lyrical about some strappy red heels in the window. You'd only need one shoe after you'd forked out an arm and a leg for them, he'd gruffed and Beverley had gone silent, shut down on him. He'd looked into the shop and seen Rachel Windrush trying two different pairs at once, strutting across the shop floor from mirror to floor-length mirror, all the assistants on their knees.

Beverley was wearing Swedish clogs and wiping clay-dabbled hands on a big butcher's apron. Her hair was thrown up anyhow and stabbed with a pencil. She'd got slip dried onto a cheek, Persian Green she said it was called as she swiped at it with the back of her hand. He sat at the enormous table in the kitchen. A big black range was giving off heat and a cat was nesting on a cushion by the bottom oven.

Detective Inspector Fry thought he'd never seen his wife look so beautiful. He watched the high, round-apple cheeks of her arse as she moved between sink, dresser and range and was caught looking by Beard, who stood in the doorway suddenly, winking at Fry.

He was genial, this potter man, and he knew how to make stuff. Fry had taken the time yesterday to visit the new gallery that had opened down at the old mill. They'd got a selection of Beard's pots. Practical. Good-looking. Ray Beard. Of course you could wink when you'd won her.

'Liquorice?' Beverley mused as she took another square of shortbread from the baking pan and slid the rest towards Fry for seconds. Or was it thirds by now? 'Not almonds?' She gave it very serious attention, her lips, as always when she was thoughtful, pinching themselves into the shape of a prune. Her eyes, he saw, flecked with a hint of that Persian Green.

Then, wiping her sugared hands on the butcher's apron she said it all aloud, just as it was in the back of his head.

His instinct knew the grandmother had done it. Jealous or desperate, or both. But he couldn't get over the little kid. He believed her and yet the liquorice threw him. He knew it wasn't true and yet . . .

'Consider her options if you got her grandmother for it.' Beverley resolved it. 'Consider that, Fry, and I think, just now, you can live with the lie.'

He nodded, and then, 'But can they?'

As he stood to leave he handed her the Russell Wantage bag. An imperious purple with burnished gold lettering, he'd kept it behind him at the door, placed it at his feet as she'd made the tea in the kitchen.

'What's this?' She looked at him. He nodded for her to take the bag.

The shoes were gold, high-heeled, a cobweb of straps across the instep. The assistant had gone on about kid leather but he'd already been convinced just spotting them in the window as he'd walked past.

'They're the right size.' Beverley was amazed, held the shoe up where the leather caught the sunlight. Looked at him. Touched.

'Sorry,' he said, and she knew he meant it.

Dr Windrush did not ask Grace to stick out her tongue and say 'ah' or lift her jumper so she could listen to her heart with a stethoscope, like Dr Bannister. Grace was relieved, convinced that just one glance into her throat would reveal all, the memories and the lies piled in on top of each other like the contents of a dustbin. It was all tapping out in the morse code arrhythmia of her heart. Since The Day it had taken to lurching about or racing too fast for itself and then seeming to tire so drastically that she thought it might stop. She began to think of it as a sort of bird she was keeping safe behind the bars of her ribcage. It twittered about and frightened her but it was special, rare. It was all she had left.

Dr Windrush's office was soft and cool and dangerous. Grace's insides felt thick and woolly as she waited to be tested. She remembered going over and over page seven in the maths workbook to please Mr Pownall. That was what she must do now. Everything she said had to be as sure as pen, inked in permanently so that they would let her go.

She saw her mother in the kitchen in a boat on a red lake, her voice echoing across the surface, *Grace*. And the rooks coming from the treetops, twenty, thirty – she lost count as they spurtled upwards, a black cloak of feathers rising above the red lake, the grey rill of road in front of their house. *Comecomecomecomecome*, the cries crawked out into the sky, pulling the grey clouds down close. Thick, black, battering until she could see only cuts and scrapes of sky among the purplegreen blueblack. Beaks speared into her clothing, claws took hold. As they lifted her, her legs did not ache, did not dangle uselessly, they folded neatly beneath her and she soared.

Into the topmost tree, into the highest part of the rookery. A rattling, crackling sound around her shuttered out the world beyond those branches. The boughs sawed and bent with her. The rooks' beaks and claws weaving and teasing the nylon threads from the ugly blue horrible of cardigan, unravelled it, snaking it away from her, her hair tugged and furled. They made a nest of her. Warped. Weft. They settled inside her, a comfort of black beaded eyes reflecting water, the sun off the jetty, the silvered green of lake weed. Up. High. Far. Smooth white swords of beak arranged around her, protection and weapon.

8

BLINK AND YOU MISS IT

Rugeley, a bull of a burglar, shoulders like sides of beef, had commandeered the top bunk and Alec spent each night feeling more imprisoned in the tiny cage of bunk-bed frame. He entertained Rugeley with his nightmares.

'Can't you just fucking sleep?' Rugeley growled one red-eyed slop out. 'I'm grumpy enough in the mornings as it is, Lecky.'

In another life Alec would not have cared for the nickname but, issuing from Rugeley's mouth packed with cared-for teeth, it soothed him. Rugeley was pernickety about his toothbrush and toothpaste.

'My wife makes me and the girls go to the dentist every six months . . . well, not in here, like . . .' Rugeley ran a hand around his vast face. 'Yep. Got to keep me handsome, she says.'

Alec listened to the rasp of razor against Rugeley's hide.

How Rugeley ever fitted his muscular frame through anyone's carelessly left open window was a mystery to Alec. Less of a mystery was Rugeley's home life. Rugeley did not begin sentences with 'I', instead it was always, 'My wife . . .'

'My wife keeps the books, see . . . Got it up here,' Rugeley confided, tapping at the carefully stubbled surface of his rock-like head, '. . . and here . . .' He grinned, making breasts with his hands.

Alec had never had a visitor and had therefore never had the opportunity to see Rugeley's wife across the visiting room. As their confinement continued and Rugeley told more stories of his home life, Alec began to imagine her. Small and sparrowish and not beautiful, Alec gave his own personal Mrs Rugeley an interesting face, which he looked at in his mind each night as he searched for sleep. He closed his eyes and saw the slope of her cheek, his thumb traced the line of her lips. He felt guilty in the mornings for the infidelities he'd let her commit.

If he woke from a nightmare he imagined Mrs Rugeley beside him, crackling in the nylon nightie that Rugeley was fond of.

'Nothing like a bit of static . . . if you take my meaning.'

Alec struggled to remember the last time he had slept with Cherry and when the memory surfaced it was not good. The fracture between them then was clear to him now.

'My wife, see, is my partner . . . my team captain.' Rugeley was avuncular, dishing out advice to a fellow inmate, Trev, as they played half-hearted dominoes. 'You lads as diddle around, can't make your dicks up, dipping it here and there . . .'

'I wish.' Trev grimaced.

Rugeley creased his face, shook his head. 'You're missing the point.'

Alec understood. Alec had nothing, just prison, a list and lies, Rugeley had everything. He had three daughters.

'Know what it's like to live in a houseful of women, Lecky?'

Rugeley offered as they played rummy at association one day. Alec thought of his mother and the quiet of their house. He shook his head. 'I tell you. It's women as wear the trousers these days. My wife, I'm not kidding, she could take on any of these managing directors in their Jags. Run rings round the lot. Organized. Clued-up. Only the other week she . . .'

And Alec lost all concentration, saw nothing on his cards except the scenes of Rugeley's story. The Adventures of a Family Man. Alison, his eldest daughter, her success at college being threatened by interest from an unsuitable young man. His youngest daughter and her problems standing up for herself against a bully.

'My wife can't get over the fucking injustice. Our Samantha lamped her 'cause she's a fucking bully bitch. Do they deal with that? No. They punish my Sammy.'

Alec had a great deal of sympathy for Sammy. He saw her in the playground, pigtailed.

Rugeley began to sort his cards. 'My wife's going into school tomorrow afternoon. I tell you, Lecky . . . She's like a lioness, my wife.' He laid down a run of hearts. 'They'll wish for death before she's finished with them.'

Pride in Susanne, his middle daughter, and her skill at dressmaking.

'Like that Zandra Rhodes, she is,' Rugeley bragged, keen to share the Polaroid photos of a school fashion show.

For a year, Alec's days were filled with family. Then Rugeley was moved.

Alec's fantasy Mrs Rugeley packed her nylon nightie and

vanished from his dreams leaving him to a nightmare taking place in the hotel. Mr Shearwater was in the lift with his mother. The door shut upon Alec; he saw Mr Shearwater press the button to make certain. However hard and frequently Alec pressed the button the doors wouldn't open, the lights flicked upwards.

He ran up the stairs, Escher stairs, twisting and confusing him, and finally someone opened a firedoor into his face, waking him. Shouting. Sweating. He would realize he was in the birdcage bunk bed. The tiny window showing a fake square of light at the opposite wall as if, could he just stand on the top bunk, he might be able to, yes, stretch, on tiptoe, and he was leaning out into sunshine.

The sunshine of Bournemouth, blazing through the window at the far end of the corridor. All the doors were closed. He needed to get to his mother, to the right door, to save her from Mr Shearwater.

Each night, it ended when Mr Shearwater locked the door and threw away the key.

The cell seemed as broad as a savannah without Rugeley and his family to fill it. Attempting to break his nightmares, Alec moved to the top bunk. From there he was just able to see the view through the high eyeblink of window, and he looked outwards, took in the postage-stamp vista.

Along the wall was a haze of barbed wire that, from here, looked like a veil on a hat. Beyond that almost nothing moved. It was farmland, ploughed over and frosted hard. He looked forward then, to a day when he might be up here and catch the tractor or the harvester. Further still on the top edge before the next field was a stand of trees, gnarled and ancient-looking black poplar. The rookery was caught in the branches. Alec could see the tangles of nests. Five, seven. He didn't know much about birds, did rooks fly anywhere for the winter? As if in answer there came from the grey of the sky, the dark dagger of bird, wings angling like ailerons to balance on the wind. The rook landed beside a tangled nest, swayed under the wind and stood lookout.

He watched five of them settle into the tree before he felt brave enough to go down to the hotplate and chance breakfast.

9

INTARSIA

They had tried to stay in the old house but it didn't work. Lights on, lights off, Nan couldn't sleep. Grace fought hard not to sleep at all, tried to keep watch with the carpet wolves, and then would wake in a flood-sweat from a dream where the carpet wolves licked a terrible blood-red, Flat Stanley sort of Mum from the kitchen floor, sticky sinews stretching like toffee.

On the morning of the move Grace had to go to school and then later she was to go to Dr Windrush's office for her appointment. She awoke that morning from a tiring running dream to the sound of Nan vomiting.

'Are we not going now?' Grace asked as Nan swilled her mouth with cold water. 'Will we have to wait?'

'Get dressed.' Nan spat into the sink.

She wasn't sick again. She dragged through two cigarettes as Grace ate breakfast. They ate in the dining room now, although today the table was hemmed in by boxes. There were marks on the walls where the pictures had been, a bare floor, the rug rolled up with string behind the door. When Grace finished Nan flung the cereal bowl and spoon into the bin outside. Grace watched her through the French doors in the dining room. She couldn't remember when they'd last been opened. It had been in the summer and she knew it was connected to Mum because when she tried to think of it, tried to see Mum's face that afternoon, it was as if a curtain fell, just like in a theatre.

Grace added another layer to her fear today. She had no idea where the new flat was. She wondered whether, after her time with Dr Windrush finished, Nan would be there to collect her. She couldn't speak, her mouth tasted of milky glue. If she asked, Nan would be angry. Maybe, if she hadn't already decided to leave Grace, then annoying her with questions would sway her decision. She would shut the door and they would never see each other again. Grace's guts twisted and she reached the sink just in time.

The water washed the vomit away. Nan reached for the bottle of bleach she had left in the sink cupboard and tipped the last splash into the sink. It was like breathing in nettles.

Later, after Dr Windrush had asked questions and Grace had busked a variety of whitened lies, Dr Windrush opened the door to dismiss her. Nan was sitting outside in one of the boxy armchairs in the book-lined waiting room.

The flat was in a small block landscaped by trees and graced with a half-moon one-way drive. You entered at the left gate by the lions' heads and you exited from the right gate by the eagles. 'Springfield Court' the sign said in plastic letters. 'Nos 11–17' said a smaller white and black arrowhead sign that pointed down a small fork in the driveway. Nan steered the runabout around the back of the building. Grace noticed that each flat had square floor-to-ceiling windows that slid open onto a small balcony.

There were potted palms and spider plants softening the edges of the concrete stairs and a man in a brown shopcoat was buffing the brass doorware with a soft yellow cloth. Beside him was a neat workbox of cleaning stuffs.

'Afternoon.' He nodded. Nan nodded back tugging Grace up the flight of stairs. She was already taking the new keys from her bag. She handed two keys to Grace. They were on a fob, a freebie advertising Fran's salon.

'Open up, then,' Nan snapped. The number on the door was '11'. Grace looked at the keys, both Yale. Nan's claws scratched at them.

'This one. That one's for the door downstairs so you can let yourself in there.' Grace wondered how she would ever tell them apart. She reached up, on tiptoe, fitted the new key into the lock.

The downstairs-door key's teeth were a miniature mountain range jutted with peaks and edges. The front-door key was a croc-odile jaw. She never confused them.

Each afternoon, except for Dr Windrush days, she would arrive at the flat and be greeted by Mr Eatoff's polite but unsmiling nod.

'Afternoon,' he would say, as if she was a grown-up. Sometimes he held the door open for her the way he held it for other resident ladies, like Mrs Brant, a divorcee on the ground floor with hair as thick and black as ink.

'Not natural,' Nan spat her decision from their balcony one evening as they watched Mrs Brant climbing into an open-top sports car. Then there was Gemma, some sort of nurse or beautician who lived along the hall from them and wore a white uniform and white shoes and was so beautiful Grace couldn't believe she was real.

'Masseuse at the Spa, my arse,' Nan delivered the verdict. 'That fucking white coat isn't fooling anyone.'

'Stuck-up cow' was the sentence passed upon Miss Loftus who lived above them.

Grace secretly liked Miss Loftus and the plants that trailed down to their balcony from hers, the three-pointed stars of ivy, the tiny blue flowers and fizz of leaves on her Swann River daisies. The Black-eyed Susans.

'*Thunbergia alata*. Aren't they beautiful?' Miss Loftus's fingers were delicate behind the vivid orange-coloured blooms as she turned their black faces towards Grace.

Grace had been locked out. Left her keys on the worktop in the galley kitchen. Miss Loftus had let her in, offered a cup of tea while she waited, wedged the door to her flat open with a statue of Buddha so that they would hear Nan on the stairs.

'What did you say to her?' Nan couldn't shut their door fast enough. 'What fucking sob story did you spin?'

At school, Grace was alternately pitied and picked on. Everyone knew about 'the accident' and most chose to shut their traps the way Grace did. She had found a way to be invisible, to keep as still and as quiet as possible and go unnoticed. They were scared of her, of what she had done. One playground spat ended abruptly when, taunted to her furthest edge, she yelled at Michael, 'Watch I don't stab you.'

She was whisked to the staff room. She hadn't wanted to say anything but Michael had been mean, had pushed and pushed and pushed and before she could control it the bile rose in her, her face flushed white-hot and the words came out.

She had expected the slipper, a few quick slaps of it across her outstretched palms. What she got was a cup of tea and, some time later, a forced apology from a tear-stained Michael.

As Grace expected, Dr Windrush had spies at the school for that very afternoon she asked questions about the incident. Grace waited to be tested, to be tricked and tripped up but Dr Windrush did none of those things.

Grace liked the creaky leather chair that sat at Dr Windrush's desk. Outside, there were trees with tiny leaves, and when the sun shone inside it cast myriad shadows. Grace loved the shadow afternoons, always sat in the chair that faced the window so that the shadows would pattern her. If only Dr Windrush would go. She knew Dr Windrush was a test, they were waiting for her to forget the true lie. Waiting to catch her.

In the summer holidays there was nothing to do all day, with Nan at the shop. Grace headed to the library most mornings. She could sit among the books and not be noticed. She could wander into town later, careful to avoid Nan's shop, and, weather dependent, swing in the park until she grew hot and tired or cold and wet. Then she could dawdle back to the flat. In the garden one afternoon, she remembered her binoculars, they would still be hidden in the caravan cupboard, folded into her smelly T-shirt.

After three weeks of aimless mooching, Miss Loftus caught her sitting on the stairs one afternoon. Grace had been watching a spider weave a web in the leaves of the tallest palm.

'Locked out again?' Miss Loftus smiled as she pattered past. Grace made no reply. A few moments later Miss Loftus was back bearing a frozen lolly and a packet of seeds.

'Here you go,' she said, her voice soft. 'Meant to drop these in with your nan. You have to soak them in water for twenty-four hours. Just pop them in a glass on your sink top for a couple of days and then you can plant them. Softens the casing, you see. D'you want to do that? Would your nan mind?'

Grace looked at the blue packet, at the deep blue flowers depicted amid deep green tendrils.

'*Ipomoea*,' Miss Loftus intoned, 'Morning Glory.'

Next afternoon, when Grace dawdled back from a day mooching around the market, she found Miss Loftus in a deckchair on the back lawn. Mr Eatoff was putting up a huge umbrella for shade.

'Thanks ever so, Ken.'

Mr Eatoff nodded to Grace with the greeting, 'Afternoon.'

'Hello there.' Miss Loftus smiled. Grace had her keys in her hand this time. 'Lovely day. Got your keys, I see.'

Grace nodded. Miss Loftus had a vividly coloured fabric shopper open beside her. Inside, was a tornado of colours, wools, all textures ravelled together. A pair of thick wooden needles jabbed into them as if they were skinny arms in a lucky dip. Miss Loftus's hands were busy, a pair of thinner needles clicking wildly in a confusion of points and yarn and fingertips.

'Do you know how to knit, Grace?' Miss Loftus looked at her over the bright silver frames of her glasses. They were on a chain around her neck, the sun catching the metal and making sharp stars. 'Here. Let me show you. It's not hard.'

Miss Loftus dived a hand into the lucky-dip bag and came up with another pair of needles, a ball of yarn in a deep forest green. Something in Grace's stomach twitched at the green, made her memory splash cold with Coniston Water.

It began with a loop no bigger than her fingernail and as her needles duelled with her fingers it grew, lengthened, each after-noon. Sometimes they sat out on the lawn, sometimes on Miss Loftus's balcony.

After a week Nan asked the questions but by then Grace had had nearly seven days to think of the true lie she would tell.

'What have you been doing with yourself?' Nan enquired, taking her mug of coffee and her cigarette out onto their balcony.

'Been at the library,' Grace answered. She saw Nan raise her eyebrows skyward as she folded herself into the low wooden deckchair, a bargain buy from the junk shop on the corner. Nan's eyes clocked the trailing plants that were winding their way up the side trellis, tall, beautiful amid the stunted conifers and pots that Nan had placed there.

'Where the fuck did this come from?' She peered upwards to Miss Loftus's balcony. 'Did you plant this? Have you been talking to that stuck-up cow from upstairs?'

'No.' Grace was not lying. First, Miss Loftus was not a stuck-up cow, she taught needlework and textiles at a local college. Secondly, they hardly ever talked. Just knitted.

As the summer wore on, Grace became more skilled. Her stitches neatened and she tensioned properly. Miss Loftus taught her moss stitch, how to cable, how the patterns and possibilities were endless. She learned to tie in the intarsia of colours and yarns to make something spectacular and textured.

'I think you like green. It's your colour,' Miss Loftus noted as Grace's choices from the lucky-dip bag swerved from forest to lime to kelly. Miss Loftus watched her over the top of her glasses. Grace had edged it in chocolate and ochre because she knew that's where the shoreline was.

It was raining that last afternoon. Grace suddenly came to the end of the knitting and Miss Loftus sat beside her showing her how to cast off. 'Like a boat.' Grace gasped. The stitches sealed themselves with a twist and a turn. The scarf was finished.

Miss Loftus looked at the colours and textures for a long time, her hand smoothing gently across the yarns. She looked at Grace, draped the scarf around her neck and in a whispery, faded voice she said simply: 'Beautiful.'

It was finished in time for the new term. She was to be in Class Six this year, far away from Mr Pownall and her seat at the back. She lay awake the night before school trying to remember the room. It was at the top corner of the single-storey sixties building. It jutted out onto the car park and the playing field. What could she see through the windows? The class turned away from the garages and the trees where the rooks were. She had a tight-chested dream where her neck was in a brace, Nan clicked it shut around her, pinching the skin, and she couldn't turn now, couldn't look out onto the field. There were trees, weren't there? Just beyond the chain-link fence of the playing field?

In the end she need not have worried. She was placed up in the corner by the sink and from there she could see out in two different directions, back out across the playground to the Manchester

Poplars at the edge of the council estate and, if she turned her head left, out towards the higgledy-piggledy house where she saw instantly that a mass of rooks had gathered in the branches of the copper beeches.

'Knitting, is it?' Mrs Knightstone, the librarian, had raised her eyebrows very high up her forehead. 'I think I can help you there.' And she began to stride across the library, waggling her follow-me finger. With quick darting gestures she pulled out three volumes for Grace: a small brown fabric book, *Knitting for Victory*, another wider, more modern edition in primary colours titled *Clackety-clack Knit that Bag!*, and a small pocket-sized spiral-bound paperback, *Intarsia: A Yarn Around Europe*.

'And, of course . . . we must not forget . . .' She sidled swiftly through the shelving to a far corner, the follow-me finger waggling once more, her hand darting out to a volume under a sign that read 'Charles Dickens'. Grace took it, read the title, *A Tale of Two Cities*, and looked at Mrs Knightstone.

'You'll see.' And she winked.

It was as though a key had turned and opened her up. The book was difficult but Grace had time to persevere, and time spent trap shut, head in a book was time she didn't get on Nan's nerves or get under Nan's feet.

She hid on the balcony, curling into the wooden chair, screened from the living room by the weeping fig that Fran had brought as a house-warming gift. With the doors closed, Nan and Grace could pretend they were in different worlds. Nan's cigarette-clouded landbase could revolve slowly as Grace's small cold planet found its orbit in the universe at last. Grace was not alone, she had Madame de Farge.

She had knitted Coniston Water into that first scarf; now, befriended by Madame de Farge, she could knit everything, put all her secrets into the safekeeping of wool and stitches.

Nan never remembered pocket money and only remembered school dinner money because it freed her from having to think about lunches. Grace knew that she could not ask for the needles and wool she wanted. This year Nan had also forgotten Grace's birthday. She had been ten a month ago but perhaps, without Mum, there was no point to remembering it. Grace could not look in that direction.

On her way home from school she had come across a small side street up by the row of banks and building societies. Along the middle of it, next to a furniture shop, was No More Twist, a wool shop, the window adorned with willow baskets filled with yarns in every shade of red incarnadine. The colour pulled at her, made her eyes fill and her heart hop about, desperate.

Grace saved the lie up. Waiting. She was trying to ration the power of her true lying. She had to use up almost all her true lies during her sessions with Dr Windrush, when the intensity of telling them made her giddy, as if she'd been on the roundabout going too fast, and the taste of liquorice made her mouth feel dry and sticky.

'What trip?' Nan flicked at her lighter, finding it disobedient.

'To the zoo.' Grace had calculated how much she needed and how much she could feasibly ask for.

'You'll have to wait. I've no cash. Remind me tomorrow.'

*

She was shocked on the Saturday morning. She had been up early, needing a drink to take away the taste of liquorice that had begun to permeate her mouth in anticipation of reminding Nan of the true zoo lie. As she sat at the table Nan pulled a five-pound note from her purse and handed it to Grace.

'Here. And take this an' all.' Another pound was unfolded, examined as if it was counterfeit and chucked at Grace. 'Enough for the zoo and you can go out today. I don't want to see you back here till after eight. Understand?'

The wool shop was filled with all sorts of different treasures. A long oak table groaned with baskets of ribbon and findings, clasps and buttons and horn toggles. There were knitting bags with zips or clacking wooden handles. Dark wood shelves insulated the walls and a dresser at the back was stuffed to bursting with wools and silks. There was a soft, warm smell to the place. Grace felt a rush as she stepped through the door. Her heart was flacking against her ribs as she moved past the long table. The wools were colour-coded: greens, browns and, at the far corner, oranges, yellows, reds.

She bought herself a pair of small-gauge needles. The selection of three balls of wool was not choice, it was compulsion, the red yarn drawn to her hand. As she made her way, hardly breathing, back to the counter at the front of the shop her eye snagged on a small bleached-out basket on the floor: 'Ends of Line 25p'. Among the balls and skeins was a tightly wound silver, dart-bright and cold.

She sat at the back of the library in the small bucket chair by the shelf marked 'Charles Dickens' until Mrs Knightstone approached, waggling her follow-me finger once again.

'This way,' she whispered.

She took Grace through a door marked 'Staff Only' into a short corridor and then a room full of sofas and a kitchen corner. Mrs Knightstone ushered Grace into the room.

Several cups of tea, two KitKats and a sausage roll saw Grace through the day. Her eyes narrowed their focus to her fingertips as they translated her thoughts for the benefit of wool and needles. Grace had tensioned the stitches too tightly, she knew; the red wool coagulated together, the silver thread harsh and nylon between.

She cast off, hands shaking, fingers aching and sore where she had jabbed the tips with the points of the needles. The stitches bared the needle, twist and off, twist and off, until the red flag fell into her lap. Let go.

It was six-thirty when Grace arrived back at the flat. Mr Eatoff was not polishing brasses or buffing the flooring and the stairs were very quiet. Grace opened the door to number 11 to find it dark inside. Nan was nowhere to be seen. Grace foraged in the fridge for a squodgy tomato and the last of the plastic cheese slices. There was enough bread for one round of sandwiches.

She had no idea when she had fallen asleep. She had been dreaming she was on the jetty, her binoculars pinned to her face. In the morning she got up to pee and found Mr Eatoff already there before her. Instead of his usual brown shopcoat he was wearing Nan's gold kimono, a black dragon snarled up the back. Mr Eatoff's legs were revealed beneath its knee-length; they were old-mannish, half hairless.

At the wool shop on Monday after school Grace found all the browns and golds and blacks she needed.

THIS IS NOW

1990

10

ROADKILL

And the rooks came, as surely as guardians, resting in the boughs of the oak in the expanse of field beyond.

Grace had asked Maisie to drive her over there, had looked out of the window like a rubbernecker at the point on the dual carriageway where Nan had become roadkill. They had pulled up onto the hard shoulder a few yards from the first tyre scorches on the tarmac.

'All right?' Maisie asked, already knowing the answer. Grace felt cold and white. She reached for the door and stepped out into the light drizzle.

Tyre tracks were gouged in the banking, tearing through a rent in the hedge. Grace climbed the slippery ground, slithering but determined. The rain pattered among the leaves and she saw where branches were broken, their sappy insides showing, and on the right-hand side the burnt part where the car had caught fire.

Her heart, which had kept good time in recent years, began to jitter and explode. *Now. This is it. Now*, Grace said to herself. But the tears wouldn't come. They were sealed into the tomb. In the cold and damp her body juddered as if Nan was shaking her.

Nan and Ken had only just flown back from a trip looking at property in Spain the week before.

She had not wanted to go to the funeral. Hugo had offered to come with her. 'For immoral support,' he joked, assuming, as always, that his charm was the cure-all.

'My nan's funeral, Hugo. Our first date?' But that had only given him hope.

Grace had taken the day off work and had woken at about five. The early spring sunshine flooded in through the kitchen window of her rented flat as she tried to drink a cup of tea. She had puked moments later, running the water into the scruffy stainless-steel sink.

The voice whispered in her head: 'Are we not going now? Will we have to wait?'

'Get dressed.' Nan's voice in the old house.

Grace had changed three times, had walked down the thin stairs to lock and then unlock the front door. She had sat for a long time on the top stair, keys in hand, ready, but not ready to go.

In the end she had arrived at Springfield Court just as Nan did, in the back of the hearse. 'You're late!' Ken, looking strangled in his shirt and tie, hissed as he pushed out of the doors. 'We've been ringing and ringing . . .' Fran, puffy-faced, was behind him, Debbie sombre in something borrowed from the shop.

For the following few weeks, Grace had put off coming back to the flat but Ken had pestered her with phone calls. Now, today, after she'd found the courage to come after work, he greeted her with characteristic sharpness.

'Well. You're here now. Shame you never popped round when she was alive.'

Ken, she could see, was tearing up and she did not have the hard heart to tell him of how she was always the unwelcome, the unwanted. *'Long as you're out of my sight.'* She heard Nan's voice from the kitchen. Grace didn't know why she was here. She wanted to run away from the responsibilities of Nan's demise, from everything she felt at this moment, standing on the old carpet, wishing she could step onto the balcony and shut the door on Ken and his grief, on old times.

'What about her clothes and stuff?' She could see Ken struggling as he looked towards the bedroom. He no longer wore his brown shopcoat. He had retired earlier in the year. The house in Spain was going to be their first place together. Grace wanted five minutes of vision through Ken Eatoff's eyes, to be able to see her grandmother in another light, a quite different, other Nan.

'I'll sort it out. Is there anything you would like, Ken?' Grace offered, standing in the living room.

'Yes.'

He turned on her suddenly, drawing himself up straight, the way he had always done when he opened the door for residents. 'For all you didn't get on, I'd like you to think about everything she did for you. For you and for your mam.' She heard 'before you killed her' echo from inside his head and Grace snapped the lid shut on herself. He hadn't finished. 'I'd just like you to remember those weekends when she visited you at university.'

Grace heard the words and struggled not to look bewildered and shout, 'What?' at the top of her voice.

'The fact that, however small you might consider it, however much you didn't care, she cared enough to make the effort those few times. She was still, even after everything, your nan.' Ken was righteous, indignant. He looked at her with eyes that suspected she was a cold-blooded killer. Grace envisioned herself with a remote control at the roadside, swerving Nan's car from the inside lane.

Nan had only been once to the university, on the first day, to dispose of her. She had never visited again, not even that last terrible week, part way through her second year, when Grace had dropped out and struggled homewards on the train with all her worldly goods in suitcases and carrier bags. Grace had no idea where Nan had been on the weekends Ken spoke of. She wondered how many weekends away 'a few' was and who Nan had been with. Someone else, someone she did not want to guess at, someone that Ken did not need to know about. Grace wondered if her silence counted as a true lie.

'Think on is all I ask, Grace.' And he left her then.

Grace stood, unmoving, for nearly an hour. There was a tarn deep inside her, cold and black, but it did not empty.

From the payphone in the hallway she called a house clearance firm.

She had parked, purposely, at the DIY store so that she would have to walk into the shopping precinct the long way, through the market. She was dragging her feet. Now, she had walked past the shop front and seen Debbie inside, busy with a mother of the bride judging by the elaborate turquoise hat that was being tried on with a variety of colour coordinated outfits. Grace felt just as she always had in the concrete shopping tunnel, as if it was forbidden. She couldn't bring herself to walk down towards A Cut Above where she knew Fran would still be madly twirling brushes into wet hair. Grace was not brave enough to face the warm welcome, Fran's tears and the consoling cup of coffee.

The shop was empty when Grace pushed the door at last. Debbie could be glimpsed in the back room talking on the telephone, her hands busy with invoices, sorting out deliveries. The bell rang out, a few bright tinkling notes that made the hairs rise on the back of Grace's neck. Nan would catch her. She'd be in trouble.

Which was exactly the look mirrored on Debbie's face as she turned from her phone call. Debbie, now in her thirties, was more stylish than Nan had ever given her credit for.

'Oh. Hello.' She greeted Grace with a wavering smile. 'I was just on the verge of tilling up.' Grace saw how nervous she was as she stepped up to the counter.

'I don't know what your plans are, Debbie . . .' Grace was tentative, not wanting to put Debbie on any more of a spot. Debbie gave a quick and fakely careless shrug, cutting across Grace.

'Oh, don't know really. I'd be happy to stay on but that all depends on . . .' Her voice trailed off. Grace saw the tears well in Debbie's eyes and hurried to save her.

'I want to sell you the business.'

The tears welled deeper but brighter. 'Seriously?'

'If you want it?'

Debbie couldn't speak, took a deep choked breath inwards, breathed out through her mouth and the words came out calm at last. 'Oh. I want it. I want it, Grace . . . I've spoken to the bank . . . about arranging a loan . . . If we agree on . . . you know . . . I can speak to Amy tonight . . . she works at the bank in the small business—'

'For a pound,' Grace stopped her.

Debbie couldn't speak or breathe, her face shocked. Her shaking hand reached for the steadying influence of the familiar glass display case. Keys on her hip clattered against it, breaking her thoughts.

'But . . . Grace . . . I—'

'My final offer.'

'Grace, it's worth much—' Debbie couldn't continue, pressed her lips together.

'I know what it's worth.' Grace knew what was worth more and held Debbie's gaze until she understood. Debbie took a moment to master her emotions. In the silence they could hear the noises from the precinct, heels and cars and babies.

'Why, Grace?'

'You've earned it.' Grace's own voice failing at last.

After that last visit to the old Springfield Court flat with Ken it came as a relief to put it on the market. With the shop in Debbie's rightful hands Grace knew there was nothing that should hold her here. She thought back to that day so many Augusts ago when Mr Keene had handed her the slip of paper with her A level results printed upon it, the four-letter escape code she had so desperately wanted. She had a summer job at Fran's, washing hair and sweeping up, and it would only have been a few steps down the way to nip into the shop and tell Nan the news that they would be free of each other. But she had not taken those steps. She had gone back to the salon and kept her trap shut.

The day she left, Nan had piled all Grace's stuff into the back of her latest car. No more runabouts. Now Nan had a flashy coupé. But it didn't matter how many bags they packed, how much they tried to prise themselves apart, the liquorice of the true lie stuck to them. Nan had cast a cursory glance around the university hall of residence before lighting up in the car park. Where others had parted tearfully or cheerfully with waves and kisses, Nan simply ground out the stub of her cigarette and slithered behind the wheel.

'See you then,' had been her parting shot. She'd reversed out, the car wheeling backwards, and then as she arced forwards towards the exit she did not, like other parents, toot the horn, wave or wind down the window for a last-minute declaration of love disguised as a checklist of personal belongings. Grace had known then. They were each other's sentence.

After the university disaster she had learned to touch-type and taken the temp job at FRJ. She told herself that it was her friendship with Maisie that was keeping her there now. The job was not demanding, it paid the rent and then some. But it was worse than that, worse even than a simple lack of ambition. She had no idea of what else to do. And she needed to do something.

'Get out of that flat,' Maisie advised in the coffee shop, shovelling sugar into her mocha. She had that wild-eyed look that was part passionate feeling and part a consequence of wearing contact lenses. 'Buy yourself a place. You can afford to.'

Grace felt somehow that the money from Nan's flat was poisoned.

*

She had a sense of flight, of wanting to stretch out her wings, purplegreen and blueblack. But she did not know where to fly. It seemed Hugo would crystallize things for her.

She knew she was being cornered the moment Hugo made the excuse that James needed the computer in Hugo's office and shunted her into the absent Don's broom cupboard of space. There was a long thin window that overlooked the inner court-yard of the building. A slimline view of brickwork and, just at sill level, the topmost branches of a stunted tree.

'Sit yourself down then, dolly, and we'll draft this letter.' Hugo, big and bluff, swivelled himself towards her in Don's power-crazed leather chair. It was the same every day, like facing a lion on a footbridge. 'Hup two, hon, park that arse here,' and he slapped at his lap.

'"Hup two?" Hugo, what am I? The vice-captain of your hockey team?' she said, planting her arse firmly in the skinny swivel chair. He winked at her, his bear brown eyes flashing warmly.

'My *vice* captain.' He gave a laugh, the one he thought was masculine and seductive, and Grace couldn't believe she'd handed that to him.

'Can we just get on with the letter?' She turned to the keyboard and, as usual, he leaned forward, the deep V of his spread legs pegging her into the corner of the desk.

'Dear Bastard Joe Broughton . . .' Hugo began. Her fingers had flinched ready to type and she glared at him, his face too close to her shoulder. 'Bastard should be capitalized, Gracie, it's a title.'

'If you're going to fart about—' She tried to push her chair back but Hugo's square pork chop of a hand blocked her.

'Don't, Gracie, please.' His voice was soft behind her ear. 'I need your input, you know what an illiterate I am. You've got the words. Help me out? Pretty please . . . with nobs on?'

It was the final 'You're making it very hard for me' that snapped her. Hugo expected her to fold, sighing, into his butch embrace, instead Grace wheeled around, fist clenched, clipping him on the edge of his jaw. His head snapped upwards, Hugo grunting as he bit his tongue. He backed away across the cramped floor-space, blood seeping from his tongue, his hands raised in mock surrender.

In Carmel's office later, she tried to complain.

'He's like that. Ride it out till he gets bored.' Carmel shrugged.

'He's been to my flat. Uninvited.'

'Not my problem. Once you leave the building I don't have to give a stuff.' Carmel offered a biscuit from a newly opened pack. 'Look, if you're so determined . . . Is it just verbal abuse and stupid joking around or has he touched you?'

'He's always too close.'

'Listen to the question. Has he actually, physically, sexually touched you?' Carmel's tongue moved inside her cheek picking biscuit out of her jawline. Grace gave up. She had punched Hugo, had made him bleed. If anyone had a case, Carmel commented, it was Hugo.

She let the doorbell ring and ring and ring, sitting at the kitchen table, unable to make a cup of tea, feeling instead a terrible urge for a cupboard under the stairs, a rubber torch and a glass of Tizer.

'I know you're in there,' he called through the letter box. Grace half-wanted to laugh at the police-raid tone. 'For Pete's sake, Gracie, open the door. Look. I can see you from down here. I can see your foot.'

She looked down at her foot. The bell jangled on. Upstairs she could hear Barry yell, 'For fuck's sake let the bastard in.'

Hugo leaned to the letter box again, this time as he flapped it open Grace looked back at him.

'You'd think you'd get the message, Hugo.' She tried to sound haughty, raised a sarcastic eyebrow.

'I can't believe you went crying to Carmel. This is us, Gracie. Me and you. We can sort this between us, can't we?'

Grace said nothing, stood to go back up the stairs.

'Wait. I'm sorry. I'm really sorry.'

Two hours later in the pub around the corner ('Thank Christ for that,' Barry had yelled from his upper window as they left), Grace felt sick and dizzy. She did not want to be here. Hugo had bought drinks and mouthed apologies and attempted to recover lost ground with jokey stories and charm-soaked smiles. But the drink blistered his surface, peeled away a layer, and Grace didn't want to listen to tales of the rugby club in Amsterdam shoving lemons up their arses. Hugo laughed with a big red mouth, black fillings here and there, spit spattered onto the shiny top of the table. He was careful not to touch her but his physical bulk took up all her space, his arms windmilling with the actions of his story, pinning her.

She excused herself as he headed back to the bar. 'I'll get you a short. What do you want? Whisky? Vodka?' He didn't wait for her answer, gave all his attention to the change in his hand.

As she moved towards the toilets the corridor closed in on her, brown and beery. A door opened suddenly on her left and a man carrying a huge stack of steaming plates almost barged her.

'Sorry, love.' He turned and pushed through another door revealing a kitchen, wildly busy, fogged with smoke from a steak-loaded grill, and beyond, a door.

As she drew up outside the flat she was ashamed to see Hugo. Triumphant.

'You're no lady are you, Grace?' He shook his head in mock dismay, 'Tut, tut.'

'What are you doing here? Apart from nicking my parking space.' She looked through the wound-down window, managing to make her features seem harsher than she felt.

'Looking for an apology. Thinking of ways you can make this up to me.' Hugo slapped a hand on the roof of the car. 'You know, I just want a bit of fun and a fuckaround, Gracie. It's that simple.' He leaned in through the window as if to kiss her.

Grace was pleased at the squeal the tyres made as she drove off.

She thought she'd give him an hour to clear the area and if he was still there when she drove back she would crash at Maisie's little house by the canal. She drove past there first, glad to see the light on in the tiny front window. It was a cosy-looking terrace. Maisie had painted the living room Imperial Purple and the kitchen behind a deep Dragon's Blood red. The kitchen gave onto a tiny terrace of garden. They had sat out there last summer, tea lights glowing like fairies. Grace thought about going back to her flat and its horrible yellow-painted kitchen and the white melamine of the crappy cupboards, that fusty smell in the bathroom, the crack in the toilet seat.

She snagged herself in the one-way system and, in order to unsnag herself, she took a left turn. This part of town was Monkton but everyone called it Leafy Heights. It was a 'sought-after area', full of mature gardens, that she had never visited before and, hopelessly lost, she took a random turning, the next right. She saw the sign, draped with ivy from the wall behind, 'Ruskin Road'.

The road was wide and sweeping. On either side Edwardian villas cosied into their gardens behind beautifully laid brick walls and wrought-iron gatery. The trees that lined the street had been recently pollarded. Mid-range cars were parked two or three deep in driveways and the place gave off a sense of tranquillity. It seemed to Grace that suddenly she couldn't hear the engine any more, she could hear the wind in the trees, the birdsong. The house was in the middle of the right-hand row. The smartest thing about it was the 'For Sale' sign hammered into the overgrown wilderness of the front garden, where a ceanothus was in full deep blue bloom. Before she thought about it Grace was pulling into the driveway, getting out of her car, not even closing the door.

She stepped up to the windows. The house was in darkness. Inside, the rooms were bare. Waiting for her.

The next morning she took a sick day and was at the estate agent's before they opened. By lunchtime on Friday she had watched them take down the For Sale sign and spent an hour at the solicitor's going over the paperwork.

A house. The house. Her house. Home.

11

AS GOOD AS HIS WORD

Alec had been at the open prison for just over two years. He had been transferred here and taken it as a sign that he would be paroled, a promising first step back to civilization. It began well. His room had a window that looked out across the prison garden. In the two years since he had arrived rooks had built five nests.

But he had been denied parole. He had, he knew now, foolishly anticipated someone reading his file and his prison record and deciphering the truth. He said nothing, not a complaint, no outburst against the injustice of his sentence. He did not breathe too heavily. He had hoped, vainly, that it would be over.

He did not, could not, say he was sorry. They had already decided 'No' before they even met him.

Now, a year on and due for a parole hearing again, Alec was settled in a three day a week gardening-handyman job at the local vicarage. His position was voluntary, a proving ground, he had been told, with a view to paid work and a reassimilation into society. But it had never progressed to a paid job and Alec didn't care. He valued the walk to the bus stop, the ride through town, the time spent at someone else's home, more than any cash. He had nowhere to send cash, nothing to spend it on in prison except perhaps an extra KitKat. But he could cash in the experience; each night, even when he had not been at the vicarage, he could walk around the extensive and overgrown garden in his head and find sleep.

He had been placed there at the request of the governor himself. His daughter was the vicar's wife and he was disturbed by the pauper lifestyle to which she was having to become accustomed. She had been married for eight years and had four babies with another on the way. As the governor put it, the Church of England expected his daughter and her husband to heat and maintain the vast Gothic vicarage on 'tuppence ha'penny a week' and, he had concluded, 'If God won't provide, I have to.'

Alec got the position because he had done a plumbing course, a carpentry course and was a fully qualified mechanic. On that first day, Ruth Standforth had looked pleased to see him; that look never faltered and he saw he was her sigh of relief, a helpful stranger. After she had seen the dire state of the prison packed lunch he'd brought along on the first day, she insisted on a slice of quiche, a slab of cake, a pot of tea. When she found he could cook he took on some of those duties too. She wrote out his cake recipes, the ones his mum had taught him, and kept them in a file in the kitchen. He made curry, a dish including vegetables that the boys ate, unawares, mopping it up with naan.

As he fixed the Standforths' lumbering estate car one afternoon he found himself talking to Ruth Standforth about his A levels and the degree in English he'd done in prison.

'Ha. P'raps I should go to prison. Might finish my History of Art,' Ruth mused.

'Finish it? You started, then?' Alec pictured her on campus, arms full of books.

'Yes. But his nibs was doing Theology. And then, of course . . .' She patted her filled-out bulge.

'Biology,' Alec finished it for her. Each saw the other's thin sad smile perfectly mirrored.

With each day and each cake Alec found himself running off at the mouth, talking about growing veg when he first came to HMP Meadowbridge and how he had rowed to Iceland.

'For fun. And charity.' Alec rolled himself out from under the car where he was replacing the sump plug. He neglected to mention that it had staved off insanity for a while. Ruth handed him cake.

'Dorset Apple.' She took a napkin from her sleeve. 'They let you go to Iceland? Isn't the sea a bit rough after Greenland?'

Alec laughed, a crumb of cake catching in his throat. 'Indoors,' he spluttered, 'on a rower. With pins tracking across a map.' Ruth's thin and bitten fingers filched a broken-off chunk of cake from the plate. 'They didn't let anyone out of the Dogs' Home.' He was sorry the second the words came out, but the name was as familiar to him as 221b Baker Street or Sesame Street. Ruth looked at him, broke off more cake.

'The Dogs' Home? Is that what you called the other prison?' Ruth cradled her cup, her pregnant belly protruding under her worn-out sweater, her perished leggings stretched around it.

Alec was quiet then, thinking of the razor-wired landscapes of the seven different prisons he had occupied. He had kept the snapshots in his head, trying to fling wide the doors of his mind so it would not matter where his body was. But this job at the vicarage was picking him apart. Each day Ruth Standforth's kindness, her reliance, coloured him in for a while but it was only with watercolour pencils. Each day when he returned to prison he was rubbed out again.

Ruth spoke into the silence, her voice tentative. 'What did you do, Alec?'

But there was rain coming. Alec looked up, away.

'I should do the gutters.'

He saw from his various perches on ladders around the vicarage, that Ruth was the one who should be ordained. She was the engine of the parish, meeting the Parish Council, refereeing the infighting and politics between the organist and choirmaster. The vicar did not take over the running of the Brownie pack when no other volunteers were forthcoming. He did not spend two days baking for the Sale of Work. He didn't organize jumble sales, flower rotas, beetle drives or the Whit Walk. He didn't photocopy the flyers for the Easter Services or the Harvest Festival. The vicar sat in his study at the back of the house and communed with God, who surely could be seen through the rotting French doors he spent his hours staring through. God, it seemed, had chosen the names of their boys – Joseph, Jerome, Job and Jonah – channelling his choices through the vicar with his divine right to christen them, and allowing the vicar his still more divine right to ignore them. God liked jazz and locked doors and smokes. God was also, it seemed, to be found at least three afternoons a week on the country club golf course.

'Can't you keep them quiet?' Reverend Standforth demanded one afternoon. He was trying to compose a sermon from his jazz-imbued mount as the boys burnt off energy that had been suppressed all day at their infant school.

'Can't you buy earplugs?' Ruth had rejoined. She was about to counsel a wedding couple. Alec wondered if their glimpse of vicarage wedded bliss would put them off.

'I couldn't ask you to watch the boys for half an hour, could I? Only I have to speak to Mrs Wickham about the flower rota and they're playing up this afternoon.' Ruth Standforth was eight months pregnant now and did not look healthy and glowing and fecund. She looked dark-circled, scrawny and rattish. He noticed that lately her smile had been like a mark someone made with felt-tip on glass. 'Would that be all right, Alec?' Alec wasn't sure. He seemed to have forgotten how civilization worked. He had regressed to a schoolboy, certain only of punishment.

In the kitchen he sat the boys at the table and taught them Muggins, a card game his dad had taught him. Without warning, the shuffle and deal brought back his father more vividly than any photo, sharper than any of his other memories. As the boys' small hands and eager eyes darted through the game Alec was suddenly aware of who he was and who he wasn't.

He was going to be forty in a few months. He was not a dad. He had no one. His life was a lie told by others.

With another parole session scheduled Alec struggled not to think that he might spend his fortieth birthday on the outside. It dogged him. He saw, at last, that the parole committee were just the scientists, out to snare Fraser Halls. They sat behind their long table with his file, fat now with all he had done. It might even look like a life, a steady climb of self-improvement. But he had to focus on their purpose. They were out to get him.

It had blurred for him this last year, the line between the truth and the lie. He had kept his list so long in his head it was dog-eared and now he found that, as he lay awake in the night going over the details, the lie sometimes slid into place because he had imagined it so often. He seemed to remember seeing Debbie Winstanley dead on the balcony. He saw himself locking the door, only sometimes he was on the inside, locking the door as a prelude to murder.

She had let someone in later, he knew that much. He had listened very hard to all of the evidence because so much of it was new to him. While they all believed he had been the murderer in her flat, Alec knew the man with the gold ring and the leather jacket had followed on their heels, had bided his time. She would let him in. Why wouldn't she? It was clear in the pub they were part of something, even if it was only the parting of company.

Perhaps she wasn't called Debbie. Perhaps he had misheard it and they had actually called out 'Cherry'. Perhaps he had not just battered the door that last evening and now this was his madness, his punishment, his ludicrous belief in his own innocence. Gold. Blonde. Was that how it went? Sour. Dark. Smoky. Yes. Hold on to that, Alec. And the last. Her tears.

'It strikes me, in our brief conversation here, that you don't yet express any remorse at what you have done.' The Chair was tall, her clothes just too short for her so she was all wrists and ankles. Her skirt rode up and revealed thick, hiker legs under the desk. Her hair was set into place in a practical short style, her blouse as crisp and white as a napkin. She was a magistrate. It occurred to him that the other two committee members could not look at him, kept their eyes firmly on the paperwork before them. Alec looked at the tall woman, his face trying to take on the quality of stone when in fact he wanted to liquefy, was destroyed.

'Have you understood what I have just said, Mr Holm?'

Alec nodded.

'And yet you have nothing more to say?' Her pen hovered in her hand. Alec could feel the ink shifting beneath the force of gravity, drawing down to the box marked 'No'.

'I did not kill Deborah Winstanley,' he managed at last. She looked at him, unblinking, for a few long moments.

'You have been in the prison system for fifteen years. That's a long time to look over what you have done, is it not?'

Alec was silent. It was a longer time to look over what he had not done. The days flittered like butterflies in his head. Days and days.

'Can I go now?' was all he could whisper.

Alec had been up and down the ladder for most of the morning. He had determined to find and repair the leak in the roof of the single-storey kitchen.

'I'm tired of these buckets,' Ruth had said yesterday. He had not let her empty them. He saw she was tired of everything, growing thinner and darker each day.

'Sit down.' He'd commanded, tipping the brownish water into

the sink. Ruth looked as pale and insubstantial as a ghost. She looked up at the speckled black mould on the sagging ceiling. The leak was Alec's priority.

This morning he had located a broken tile beneath which feral pigeons were nesting. He shooed them, cleared the nest and then tugged the tile out of its place. There were no spares in the garage or the shed but, as he passed the compost heap by the back fence, he spotted three good tiles half hidden under the ivy.

Ruth had been attending her latest antenatal appointment. The vicar had been sitting in the kitchen in his pyjamas all morning. Alec, muscles twanging with effort, hitched the tile into place and cleared out the gully. As he started back down the ladder the kitchen window opened and bitter smoke furled out.

'You can't say no, Ruth, you're the vicar's wife.' The vicar was delivering his usual sermon.

'I'm not the vicar, though.' Alec could see Ruth now at the sink, making a start on the washing-up.

'Hm?' The vicar was at the table. 'Does a man have to pray for a miracle to get a cup of tea in this house?' he moaned.

'He has only to put the kettle on.' Ruth spoke as she moved to fill the kettle herself.

'Hm?' the vicar, deep in a crossword.

'Anne was worried about my blood pressure.' Ruth sounded casual, as if talking about the weather.

'Anne?'

'The midwife. Anne.' Ruth was too weary to be snappy. 'Dr Sandhu is concerned about where the placenta is. Had a good old prod around.' Ruth was self-mocking. 'He thinks it might be a bit forward.' Alec saw her hand glide anxiously across her belly.

'Said it might be "a bit in the way on the big day". Said I need to rest.'

'Hm.' A rustle of newspaper.

'They want to keep an eye on me.'

A page turned. And another.

'Any chance of that tea, Ruthie?'

The next day the bus was late and so it was a thick, red lake in which Alec found her. The baby was still within her although Alec had no idea if it was alive or dead. Ruth Standforth grabbed for his hand, her own cold, sticky with her blood, the midwife's number clutched in her fingers. The midwife was no help now, Alec could see. The dark circles beneath Ruth's eyes were gone, replaced with a chalk white.

'Boys. The boys,' she hissed out. The boys were at school, someone would have to pick them up. The telephone was tipped from the table, just beyond her reach. Alec leaned towards it but she wouldn't let him go. 'Boys,' she insisted. There was no time for an ambulance, Alec could see that, as her breathing shallowed.

He laid her on a blanket on the back seat, shoved all the bags of jumble for Friday's sale, over into the boot of the lumbering estate car and drove as if it was a getaway.

At the hospital life and death were red and white. The red of the gallons of blood she and her child had poured, the white of her skin, her eyes closed now as he carried her through the doors.

'Help.' His voice was sharp, a command. Gurneys, people, doors, all rushing at him, rushing her away. He gave the details of her community midwife, of what he had overheard about her ante-natal appointment and the doctor's concerns. He remembered that arrangements must be made to collect the boys. The woman at the desk turned away to deal with all this. He saw the rooks then, a crowd shooting upwards from the trees at the far end of the car park. Leaving him behind.

He stood in the waiting room. He knew that this was something complex and obstetric, nothing to do with him. He had only wanted to help. But he felt he had been here before. He was a convicted murderer. He was covered in Ruth Standforth's blood. She would die. The baby would die. He would be held responsible.

In the car park he sorted through the jumble bags in the boot and found clothes. An old sweater smelling of garden and new wood. A pair of dark jeans reeking of tobacco and old beer.

He had no idea who he was. He only knew he must walk away.

12

THE TRUE LIE

Carmel didn't just admire the sweater, an old favourite Grace had knitted last autumn, she clutched at it, was greedy for it. Grace had pulled it on this morning as a colourful safety blanket against the daily onslaught of Hugo. Yesterday they had been trapped together in the lift. It had been possibly the longest three hours of her life, Hugo peeling off layers of clothing as the lift grew hotter and hotter and eager to play a porno version of I-Spy. 'Something beginning with N? Nipple.'

So she had tugged the sweater over her head and it had failed her. Now she was hiding in the staff kitchen, squeezed in by the sink, trying to make her mug of tea last until knocking-off time.

'You knitted it? What? With needles, you mean? Like a granny?'

Grace nodded, feeling that after a morning with Hugo she didn't need an afternoon with Carmel. Carmel, Grace noted, had not taken her hand from Grace's sleeve, was pawing, kittenish, at the wool.

'Shit, Grace, wish I could turn my hand to something creative. God, the hours my granny Sheila wasted trying to teach me.' She looked, Grace hardly believed it, wistful, as her fingertips caressed the sleeve of the sloppy joe. 'Couldn't try it, could I, Grace?'

Grace took a deep breath and then, with the thought that this interaction would delay her having to return to another round or two with Hugo, she peeled off her favourite sweater. Carmel was already out of her smart tailored jacket and, disconcertingly, was now unbuttoning her crisp white shirt to reveal her silk camisole and beneath that a sculpted and pristine white lace bra. She pulled Grace's sweater over her head, careless, for once, of her hair. She gave a little sigh.

'Oooooh, Grace – I love this!' Grace realized she was whispering, reverential. Carmel's face, usually washed out by a harsh palette of black and grey suits and heavy foundation, was warmed up by the burnished oranges and earthy browns of the knit. 'Oh, it is soooooooooooo beautiful.' Grace had never seen Carmel like this. Something prickled inside her. Had Carmel ever smiled?

'Keep it.' Grace tipped out the last of her tea, rinsed her mug. She was smart enough in her long-sleeved T-shirt and there was a jacket in the car.

Carmel was stunned. 'No . . . I couldn't . . . Here –' she reached into her bag, took out her purse and fished out two fresh-from-the-cashpoint twenty-pound notes – 'I'll buy it. Is forty enough? I can always nip out and get more.'

'Carmel—'

'Seriously. Take it. Craftsmanship is worth it.' Carmel shoved the money at her.

By the end of the week she had orders from two of the women in admin for the same sloppy joe in two different colourways. She began work on them the following Wednesday evening.

Grace had settled quickly that the small ante-room off the kitchen would be her workroom. Before she had bought a bed or even a chair she had seen the dresser in the junk shop and it had been delivered and stacked with her yarns and needles before nine o'clock that same night. Over the next few weeks a sagging leather armchair and a slightly wobbly scrubbed elm table had joined it.

She wore the scarf one morning when the weather cooled. By lunchtime everyone wanted one. Maisie took Grace out for lunch that Thursday. They had been heading out to their usual haunt, the Greenhouse Café, but Maisie took a slight detour towards 'Archie's Market'. 'Get it?' Maisie asked with childlike delight. 'Arches . . . Archies . . .'

The market was based in and around the disused railway arches and defunct station. They ate lunch in the Waiting Room Café with Maisie's Swedish friend, Elke, who had a stall and ran up her own clothing designs from vintage fabrics on an antique Husqvarna sewing machine.

'I'd love to sell this . . . the colours, the textures . . . you have an eye for this. All these tones will tie in with my new autumn pieces . . . we will go over to the stall now. I'll show you.'

Elke and her many-ringed hand had tugged Grace and her scarf outside and across to the cosy stall underneath the furthest arch. Elke showed off her latest creations hanging on silk-padded wooden coat hangers. 'And these . . . are coats and jackets . . . new for me . . . from these curtains . . . so glamorous . . .' Grace loved the fabric, the slightly aged colours, the richness of the jacquard and damasked weaves. 'You have more scarves?' Elke sniffed deeply at a bale of curtain fabric as if it were chocolate.

'Some more.'

'Ten? Twenty?' Elke looked expectant, eyes bright and wide behind the slim black plastic rectangles of her spectacles. Grace had a hamper in the corner of her workroom. She could visualize it, all the strands and lengths she'd knitted together over the last four or five years. She could see clearly all the new pieces and swatches she'd been at work on since breaking free of the yellow flat. It would do her good to find homes for them. To be alive they needed to be worn.

Now Grace often found her footsteps heading to Archie's Market to see Elke on the pretext of asking how her scarves were doing. They had done very well. Once or twice she'd minded the stall as Elke headed off to the bank for more change or grabbed a sandwich from the Waiting Room Café.

She was there today, reluctant to go back to the office, already fifteen minutes over her allotted lunch hour and not caring that Elke had said she would be half an hour tops and was now pushing into a second hour away.

She was pondering what true lie she could tell Hugo to get him off her back, or, more precisely, to keep his hand from her bottom, his thoughts from her knickers. She was so tired of him she could hardly bear it. Nothing she said affected him; if she was sharp and aggressive he might back off for a day only to come back next morning, refreshed and ready for the fight. After the day in Don's office when she had punched him he had cornered her in the ladies' toilets and asked her to punch him again. 'You know you want to. Come on. Fight me.'

Carmel had been uneasy about the situation and dissuaded Grace from 'causing trouble'. It had outraged Grace.

'Causing trouble? For Hugo? Isn't that the point—'

But Carmel had shushed her. 'No, Grace, I meant causing trouble for you.'

Grace knew a lie was necessary. She had thought of the obvious, 'I'm a lesbian', but having heard most of his rugby club stories she realized that was less a true lie to get her out of difficulty than a gauntlet thrown down. She wondered how Mum and Nan had got away with it, how they had juggled and slapped down and teased. And then she didn't want to think about it, how Nan would have had Hugo, pants down in the photocopy room, wiped her mouth when he was done and that would have been that.

Had Davey really been what Mum had wanted? Or was he just the special offer, the last scraping from the bottom of the bargain bin? Davey, one of the great mysteries of life, a man she sometimes thought she might have made up.

That was when it occurred to her. She saw, quite clearly in her mind, the man she would like to meet. She could see him smiling from the top of a step ladder as he fixed that curtain rail she'd so hopelessly botched. She was standing at the bottom of the ladder offering tea and cake. She could see that someone like Carmel might scorn her vision of a future. But he stayed in her mind, a lean and muscled man, older, wiser, snoring as they spooned in bed. She saw the slight redbronze sheen to the hairs on his forearms as, sleeves rolled up, he put a cup to drain at the sink. She saw his fingers, hard-worked, the curve between his neck and collarbone and, as he looked up, a kiss in his eyes. Grace looked up too, and saw Elke.

'You were many miles away.' Elke smiled and offered Grace a takeaway coffee. 'Travel somewhere good?'

'You've never mentioned this bloke before.' Hugo towered over her in the confines of the staff kitchen. She'd chosen a poor spot, wedged in between the worktop, the stubby fridge and Hugo. His arms were either side of her, hands knuckled into the worktop. Hugo, trying to look hurt. Or make her feel guilty. Her tongue felt black with liquorice.

'I always hoped you'd get the message. Anyway, it's private. It isn't really your business. You're not my—' She was going to say 'mother' but the word wouldn't come. Family caught in the back of her throat too. Hugo shifted his weight, thoughtful.

'What about at the pub a while back? You came out to the pub that night and not a word of loverboy. What did you say his name was?'

Grace realized she hadn't. She saw a carrier looped on the back of the door, some tights Carmel had bought in town in her lunch-break. House of Fraser.

'Fraser.'

Hugo gave a scornful snort but he was convinced. He leaned closer, whispering in her ear, 'You were just stringing me along, Gracie. How could you?'

'I didn't want to hurt you, Hugo. I just didn't know how serious things would get between myself and Fraser. I've been hurt before . . .'

The lie was working. She could see his eyes glazing over.

'Hey, I said straight up then, a fuckaround, a bit of fun, no strings . . .' Again he raised his hands in mock surrender. 'That offer still stands, if Fraser fucks off.'

'We're getting married, Hugo.'

He backed off at last; the word 'married' seemed to set off an allergic reaction in him. Perhaps that is what she should have said, months ago: *Hugo, I love you and want to marry you and have your babies*. He was looking at her now as if she might be contagious.

'All right. Well. Wish you luck and triplets and all that.'

And he was gone.

She introduced Fraser the Fiancé at the Neighbourhood Watch meeting that week.

Her left-hand neighbours, Jack and Hazel Spring, had been welcoming and friendly but had also respected her privacy and, she knew, expected that she would respect theirs. She had left a key with them for emergencies. Mr Denton on the right-hand side, however, had dogged her every footstep. He had complained in quick succession about the apple tree, the hedge and the tumbledown garage, all of which leaned or drooped or blocked the side access on his boundary.

'I assume you discussed the boundary responsibilities with your solicitor?' he said when he had cornered her at the last meeting. She knew as she walked up the path to Jack and Hazel's house that he would pounce again at this meeting. She had not lopped or trimmed or demolished and now, to compound matters, she'd had a skip delivered, ready to receive her ripped-out old kitchen.

And then there was Mrs Hadfield who lived opposite. Slim, grey-haired, in her late sixties, she had a habit of staring at Grace with no idle, dreamy look; it was hard, calculating. Grace tried not to look at her, to imagine that in fact she wasn't there.

So when Mr Denton did indeed corner her in Jack's conservatory, Grace was prepared. She saw her imaginary true-lie love in the garden, expertly pruning the apple tree.

'Oh.' Mr Denton was halted. He considered a moment. 'When might he get around to it?' Mr Denton, it was clear, felt much happier at the idea of dealing with a proper stout-hearted man rather than some woolly-headed girl.

'He's away, abroad, at the moment.' Grace saw him busy in an office, somewhere temperate like Stockholm. In a meeting. At a long black table. 'I'm calling him later tonight so I'll mention it. We can start that ball rolling.' Grace was feeling smug at having shoehorned one of Mr Denton's favourite phrases into her true lying. And it was true, if she had possessed Fraser she would have asked him, would have joked about Mr Denton over a glass or two of wine and some delicious chicken. He might have baked bread, soft, white and yeasty, to dip into the juices. She stopped herself as her mind's picture showed him reaching with sticky, roasted-chicken fingers to—

'You're getting married?' Mrs Hadfield sounded snide.

'Yes. Next year. We're going to finalize the date when he gets back.'

Mrs Hadfield stared hard over her sip of wine but just then their community police officer, Ged, arrived and Jack called the meeting to order.

Later, after supper, she finished the second of the sloppy joe sweaters as she sat in the leather chair. After she'd cast off and begun to stitch the sleeves to the body she fell asleep in the moonlight that shimmered through the French doors. She dreamed of the carpet wolves at the old house, dreamed they were wandering through the night streets now, trying to catch her scent.

13

MAN, TRAPPED

Alec had kept track. He knew it was a Thursday at the furthest edge of September. He felt edgy still, wondering when he might turn a corner and find a prison van waiting, officers armed with nets and tridents like blue-uniformed gladiators ready to trap him and, he knew, take him back to the Dogs' Home. He had seen the newspapers, flicked through them in a supermarket, picked up a discarded one here and there. There had been nothing about him. No 'Have you seen this man?' and a cobbled-together jigsaw picture of him, no mention of a dangerous criminal absconding from an open prison. Perhaps he was scheduled to be on *Crimewatch* and even now actors could be re-enacting his hospital dash with Ruth Standforth. He thought about Ruth every day. Thought of the last precious minutes of Ruth and the baby's life that the delayed bus had ticked by.

Now he had reached the edges of this new town he wondered if the rivers or canal here would offer a feast. His diet had been fish-based for a few weeks, Alec eternally grateful for Mr

Tweedy's lecture on coy fishing on that distant day in Bournemouth. True, the fish tasted muddy but that was better than scavenging in bins.

He had kept himself clean in rivers and ponds. He'd been picking potatoes, pretending to be foreign and sleeping outside instead of in the caravans. He found, after fifteen years of gates and walls, he liked the open air. At the caravan site he had got out of the habit of the rivers and streams, using the makeshift showers instead. Yesterday he had walked all the way from the farm. Very early this morning he had rolled in a shallow woodland river. He had relished the cold knives of water and was Robin Hood again.

The little high street was clearly on the up, a coffee shop, a glittering interiors store and a small cookshop being fitted out in among the usual charity shops. He had cash from his vegetable picking, so he entered the coffee shop and ordered.

He sat at the back with his sandwich. A terrible melancholy fizzed through him at the first bite of soft, fresh bread, the savoury meat flavours of the ham, the prickle of mustard. Could he just keep going like this? If he continued walking he would reach an edge somewhere, a cliff, a coastline, would he double back? If he was going to keep walking he would need newish boots from the charity shop. That was enough of a decision for now. The newish boots might last him long enough.

Long enough. He thought of Fraser Halls unable to return to his home because the search was always on. He'd spent a few episodes in Dr Grace Storey's attic where they had become trapped together for a night in a murphy bed. Alec thought of his old flat, of the couple who had bought it, thought of his old room at home with Mum. He thought of nowhere to go to and drank down his coffee to distract himself.

Later, the policeman and policewoman strolling the length of the high street jolted him and he found himself taking a random turn past an ivy-covered street sign he only half took in. All he knew was that the road filled the periphery of his vision with gardens and green. But the police turned in behind him, their radios crackling with messages.

He looked very different now, he knew. The beard that he had so carefully scraped off each morning in prison had grown well and he kept it scrupulously clean and trimmed. The last thing he wanted was to draw attention to himself by being a scruffy, dirty vagrant. He walked past the houses, disturbed, as he turned from the kerb to cross the road, to find the police officers were still following him. He felt the panic trying to land and struggled hard to prevent it. He could feel his legs starting to fail him at last. He was about to stumble when he heard the *crar* behind the house: a rook in the tallest tree. There was no choice. He must step through the gate.

There was a skip parked in the driveway and as he edged past it he could already see, beside the tumbledown garage, a wrought-iron garden gate, just ajar. It groaned as he pushed through.

The garden was cool and green. His senses couldn't take in all the scents and sensations, the climbing rose that grappled at his sleeve, the rich earth must from under the shade of the overgrown hedge on the boundary, the froggish water in an oval pond. Vaguely, in the back of his head, he heard the police at the front exchange greetings with a man and his dog. He heard the noises of the dog being petted, chucked under the chin, some mention of the vet. Community policing. Five minutes. A breather. That was all.

He saw that the houses backed onto an overgrown lane and beyond that a disused factory strangled by ivy. If he could just haul himself over the hedge and drop down on the other side . . .

'Hello.' The cheery voice startled him. Alec spun round, prepared to be a Jehovah's Witness, but there was no one in the garden. 'Sorry, didn't mean to startle you . . . Up here . . .'

Alec's gaze was caught by a man's head, just visible above the dark ivy and pale pink clematis that scrambled over the tall garden wall. The nubs of a ladder, a large pair of secateurs. 'You must be Fraser.' Alec startled at the name. Had he heard right? 'I'm Jack. She didn't mention you were flying in. Going to surprise her? Hang on a tick, you'll need the key.' The man turned to yell, 'HAZEL? Hazel, Fraser's here.'

The kitchen was half torn out. A new free-standing oak sideboard was waiting. There was a marble-top wooden table by the sink unit and Alec, aware of the neighbour, Jack, still atop the wall with his gardening gloves on, reached for the kettle, filled it and tried to look at home. As the kettle rattled to a boil Alec moved through into the long living room. He was still visible from the garden through a set of French doors. He kept moving forward, aware of the pots of paint, the newspapers and dustsheets. He made his way to the front of the house, hoping to make his getaway through the front door but it seemed the community police were dog fanatics. It looked like a meeting of the Kennel Club with the man and a golden retriever having been joined by an older woman and her white-haired Westies and now, from across the road, a middle-aged woman with dyed-orange hair and what appeared to be a pack of deerhounds.

The kettle had clicked off. Alec saw nothing for it but to make some tea. 'She' had left a key and wasn't expected back any time soon. He could enjoy the tea and he could leave some spare change lying around, a couple of quid down the back of the sofa perhaps. Only, as he saw, there was no sofa.

He stood in the kitchen, his hand reached to smooth at the surface of the oak sideboard. It felt warm and he could see how the light through the kitchen window would make it glow golden once it was in place. The tap dripped at the sink. He pushed at the lever but the drip continued, slow and steady. There was a toolbox by the partially demolished cupboard units. It would take half an hour, he'd look busy instead of suspicious. He opened the first drawer of the toolbox – what had she got? Rawlplugs, fuses . . . washers.

Later, in the bathroom, as he fixed the dodgy toilet flush with wire and a jubilee clip, he wished he was Fraser. The bath was edged with candles that gave off a scent of bergamot and beside them shampoos and a bar of lemon verbena soap. Lucky the man who spent his time with her. Then it struck him. There was nothing masculine in the bathroom. No razors, no toiletries.

The front door went with a sharp bang. Alec felt his guts lurch. He opened the bathroom door, glanced quickly down the stairs and saw movement, a slight figure slinging down a bag. That was when he saw the wedge of darkness and within it the narrow, steep stairs rising away from the main landing up towards a wooden door. Downstairs he heard the kettle being filled so he took the five quick steps up to the attic.

It was a rectangle of space, one corner filled with discarded storage boxes and a dank sunlounger mattress rolled into a corner by a heavy pile of violently coloured curtains. He reasoned that she would have to go to work in the morning, might even go out later this evening. He could just bide his time here in the attic. She would never know he had been there.

The floor was dusty but did not creak as he picked his way carefully, trying to synchronize his movements with the noises she was making downstairs. He sat cross-legged behind the storage boxes.

He woke with a start from somewhere deep and dreamless under his nest of curtaining. It seemed the voices were in the room with him. He lay still and petrified, listening.

'. . . did you mix this colour yourself?'

Grace wasn't certain of Maisie's mum, Renee. Renee always had a hand trailing into your things. Here she was now, in the master bedroom, opening the tins of paint. Not that Grace said anything, it would seem churlish and ungrateful after she and Maisie had arrived unannounced with house-warming gifts. 'You know, my nephew's a plasterer, I could get him up here, he'd take a look for you . . . Cash in hand, of course.'

Downstairs, later, squatting on assorted deckchairs, Grace had opened the hamper of gifts: her favourite kind of mismatched plates and a set of cranberry-glass goblets. She was touched.

'These are beautiful, Renee. They look antique.'

'They probably are but I got them cheap. I carboot.' Renee winked and tipped the dregs out of the wine bottle. 'Oops, time for a refill, Maze.'

'We can christen the glasses . . .' Grace suggested.

In the kitchen Maisie tugged another bottle of wine from the cardboard carrier they had brought with them from the new wine shop at the end of the high street as Grace rinsed out the glasses.

'You know, I should be hurt really.' It was clear from Maisie's face that she was upset. Grace was puzzled as to what she'd done. 'You never said one word about this bloke of yours.'

Now she knew. Panic blared inside Grace.

'He's the reason you wouldn't come out with us lately, I suppose?' Maisie turned to the drawer to find the corkscrew. As long as she was busy with the wine Grace knew she could lie to her. Liquorice and wine, what a horrid combination.

'You know what it's like, Maisie. I didn't want to make it all public. Not till I knew how we both felt. I'm sorry if I hurt your feelings.'

Maisie cracked a smile, chinked glasses. 'Forget it. Men, eh? The things they make us do.' And they headed back to Renee.

'So when do we get to meet this Fraser, then?' Two bottles of wine and the better part of a lemon butter-cream cake had given Maisie courage. It was obvious she had talked this over with Renee before they arrived. Grace saw now that they had probably come over to meet Fraser, not simply to warm her house.

She saw Fraser in her mind's eye, could taste the liquorice bitter and dark against the sweetness of the lemon cake. She recalled the documentary on the radio last night, while she was tearing out the kitchen. 'He's away. In the Arctic Circle. At the minute.' She drank some wine to wash down the liquorice of lying.

'Blimey,' said Renee.

Maisie was goggle-eyed with genuine surprise not just contact lenses. 'What does he do?'

'He's a husky.' Renee splurted out laughter, jolting forward, spilling wine down her trousers.

Grace was trying to remember, trying to revisualize the frozen wastes the radio programme had conjured for her.

'He's a mining engineer. He's working in Kiruna up in the north where Sweden meets Finland. They mine iron ore there.' She sipped her wine and saw the snowstormed town in her head, saw the man too, the man with gingered forearms and a smile for her. He was decked out in cold-weather gear, the fur-lined coat giving an impression of a man shifting shape into a wolf, because she saw now that he had a beard, trimmed, flecked with bronze and maybe even grey. Like his eyes, the green-grey of the sea in September. And in her mind he turned, looked back at her as if he was thinking about her too, his mittened hand reaching out across the Arctic snow.

That night Grace slept at last in the new bed under her old duvet which smelled, disconcertingly, of the old yellow flat. She dreamed she lay on wolfskins in a room aglow with salt lights, and her made-up true lie love spooned against her, his soft chest hair an insulation, his arms folded around her, keeping her safe. But as the moon rose and shone through the window onto his face he howled and she woke with a jolt. She headed downstairs to the kitchen. And fell asleep, much later, in her leather chair in the dark of the workroom.

14

POSTCARDS FROM GOD

In the morning she left early. Alec lurked in the bathroom having a last civilized pee before he returned to the slash-in-the-hedgerow life he'd been leading. He had to go, he knew it. The genuine Fraser might sled back home at any moment and he'd be doomed. He could imagine the scenario if she came home to find him here and what the police might say. Convicted murderer lurking in woman's attic. It wasn't going to look good and history had taught him no one ever believed a word he said.

But oh, he was tempted just to hole up here. He had listened last night to the symphony of this woman's life, not just the chat with her friends but the solo sounds, her singing as she listened to the radio, the clatter of the kitchen, her feet on the stairs, the running water of the shower, the brushing of her teeth. Prison had smelled like school after someone has been sick, that glassy disinfectant odour with a slight tang of mopped-up pee behind it.

He was mad to contemplate it but the white light of realization that he had nowhere to go and no one to go to had shone with a glare into his head. His legs felt weary at the idea of walking away. But he must go. He should head north, find work at a hostel or in the forestry service. He'd heard Kielder was beautiful, or he might try the Lakes. He could coppice and pollard and live in the woods.

He had decided to leave via the front door instead of being seen sneaking out of the back. If the community police happened to be strolling by then they might simply wave and he'd wave back and they'd say: 'You must be Fraser, the fiancé.' And he could smile and nod and it would seem he was on his way to work.

As he reached the bottom of the stairs he was startled to see a figure approaching. It was unclear through the stained glass but, yes, someone was definitely coming. A visitor. Alec backtracked, tripping himself up, clonking his shoulder against the banister. The letter box opened, a fan of letters was shoved through, then a slither of pizza takeaway flyers and insurance offers. The figure retreated.

Alec laughed to himself, massaged his stinging shoulder and breathed easier. Postman, that was all. He sat for a moment on the bottom stair gathering his thoughts again, readying himself to go.

It was then that he saw the name, typed in neat black on crisp white, just visible through a little window in the brown envelope. There it was again, black on white on her gas bill. And again.

Ms Grace Storey

He could not touch the letters in case the name vanished, because he knew, he was absolutely certain, he was dead or dreaming.

*

The attic had two skylights, front and rear, and at the side a small square casement window that looked down the length of Ruskin Road as it strolled towards the high street. He had no real plan now; he felt that other plans were being made for him. He had chosen his steps at random, with only the idea of walking away, but those steps had brought him here, brought him to Grace Storey. He knew she was not the Grace from the television, she was just her namesake. All he could do was keep watch and yet he wasn't certain what he watched for. What did it mean? Would she be on his side? Was that what had drawn him here? He spent half the day trying to push away the thought that someone was looking out for him at last. He couldn't afford to think like this, and yet here she was, Grace Storey. Alec knew that if the authorities ever caught up with him he would be invisible once more, locked away in a room five feet by six feet with nothing but a toilet for company. Then, as dusk began to soften the suburban edges, a dinky green car trundled along and pulled in behind the skip in Grace Storey's driveway. Alec watched from the front skylight as two women got out. Before the key had turned in the front door Alec had slipped silently onto the landing. Standing flat against the wall he had an angled view of the hallway partially reflected towards him via a long thin mirror that leaned up against the hall wall.

He knew which was Grace Storey even before the frowsy Maisie said, 'You need to sit down. I'll put the kettle on, Gracie . . .' and ushered herself into the living room. He watched Grace for a moment, her slight figure, her dark hair. She looked strained and sad and Alec wanted to step forward now, to reach out for her. Because there had to be a reason. There had to be.

Grace followed the sound of Maisie into the kitchen, tripping over an untidy pile of snapped and bent particleboard. A jagged edge of discarded Formica worktop snagged on Maisie's dress. Grace carefully unhooked her. 'Sorry, Maisie. I meant to tidy it all into the skip last night . . .'

'No worries. Sit down like I told you. You all right?'

Grace wasn't sure what she was. She was grateful to Maisie for the lift home but she wanted her made-up man, had half-hoped she would turn the corner into the kitchen and find him there, lying on the floor beside the sink cupboard fixing that U-bend, and she would lie in the cupboard next to him feeling his muscles twitch as he turned the wrench. She could lie on his chest and his heartbeat would reverberate as if it were inside her and what would he smell of, this made-up true lie man? New wood.

Maisie was sliding a kitchen chair under Grace. 'Before you fall down.'

It was one of the mismatched set she'd got at the junk shop at the weekend, none of them were plastic. Or metal. None had splayed legs waiting to trip you onto the blade of a knife.

'He had no right.' Maisie had clearly been talking and Grace had clearly been not listening. 'What time is it in the Arctic?' Maisie offered a mug of steaming tea. 'You could phone Fraser, tell him about your monumentally crap day. The thing that gets me is Carmel, you know, her attitude is—'

'He's not real.' Grace raised her voice above Maisie's. It had to be done. Maisie was too kind and Grace had no other friend. It would be a mistake to deceive her.

Maisie stopped, thought. 'Who? Hugo?'

'Fraser.' Grace spoke clearly, decisively, looking right into

Maisie's face, seeing that today she had two different-coloured contacts in, one green, one blue. 'I made him up, Maisie. He doesn't exist.'

Upstairs, ear pressed to the floor of the back box room, Alec Holm held his breath.

'You – he – I'm—' Maisie looked at the mug of tea in her hand, sat down lightly on another chair. Yes. These things were real.

'Please. Don't tell anyone. Not even your mum.'

'No, not if you . . . But I don't get it, Grace. Why?'

'Protection. He just seemed safest, a guard against Hugo – against everything really . . . A fiancé.'

Today Hugo had been more of a bully than usual, making Grace go over the hideous rolling-forecast document, retyping, reprinting, adding in, editing out, leaving each petty decision until Grace had finished his last set of wishes, had almost finished the task. No one could fault him, he was, after all, just trying to present an accurate rolling forecast. But Grace knew. And Hugo triumphed.

'Has it worked? I mean, Hugo was a bastard today.'

'Exactly. That's what today's monkey business was all about. His revenge for me being with Fraser. He'll get over it. Anyway, he's out of the office for the next few days. It'll be fine.' Grace reasoned, 'Today was the last chapter. The end.'

But Maisie did not look so certain. 'You know, you could come out with me and Elke sometimes and the girls from the pottery class. We have a wild time. You could meet someone real.' Maisie gestured at the house, the wrecked kitchen. 'Someone practical.'

Grace curled her feet around the chair legs. 'Too scary.'

And Maisie, feeling for her friend, left it there.

That night, Alec lay under the skylight looking at the stars and listening to Grace Storey not sleeping.

He heard the church bell toll midnight in the near distance. Beneath him he heard Grace stir from her room. He noticed that she did not flick on the light, instead a torch beam filtered under the attic door and was gone and he heard the third and eighth stairs creak as she descended. He heard something clatter in the kitchen. He could be invisible, just take a look.

Grace made a half-hearted attempt to stack the kitchen debris but from his vantage point behind the open door Alec saw she was moving deckchairs on the *Titanic*, shifting the clutter from one spot to another. She swept up the worst of the shavings and scraps and dumped them into the already bulging bin. Then she took her drink and moved through the arched doorway to the little workroom. He could not risk stepping out into the kitchen and peering through the gap in the jamb, he did not wish to frighten her. As she pushed the door he glimpsed the dresser, arrayed with colours, scraps of woollen items in baskets on the shelves. The middle drawer was sticking; he saw her irritation as she tried to close it and it squawked and ground against her.

She knitted into the night. He saw fragments, the dangle of her foot from the chair, her elbow, the swift movements of her hands, all ticked by to the tocking of her needles. Her body, stooping to the hollowed footstool crammed with yarn. The way her hair fell across her face or she pushed it back behind her ears. Then, at last, the needles stopped. She tipped the lid on the footstool, her feet curled upwards into the haven of the baggy brown armchair.

She snored. A light dry sound, her mouth open slightly. Alec stood just a step or so back from the doorway and watched her.

She was not very old he saw, twenty-three or -four. And she did have a resemblance to the Grace Storey of old. Petite. Her dark hair. The soft oval of her face. He was probably old enough to be her father. She shifted, mouth closing, head turning away from him, curling deeper into the chair. Her elbow nudged the mug, balanced on the chair arm.

It toppled, landed with a smash. Before she had started from sleep, he was gone. Vanished.

15

THE TO-DO LIST

Two weeks later Grace held the letter of resignation. It seemed to tremble, butterfly-like, in her hand.

'Do it,' Maisie had encouraged with a hug.

Carmel had been running late that morning and Grace took that as a sign. Clearly Fate was employing delaying tactics, clearly Fate thought Grace shouldn't resign. But as Carmel entered, hair a mass of tiny curls, her make-up much reduced and around her neck one of Grace's scarves, Grace felt instead that Fate had opted to make an entrance.

Everyone remarked on the beauty of Carmel's hair, the colour a deep nut brown, twisted and whorled around her face. Her eyes seemed a deeper green without the distraction of their usual border of kohl.

'There was a power cut so my alarm shut off. What a disaster!' Carmel, her everyday efficiency cast off, seemed like an impostor, as if this might be her less evil twin. Grace noted as she handed over the letter that Carmel kept the scarf on and that the fine-knit cashmere top beneath her coat had been chosen to match the scarf's burnt umbers and ochres.

Carmel took a moment from her attempted hair rescue to open the missive. She looked it over quickly.

'Good. About time you pissed off,' she barked with her all-purpose authoritarian smile. 'Got anything lined up or are you just winging it?'

It was a busy first week. The stall was three arches down from Elke's. In her bid to knit up more stock and transport it all to the market, Grace realized she had let the to-do list of household repairs slip out of her grasp. It didn't matter, she would be able to finish the kitchen one evening this week, all that was required was for her to unpack the oak sideboard and slide it into place where the run of chipboard cupboards had been. Yesterday Grace had seen an ornate Victorian set of shelves at a nearby stall and instead of bothering with lunch she'd bartered for it. The stall owner, Andy, had scouted her stall that morning searching for a birthday present for his wife, so Grace offered a swap. It didn't matter that she didn't know how she would manage to fix it to the wall, she would work it out somehow. As she loaded it into the back of the car she predicted it would sit on the floor of the kitchen for at least seven months.

She found her evenings were wired. It was twofold: the excitement and relief of getting away from Hugo and the job at FRJ and the nagging sensation that somewhere, in the boiling oil pots of hell, Nan was smirking.

She had found a seamstress form, a quite battered and grey torso on squeaking metal legs, and she'd positioned it at the front of the stall clad in one of Elke's new range of skirts and her own newest sweater. It was an assymetric assemblage of textures and she'd not had time to sew on the sleeves so had hit upon the idea of fastening them to the body with kilt pins. She had been delighted with the result and it had drawn people in.

But out of the corner of her eye, it was Nan. Nan with a sneer and a flick of cigarette ash.

'You've opened a shop, have you? Calling it "Something Special", are you?'

She could hear Nan in her head when she was helping customers. 'They need a nudge,' she had advised Debbie over and over. 'Leave it all to them and the bastards'll never buy anything.'

On that first Saturday morning Grace stripped the form and gave it to Andy to sell.

Then it was a Sunday and Grace realized it was also halfway through November. Maisie offered to watch the stall so that Grace could have a day off, her first since opening the stall in October. It had been a steady drip of business, some days dragged, but she was selling all the time and she was knitting. The Celtic kilt-pin sweater was a big favourite with customers but the little knitted corsages that Grace loved and had thought would go for Christmas, didn't. She'd been considering what to do with them. Hats had sprung to mind and she was toying with shapes in her head.

The box was in the attic. She knew exactly which one. It was time to lug it downstairs.

The narrow stairway to the attic was small and cosy. Grace thought she might have loved this attic when she was a girl, she could have come up here and made a place for herself when Nan and Mum went out. The door didn't creak when she opened it.

Inside, it held layers of scent: an odd cold tang of fresh air, fustiness and new wood. She moved to the skylight at the front of the house. Gasped at the view it afforded. She could see between Gloria Hadfield's house and the Bentleys' to the primary school that sat behind them and the edges of the park and, beyond that, Coverts Wood. She moved across to the stacked storage boxes. The old sewing machine was in one of these. She flipped the lid on the first box and found a variety of old kitchen utensils, some from her university days. A fish slice that had once dished up a fried egg to Deacon Massey. The wooden spoons Nan had given her from the kitchen drawer at Springfield Court. 'I'm not about to bloody use them,' Nan had said, cigarette ash fluttering into the drawer. Grace didn't like to think how long she'd had them and not used them. Then there were old pans and storage containers. She wanted none of these in the new kitchen. She shifted the box over beside the pile of old curtains slumped under the eaves. Those old curtains. They'd been here the day she moved in, shoved up here. She'd meant to take them to the tip. Grace reached to feel the texture, soft but strong in a sort of jacquard weave, the patterns retro enough for Elke to want them. She could make coats. She pulled up the edge of the topmost, dustiest curtain, beneath which were two or three other layers, a deep purple, a wildly floral green and white. Yes. Elke would love these. She let the curtain edges fall from her hands and moved across to the box at the end of the stack. This was the one with the machine in it. She flipped the lid, tugged out the heavy old machine. She struggled to the top of the attic steps with it just as the phone rang.

As Grace skitted down the stairs to answer it Alec, sandwiched under the curtains, breathed out. His face was wet with sweat and the condensation of his own partially smothered breath. Through the weave he could see the light from the landing, the silhouette of the machine on the top step. She would return. He had to decide quickly whether to stay here or risk everything to hide himself in the small cupboard that took up the edge of the roof space. It was tight in there, a triangle of roof and joists. He slid himself out from the curtains. He could hear Grace on the phone in the hallway.

'. . . I was just thinking about you. I've found these old curtains in the attic, quite retro – you could take a look. No . . . I can put them in the car . . . If you don't like them I'll do the round trip to the tip.'

Alec wedged himself through the small door, shutting it just as Grace finished on the phone and came back up the stairs. He listened as she clomped the machine down to the landing and then returned to the pile of curtains. She peeled off the top layer, folded it; each layer beneath was revealed and folded. She carried them out, shut the door behind her. Alec stayed exactly where he was until cramp bit into every part of him.

She had finished painting the kitchen late last night, finally rinsing out the paintbrushes at about 2 a.m. Despite that she'd found herself waking early this bright and wintry Sunday morning. Already she'd fitted the shelves to the wall and the spirit level at last agreed that they were plumb. All she had to do now was move the oak sideboard.

First she unhinged the two cupboard doors and then removed

the seven drawers. Even thus stripped it was a heavy old bit of tree to shift and she could barely inch and scrape it over the slightly uneven floor. An offcut of carpet might do – she could drag it, friction free.

Outside, she was too preoccupied rummaging in the skip to notice Mr Denton's approach.

'Morning,' he greeted her with a slightly militaristic wave. 'Hard at it, I see.'

Grace was startled. 'Oh. Yes. Morning.'

'Well. Many hands, as they say. Bye.' He headed off for his usual Sunday, Holy Communion at St John's and then lunch at the Bestrewn Oak near the bowling green. Grace thought how quickly they learned each other's routines. Certainly Mrs Hadfield opposite had Grace down pat. The hairs on the back of her neck rose as Mrs Hadfield's wooden blinds slatted open. She was always watching, Grace knew, clocking her in and out. Grace considered that she should have a hide erected on that neat diamond of front lawn, a spotting scope pointed out at the neighbourhood, possibly her own personal CCTV monitoring system, or she could have them all tagged like migrating geese. The sun felt warm, the air chill and it struck Grace, as she lugged her chosen remnant of carpet through the back garden gate, that something was different.

But she was distracted. She spent the best part of two hours hoiking the sideboard onto the carpet and then dragging and heaving it into position. As, kettle boiling behind her, she replaced the cupboard doors and slid in the drawers she noticed that one of the drawer handles had worked loose. She had a tiny screwdriver in the dresser in the workroom, that would fix it, otherwise she'd forget about it until it fell off.

The sense prickled again. A difference in the workroom, in the dresser. Was it just the cold of Christmas beginning to filter in? Was it simply that she hadn't had time to stop and stare lately? The middle drawer did not protest as she opened it, found the miniature screwdriver and pushed the drawer closed. She slid it out, in again. Not a squeak or a groan. She saw there was a thin sheen of smooth wax on either side of the drawer. In. Out. In. Something else too, there was another detail winking out at her. The top pane on the left above the French doors. A little rectangular casement window had been suffused with a spider web of cracks where the light had caught in the edges in the evening, splintering itself into patterns on the opposite wall. The pane had been repaired. The cracked lustre tiles in the fireplace had been replaced and the rest cleaned of soot.

She stepped back into the kitchen and the details tumbled and spilled. The tap that didn't drip, the sink cupboard door hanging true, the curtain rail she'd botched and discarded had gone and the blind that she had pegged up with a couple of nails was battened and fixed. The tiles in the floor that had seemed dull and grey were now clean and scrubbed and a deep, inky shade of blue. The three tiles that were cracked by the back door had been lifted and replaced. All the debris, she noticed with a jolt, all the scraps of cupboard and shaves of wood and worktop had gone. When had that Formica worktop last snagged her trousers?

She went through the skip. It was all there, stacked away, and what was this? Bits of garage door? Corrugated roof sheeting? She was cursing the free and easy way in which her neighbours had dumped their detritus when her eyes lifted to her own tumbledown garage. As she looked her breathing seemed to give out, her heart began a drum roll.

The doors had been repainted and rehung and the broken sections of the roof repaired. The sagging side wall had been patched and sagged no more and the weeds and ivy that had gathered there had been cleared away from the boundary with Mr Denton. The garage had been repainted a sleek black and she now saw that the back gate had also had a coat of matching paint. It looked crisp and ornate. She struggled to think back to three or four days ago when she had pushed through the gate with the bin. There had been a subtle something then, a change that she now realized was an absence of squeak.

Through the gate, the rose that had clawed so desperately at her was now espaliered to a trellis, painted the same garage black.

The bare outstretched limbs of the apple tree had been lopped and tidied. The windfalls and the worm-eaten had been tidied onto a newly constructed compost heap. Grace recognized fence posts and panels that had been cut down and recycled into a neat rectangular box. An offcut of the carpet had been flipped onto the top of the stack of fallen leaves.

It had occurred to her only the day before that the living-room paint job she had begun on Monday evening had seemed to progress much faster than she realized. She'd slapped paint around three walls by the time she headed to work on Thursday morning but by Thursday evening, when she returned late and not looking forward to a night up the ladders, she had seen that she'd painted four walls and the woodwork and undercoated the radiator. She had felt pleased, relieved even, that for once she had achieved more than she'd realized.

The guttering on the single storey of the kitchen extension. It had leaked badly, every joint cracked and dripping and the downpipe missing. The rainwater had splattered down the wall making a damp patch in the kitchen. Did she dare look up?

'Is he in?' Jack was looking over the wall at her as she squinted up at the long line of new guttering. Grace turned.

'Sorry?'

'Fraser. He around at all today?'

Grace shook her head. 'No. He isn't.' Hadn't she mentioned the Arctic Circle? Didn't they know he wouldn't commute?

'Amazing what we turned up in that garage of yours. A real Aladdin's Cave.'

Grace was unsure of what to say. Had Jack been in her garage? Had he taken it upon himself to fashion the repairs? He had a key. What if Mr Denton had moaned to him about her? Grace was stumped, embarrassed, confused.

'That guttering was in the rafters. Obvious that Bill, Mr Mellor, intended doing it a while ago. Mind you, once Gwen left him . . . Still. Saved you a packet. And the trellis too . . .'

Grace kept her trap shut now, unsure what was happening. She was convinced that she was asleep in the leather chair, dreaming.

'Anyway, we had a lovely crumble with the apples. I've got a glut of tomatoes still from the greenhouse. I'll drop some on the doorstep if I remember. See you.' Jack's face disappeared from view and a moment later she heard the creak of his shed door.

Grace stepped back into the house.

Clearly they took Neighbourhood Watch schemes too far in Ruskin Road. She was wondering how she might wrest the key from Jack. It was handy to have a spare in a safe place but for him to use it to let himself in and finish all her little jobs? What would he want in return? Grace's head was filled with a sudden garish vision of Roberts Brothers Butchers shop and the underside of Nan's shoes, the little label, the flapping apron.

She had collected some new phrases during the week to reinforce the next chapter she was going to tell of 'Fraser the Fiancé's Arctic Adventure'. From the few neighbourly queries this week ('*Is he in?*' – Jack; '*Is Fraser about?*' – the new vicar of St John's; '*That chap of yours, is he likely to be showing his face today?*' – Mr Denton), she needed to fix him a little deeper into the snow-blown wastes of the Arctic Circle. She'd decided on a technical fault with an immense tunnel-boring piece of equipment that only Fraser could fix. She had done some research at the local Late Night Library evening before coming home to half forget it all as she knitted a new hooded sweater she'd had an idea for. She'd seen some of the local students swarming to the nearby screen-printed sweatshirt stall and picking it clean of hooded shirts, and she'd had a flash of inspiration. As she dug around in the dresser for appropriately gothic colour schemes she'd picked over the knowledge she was going to impart about Fraser's Arctic exploits. It would be enough for her to seem the enthusiastic fiancée and enough to bore them into talking about something else.

Mr Denton was playing host to the Neighbourhood Watch this month. Grace was surprised to be greeted with a glass of sherry on arrival and to see the glossy dining table opened out and spread with a china tea service and an array of Marks and Spencer cakes and fancies.

As she nibbled on walnut cake she realized she couldn't recall the last time she'd had a meal in fact, not just a grabbed sandwich or a snatched bag of crisps. She looked out of the back window, saw the hedge was newly and neatly trimmed. Clearly Mr Denton had grown tired of waiting for the mythical Fraser. If asked she could be effusive, promise him that it would be Fraser's job to trim the hedge next time.

'Took us a couple of afternoons, but we got there.' Mr Denton approached to refill her teacup. Grace turned, the liquorice of lie sticky on her lips, but Mr Denton continued, 'That garage of yours is a veritable stockroom. A stroke of luck Fraser spotting those roofing sheets.' Grace wasn't sure she'd heard but Mr Denton reiterated, 'He's a bit of a workhorse, that chap of yours.' And he moved off.

Hazel smiled from the nearby chair. 'Did you finalize the date, then? Fraser said you'd thought of next October. Such a lot of family and faff, I always think. You should take the plunge, Grace, elope!'

Grace was frozen, cup in hand, watching Hazel's mouth move and finding that all it seemed to say, over and over, was, 'Fraser said . . . Fraser said . . . Fraser said . . .'

16

MY LITTLE EYE

They were an odd couple, that's all Gloria Hadfield knew, and all these other nobodies just walked around with their eyes shut.

Of course, Grace and Fraser's weirdo lifestyle was that much clearer through the Nikon spotting scope she had on a tripod in the front bedroom. Mrs Hadfield's front bedroom had never lent itself to rest. She remembered all the sleepless nights she'd tossed through when she moved here after her divorce from Colin. It was then that she'd taken to sitting in the dark near the window and watching.

Back then there had been the foxes in Bill Mellor's garden. A vixen returned each year to raise cubs, and originally that was why Gloria had bought the spotting scope. She had been at a country fair, on a day out with a loser from the dating agency, and she'd bought the scope right there and then, one of the few things she'd ever put on her credit card. Its phallic pointiness did serve to remind her of Kevin, a man with all the equipment and no clue how to use it. She'd had to ride him like a cowgirl in the end, ride him really hard, clenching herself around him, and he'd lain there, gobsmacked. Yes. That was the word. In fact he'd been so motionless at one point that she'd half-worried she'd killed him. After that he'd been all over her. 'Ride me, Gloria,' he'd beg and it was just too much like hard work.

Gloria had watched as Bill Mellor and Graeme Denton staked out the garden and shot the vixen and the cubs in a single night. There had been no foxes since and Gloria had used the scope to watch Gwen Mellor drift away from Bill. Watched the day she packed her bags and the taxi had parped at the door. Watched Bill crumble, like a block of flats with a basement full of dynamite.

The house had been empty for a year before the young woman had arrived. Gloria had watched her snooping around one night, one hand on speed-dial for Ged and his partner in crime-fighting, PC Ella Cheadle. The cheek of the woman, pulling into the drive, strolling around the back like she owned the place.

Which, a month or so later, she did. And once Gloria found out her name she, of course, remembered. She said nothing then and she was saying nothing now as the tight little domestic drama was unfolding over the road. No, this little landscape was her private property.

As far as she could tell the fiancé lived in the attic. He was handy around the house during daylight hours but the moment the clock ticked towards six and Grace was due home he seemed to hive himself off upstairs. Gloria had a very poor angle on the skylight at the front of the house but she'd seen a light up there, movement. She thought perhaps he had trains up there, or Scalextric. Either way, you didn't see them together. Clearly his return from the Arctic had not been a happy one. Maybe that was it, he enjoyed roughing it so he camped out under the eaves.

But for an explorer he never strayed far from home. She'd seen him in the park once or twice but the furthest he'd been was B&Q with Jack Spring from next door. The edgy disposition she'd witnessed as he clicked on his seat belt made her wonder how he'd got to the Arctic when he seemed to be in a cold sweat about getting out of the driveway.

He was handsome. He was older. Gloria had him pegged for about forty, maybe more, there were creases that someone or something had put into his brow and a sad, rare smile. She wondered where someone like Grace Storey had found him.

Look, there she was now, back from that idiotic Neighbourhood Watch meeting, letting herself in with a key. Why did he never answer the door?

17

THE TWELVE LABOURS OF ALEC

Alec couldn't think what she ate. The fridge was constantly bare save for milk and occasionally the end of some plastic Cheddar cheese. A tomato had grown a fur coat in the chill of the salad drawer and he was stunned next morning to find that she'd eaten it for supper the night before. The bread too seemed to sit for days in a plastic bag, sweating itself into a fungus before she would eat it. Toasted. A scrape of butter. Once, there had been a tin of beans, but only once.

He had been watching her last night as she slept. She dreamed badly, he knew, and he had fallen into the dangerous habit of keeping watch over her, sitting on the floor by her bedroom door. Last night she had made noises, a shout and then a terrible hushed sobbing. He had been bothered by how thin she seemed, the dark circles beneath her eyes. She was working too hard – all day until six and beyond on her stall, then knitting until late. Two. Three.

Alec had been self-catering. With the last of his potato-picking money gone he had fished in the river in the park. He longed to cook something for her to come home to, to sit her at the table and hear about her day, to know all the everyday details that maybe someone who hadn't been starved of life for fifteen years would find tedious.

He vowed to help her out, pull his weight, to pay in kind for the roof over his head. The winter was creeping in and he knew he could not survive in the wilds. He'd need a sleeping bag, a mat, too, most likely. He'd found out how the ground sucked the heat from your body even on a warm night in the woods. But, if he stayed here in Grace Storey's attic, he had to repay her. So he began the tasks.

He had been picking his way through the contents of the garage that first morning. He had tackled most of the jobs inside, clearing away the heaps of kitchen that Grace moved from corner to doorway, from edge to edge. Then he'd seen the blind and was looking for some offcuts of wood to use as a batten. He'd found the offcuts and now he'd seen a bit of trellis too that would be useful for the grasping rose beside the gate.

Graeme Denton had knocked on the garage door. Alec had been careful to close it behind him but he realized he had made too much noise, clattering about amid the junk and lawnmowers.

'Hello? Anyone home?' The door creaked slightly and the lower portion of it, rotted through, came away as Graeme Denton pulled it open. 'Oh heck . . .' He was genuinely upset. Alec hopped through the worst of the garage jumble.

'Saved me a job. It was top of my to-do list this morning.' And he wrenched off the rest of the rotted wood.

'I'm Graeme Denton, from next door, thataway . . .' He gesticulated with one hand while offering the other for Alec to shake. 'I don't doubt your good lady fiancée has told you about my issues with your boundary . . .' He looked expectant.

Alec considered. What would be the issues on that boundary? 'This place. The hedge. The apple tree.' He reeled off his own list and saw from Graeme Denton's pleased grin that he had guessed correctly.

Graeme was retired and wanted to help. It was as simple as that. Between the two of them they dug out more offcuts and a few featherboard fence panels, which they bodged into new garage doors. There were a few tins of black gloss, some primer. By lunchtime the new doors rested on Graeme's portable saw-horse, whitely primed. Graeme had tugged on a set of blue coveralls; a knitted skullcap covered his bald spot and was there to be toyed with if thinking had to be done. Alec made tea and they talked as the paint dried.

'I've always wondered whether it's exciting in all that frozen wilderness.' Graeme blew across the surface of his tea. Alec offered biscuits to buy himself a moment of thought. ' Or is it just bloody boring? You know. All that snow. Great weather for brass monkeys and all that.'

Alec knew almost nothing about the Arctic but then, he reasoned, neither did Graeme. He saw instantly why Grace had chosen the landscape of her fairy story. His panic subsided like a fire quoshed by a blanket. He could lie.

'It's hectic.' Like the way his heart felt. Alec had spent his lifetime clinging to the truth and it had got him into prison. But he wanted to stay here and the way to do that was to lie. White, Arctic lies. 'Some of the downtime can be fun. The Swedes and the Finns know how to deal with winter. Snowcats. Saunas. Ice fishing.'

'Vodka?'

Alec grinned and nodded and Graeme tipped his mug to the Scandinavians.

They found the roofing sheets at the far end of the garage under another lawn mower. They had been taking a proper look at the sagging side wall, shifting the detritus to reveal where the supports had rotted through and ivy was clambering in from outside, dragging the pre-fab panel sections down.

It took them three days and they had to call on Jack Spring, who stayed with ladders and loppers for a fourth day to tackle the apple tree and hedge. Alec had slept like the dead after they had fought the hedge. 'I'm thinking we might do a half share on a stout fence instead,' Graeme suggested as they glugged tea, each speared and splintered and bleeding from the job. 'That berberis seemed a good idea fifteen years ago but it's a bit old and cantankerous now.' Alec nodded. But he liked the hedge and the birds and moths that lived in it. 'It's an expense, I know, and the hedge does the job. Specially on that back border with the bridleway and the factory – real criminal's paradise that little bridleway.' Alec felt his hair bristle at the word 'criminal'. But Graeme had not noticed, his eyes trailing over the tottering gable of the towelling factory, draped as it was in ivy and the skeleton of last summer's bindweed. 'Just a thought for you to run past wifey. Although I suppose with the expense of the wedding it might be something for the future. Eh?'

The future. A place somewhere north of him that he had almost forgotten.

He felt like Hercules. Alec could finish the work, help Grace to refurbish her house and in the doing of it would be penance. That was how he felt now. They had won at last. He felt remorse. For not having done it. For having been stubborn. For having been honest.

He had been painting the ceiling on the landing. He was not expecting Grace to return. Both Graeme and Jack had commented that the Neighbourhood Watch gatherings often slid into more of a social event. They mentioned that Ged's nose was out of joint because, as Hazel had suggested, he'd had his eye on Grace. The news of her betrothal had been taken on the chin, it seemed. Alec had been disturbed by this because Ged, the burly community police officer, looked like a man who might have wrestled professionally. Alec did not want him looking too closely. Even now his photofit portrait might be pinned to the police station noticeboard. 'Alec Holm – Prisoner 9755: Number Eleven on the Ten Most Wanted'.

But she was back. He barely had time to skim down the ladder and slap the lid back on the paint. There was no way to reach the attic so he stepped into the airing cupboard by the bathroom.

She was running up the stairs. Alec held his breath, waiting for the moment when she tore open the door to the airing cupboard and demanded to know what the hell he was playing at.

She didn't. Instead he heard her rummaging in the bottom of the wardrobe. It was a crappy junk shop find and he heard it creak sideways almost toppling. He made a note to fix that too. She ran past him again. He watched through the gap in the door. She was carrying a scarf, clutching it in her hand, greens, a brown-coloured edging. In her other hand she clutched a thick rubber torch at least as long as her forearm. The beam was bright and clear. He watched her down to the hallway and then, sure she would not see him, he stepped to look over the banisters. Where was she going? He leaned forward.

There was a decisive click and he saw the door to the under-stairs cupboard as it closed. The torch beam shone out like white piping at the door edges.

Alec, as quietly as possible, picked his way up the five attic steps and shut the door behind him. He lay for a long while, his ear to the floor, listening. He imagined he could hear her breathing. He wondered what had happened. And then he knew. It was his fault, of course: the neighbours would have talked. He felt as if the night deepened, the seconds ticking away in ultra-slow motion, pulling him forward to the morning and his departure.

18

AT LAST

He pulled the door to behind him. It had been on his to-do list, a coat of paint and refit the door furniture, especially the vicious jaw of the letter box. But he couldn't think about that now.

He'd looked out early over the back garden, seen the rooks waiting in the treetops and known they had come, as heralds this time, to see him on his way. Grace had spent the night under the stairs. At five, he'd listened for the last time to her kitchen noises, aware that this morning she hadn't clicked on the radio, had not sung.

He had watched as she started up the car, reversed out, watched her trundle to the corner, grinding out of first gear, the indicator winking. She had gone.

As he moved from the doorstep he almost collided with Mrs Hadfield.

'I've caught a mouse.' She was visibly shaking. 'I've caught one and I don't know what to do. I'm sorry, Fraser, you wouldn't have five minutes, would you?'

Alec wasn't sure. He was uneasy about Mrs Hadfield, he was aware how she watched the house. He wondered about her motives, but he could see she was far from her usual sharp self.

The mouse was in a cupboard, and as he picked up the black live-capture tube, Alec felt the creature struggle inside.

'Oh be careful, be careful . . .' Mrs Hadfield's hands reached out, delicate, her left hand touching his sleeve briefly. He was surprised by her concern.

'Where do we let him out?' Alec asked. 'Bottom of the garden?' He took a step towards the back door. Mrs Hadfield stopped him.

'No. No. We'll have to— Oh I shouldn't have asked. This is putting you out. Oh I'm sorry, Fraser, really I am . . .'

'It's not a problem.'

'But you were on your way out . . .'

'What do you want me to do with him?' Alec smiled and it seemed to work on her as magically as if he had whispered abracadabra.

'The park. Well, behind the park really, to Coverts Wood. We'll take him there. If you've time? If you don't mind?'

She talked as if the elastic had gone on her mouth. Alec said nothing, carried the mousetrap carefully in his pocket, his hand staying over it, aware of the mouse inside. Mrs Hadfield was apologetic.

'I couldn't ask Graeme. Not again,' she began and Alec thought of Mr Denton holding the trap at arm's length most likely, or putting it into the boot of his car in a snap-to plastic crate. Mrs Hadfield continued, 'He just took it out and whacked it with my meat tenderizer. Not again. Never again.'

She surprised him more as she told him of the foxes. It was

clear to Alec that she had spent a lot of time in watching the vixen and had invested emotion in her and the cubs. He thought he had misjudged her. He had slapped a sticker on her very early that read 'Nosey Neighbour – Do Not Disturb', but now as they walked to the woodland he could not label her. She was not who he had imagined.

They set the mouse free among the leaf litter and saplings. The woodland was a tiny fragment of something more ancient that had been groomed and bounded by bye-laws and railings.

'They're wood mice,' Mrs Hadfield reassured herself. 'They funnel down from here through the park and into the gardens and then they wonder what on earth they're doing in the back of some musty old cupboard. He'll be happier here.'

They walked back. Without the mouse to connect them Mrs Hadfield's conversation faltered and Alec was busy with the eeny-meeny-miny-mo of his future.

'I heard that Grace's nan died recently.' Mrs Hadfield looked searching. Alec had no information but he nodded, 'Yes.'

'Must have been a hard business for her.'

Alec agreed again. He should have learned this long ago; agreeing was smooth and easy and kept you from trouble. 'Yes. It's always hard to lose someone.' He thought a vision of Cherry would blip into his head, but he was disconcerted to relive a moment in prison: a cold green reception area, his possessions being put into a box. Perhaps their continued existence in the box might convince the authorities he was still in prison.

'But doubly hard for Grace. After her mother, you know, and all that business.'

Now Alec fumbled, he could not guess what 'business' might

mean, but he knew from Mrs Hadfield's expression that it wasn't good.

'She talk about it ever?'

Alec was unsure if she was fishing for fresh information or awaiting an opportunity to blurt out the details. He had labelled her a nosey neighbour; now that label peeled and revealed something darker.

'I remember the inquest said the stabbing was accidental. Still, must have been a trial growing up with that hanging over you. Because no one ever truly knows, do they? I mean, Grace was only nine.'

'A long time ago.' Alec heard his own voice, deep and firm and resonant.

'Yeah. Fifteen years.' She sighed. Alec felt his throat constrict. 'Long time to live with it.' Mrs Hadfield fell silent for a while. They turned into Ruskin Road. 'Still, now her nan's gone there's only Grace who knows the truth.' Her eyebrow arched upwards and Alec was suddenly reminded of an owl. They had reached Mrs Hadfield's gate. 'This is me. Well. Thank you again, Fraser.'

Had she caught the mouse on purpose, swooped and snatched it from the cupboard, squeezed it into the trap? An elaborate lure, like puppies or sweets, to draw him out of the house and donate this information so generously?

'You watch yourself, lovey,' she said, unexpected and soft. And she turned up the path and was gone.

Alec stepped towards the kerb, not towards the high street. As he glanced up, waiting for the removals van from number 29 to pass, he noticed the rooks in the tree in Grace's back garden. Three. Five. Eight. Nine.

Gloria Hadfield, quite satisfied that she had killed two birds with one mouse, watched as Fraser crossed Ruskin Road and once again, not going anywhere, opened the gate.

Grace had sold almost nothing that day. The best sale she'd made was to point someone in the direction of Elke's stall when they had expressed interest in the party dress draping from a hanger and swathed with one of her cobweb shawls. She'd knitted up a hopeful stock of them but they had failed to tempt the Christmas party-goers. She felt dismal and tired and suffocated by wool.

She was thinning down the stock, sick of the sight of most of it, clearing some display space and freeing up the hanging rack. She'd got some coats and wrap cardigans she'd been working on that she would bring down tomorrow. She'd decided they'd be more pricey and she had thought of keeping them for spring. Now she chose to take a chance on them. The words 'something special' whispered into her head and she was reminded of Nan's 70 per cent bargain rail, but she didn't care. All the shawls and the other bits were going back to the house to moulder in the attic most likely. But now she had spent three hours boxing it she couldn't face taking all the handiwork home and so it was being shoved into the furthest corner of the storeroom. There were still thirty days of shopping to be filled before Christmas, there was still time.

'Let me,' the familiar voice said and the big box was lifted from her hands. Hugo stepped by her into the back room.

'Not going to offer me a cup of tea?' He showed no signs of leaving, his square shoulders and height making the stockroom look tiny. He picked up a mug and examined its cleanliness, opened a tin to hunt for tea bags. 'Have to be a coffee, then.' His big hand reached, clicked the kettle on.

'I think you should leave.' Grace kept her voice steady. How was it that Hugo owned the world, was able to stride in like this, to make himself—

'Leave? Ha. Why? Fraser going to bash me, is he?'

She didn't want to look at him, the fakery of his expression made her feel sick. Then the thought of green-eyed Fraser reached across the snow, took her hand.

'No wedding present, Hugo?' she ventured, the taste of liquorice like a rescue remedy. Sticky black confidence began to ooze into her veins.

'What wedding?' His look was direct but Grace kept going.

'Next October.' But something was wrong. She couldn't see Fraser any more, there was just the wind blowing the snow into drifts in her head.

'Oh. October, is it?' Hugo stirred sugar into his coffee. 'Not the twelfth of never, then?' He stood, arms akimbo, like a teacher ticking her off. 'Maisie let me in on the big secret.'

Grace looked hard at him. 'Hands,' she heard Nan say, and waited for the slap around her face.

Hugo leaned close, not touching, just allowing the microcosm of space between them to fill with electricity. 'You've had your fun, Gracie. Now it's time to fuck around.'

'Grace, there's a delivery waiting for you in the market office.' Elke was behind her, an elegant, beringed hand coming to rest delicately on her shoulder. Hugo's face snapped upward like a dog disturbed at a meal. 'Oh. Hi there.' Elke smiled and offered her hand which Hugo snubbed. He barged past them, tripping, only just recovering himself. He wheeled around. Glanced down at Elke's jutting foot.

'Oops.' Elke's voice was steel enough to cut him.

He hung around the market car park for so long that Elke invited Grace to crash at her house. 'With Fraser away at the moment it seems the safest, you know.'

But Grace was afraid. Fraser was not away, he hadn't gone anywhere so he couldn't very well come back. It seemed a deep, gravish hole to have dug for herself. Then, suddenly, Hugo gave up and was gone.

Grace loaded the car quickly, double padlocked the stall and drove home the long way. Her eye was so constantly drawn to the rear-view mirror that she almost shunted three other cars. No one seemed to be following.

Whatever else Maisie had blabbed about, '. . . I didn't tell him where you're living now.' Her message sang out across the hall-way: 'I'm sorry, Gracie. He cornered me and you KNOW what he's like. I'm a hopeless liar and I'm so sorry. If you need any-thing just ring and if I'm not here try Mum's and she's got a spare room, you know, if you need it. I'm so—' and was cut off. Grace bolted the doors, drew the curtains. 'Fraser, we need a portcullis and one of those decorative Japanese drawbridges . . . What do you think? Sweetheartdarlinglove,' she joked with the air, her voice shrill and catching. She looked up the stairs then, at the fresh coat of paint, the beautiful sanding job that had been done on the banisters. As she trailed her hand down the clean wood her eye was drawn to the soft gold of the newly sanded floorboards. 'You did a great job in the hall, Frase.' Her voice screeled into a yelp. Wait. At the top of the stairs. My God. Near the attic door.

'Hello?' Grace's heart was like a sock trapped in her throat. She took in a deep, slow breath. Had something moved on the landing or was it simply a shift in the light, the shadow of a car outside? Did she want to switch the light on? If they were in darkness then she couldn't see *It* but, equally, *It* couldn't see her. The doorbell sounded like an alarm and she felt the damburst of adrenalin flood her blood. She turned in time to see Hugo push his face against the stained glass.

'Open the door, Gracie.' He spoke calmly, determined. Grace took a step back. She'd left the torch in the understairs cupboard. She regretted not buying the thick brown shag-pile carpet at the weekend. It would have been fitted by now and the carpet wolves would be rising up, snapping at the door.

The letter box flipped open. Hugo looked at her.

'Do I have to huff and puff?'

'I'm calling the police.' Grace kept her voice low and level but couldn't move a step. Hugo's eyes were unblinking.

'Yeah. Okay. Right. Ged is my prop forward, Grace. Plus, what will he make of you and your LYING. Now OPEN THE FUCK-ING DOOR.'

Grace's feet took her one step back. Hugo gave a grunt and slapped the letter box, straightened up and jabbed a finger at the bell. 'Let me in, let me in, by the hairs on my chinny-chin, Little Grace,' he bellowed above it. The bell rang out until at last it strained itself and died with a discordant groan. The letter box flipped again.

'Just open the door. How hard can it be? It's me. Hugo.

Remember? The love of your fucking life. Christ's sake, this is doing my back in.' He flipped the letter box again, tried the weary bell and then started banging the knocker.

The hairs on the back of Grace's neck prickled then and as the stairs creaked beside her she dared not look round. On the periphery of her vision he appeared, moving down, down, his hand on the finial at the foot of the stairs as he moved into the hallway and took the three steps to the door. She saw the muscles twitch as he threw back the bolts, his hand reaching, his fingers curling around the lock. The door opened and Hugo stumbled inside.

Hugo looked up with lust on his face and saw, not Grace, but a lean, muscled man of about forty with a clipped and greying beard. The man said nothing. Grace stood a pace or two behind him, ghost-faced. Hugo looked at her.

'Who the fuck is this?'

Alec took his hand from the door and willed it not to shake as he offered it to Hugo.

'I'm Fraser.'

19

DEACON MASSEY

Hugo backed out of the driveway almost colliding with the gatepost. His gears ground and bit and with a ferocious glare he was gone.

Moments ago, at the top of the stairs listening to Hugo, Alec had thought that this might be the reason. The whole mess of his life was some sort of training course for guardian angels, only ones that weren't yet dead. He could hear the sound in Hugo's voice, the metallic pinking of danger. There was no decision to be made, his feet followed his instinct down the stairs.

He shut the door. Grace was standing near to the cupboard under the stairs and for a long while neither of them moved. Alec's mind was a blank.

Grace stepped forward. She did not reach for the light switch. She reached for him. He felt her fingers trembling as they passed over his face, her thumb smoothing over the texture of his beard, her palms smooth and cool over his cheek as she reached to his hair.

One word spoke in Grace's head as she raised her hand to touch Fraser, *Conjured*. She had heard of golems, men of mud made alive with a splash of blood and a prayer. *Conjured*. She had imagined this face but here, in the hallway, made real, his eyes were a darker green, his hair more tinged with slate. He was more than she had imagined. She looked into his eyes and saw he was sadder too and she wondered at all she had done to make him this way. Would he smell of liquorice? If you cut him would it seep out of him? Did he carry all her true lies? She spoke in a whisper, tilting her head into the crook of his neck where she knew it would fit perfectly.

'It's really you.'

Alec's thoughts crashed around. He needed to touch her, to fold her into him, to lie with her on that bare-boarded floor and share the knowledge that something dark and powerful had brought them here. Perhaps this was something to be afraid of. Then Grace threaded her small fingers between his own.

She woke early and alone and aware she might have dreamed it. Where had she fallen asleep? In the hall? On the floor? Waiting for Hugo to be gone or break the door open. But Hugo had gone. Had she hidden under the stairs and drifted off and dreamed it all? What was the last thing she remembered?

Fraser. Naked. Fetching the duvet for them to lie on.

He was in the kitchen, the radio was on low as it was each morning and he was fishing broken toast from the toaster with a wooden spoon.

'You're still real.' Grace did not want to blink as she looked at him in case, on lifting her lids, she'd find him gone. He looked uncertain, which was how it should be, his expression the decoction of all that was boiling in her head.

'Will you be here when I get home?' Grace was pulling on her coat, ready but unwilling to leave for work, but equally unwilling to stay and wear out the fantasy. 'If I want you to, you will be. Is that how it works?'

'I don't know how this works, Grace.'

She wanted to kiss him now but something in the daylight prevented her.

The day seemed to pass in shards and splinters of time. The morning ripped past, a blur of customers, three of whom bought the expensive coats. In the euphoria of such huge sales she unpacked more boxes and there was a rush on the hats she had fashioned and decorated with the unwanted flowers. She saw she had missed a trick, that people wanted gift-wrapping, that her economical stripey paper bags were not glamorous enough for the festive season.

The afternoon dragged by like a slug.

The house was dark as she pulled in at the drive, and at the sight she almost reversed out again. She sat in the car for a long time until a twitch of light from Mrs Hadfield's window pushed her inside.

There was no sound. Grace shut the front door and leaned back against it, her eyes wandering to the darkness at the top of the stairs. Perhaps it was a spell she had to cast, to begin again, like last night. But there was no movement.

In the workroom she dug through the baskets of yarn for some brackish-green, the Coniston Water colour of Fraser's eyes, and began weaving it into another skein of brown, the burnished bronze of his hair.

She had never fallen in love lightly. The first time, Grace had been seventeen and found the man enticing. She'd had a work experience placement at a replacement window firm and he was the handsome, older manager. She had been prickly but he paid her attention. The way he looked at her, which hindsight showed her was greediness, lit an intense blue flame in the pit of her stomach. He had not seemed like the men Nan and Mum found. He had worn a suit. There were leather seats in his car.

He had taken her virginity like someone snaffling a cream cake. He had driven her out into the countryside beyond Coverts Wood. They had moved into the back of his car, Grace as eager, the intense blue flame hissing within her. She remembered his hands, the cologne smell of him. But then a gear had shifted somewhere and she was uncomfortable, rubbed raw, the cheeks of her bottom sticking against the leather of the seat as he pounded at her. The way he tied off the condom like a party balloon.

'What the fuck were you doing with that knicker-merchant?' Nan had demanded. He'd been at the pub bragging and triumphant about his Coverts Wood conquest. 'After all I've taught you . . . haven't you learned one FUCKING thing?' Nan was angry, her cigarette pointing at Grace, glowing, like a miniature doorway to the gates of hell. Grace let her rant. He had discarded her. It was done with.

After that Grace realized she didn't want just sex, an animal rutting, the licking of parts.

'Well, you're going to be disappointed,' Nan had sneered. But

Grace hadn't been. She had gone to university and met Deacon Massey.

She looked back and saw his dorm room, the bookshelves stacked with Celestial mechanics and quantum theory. It was so clear in her mind's eye, as boldly outlined and definite as a true lie and she sometimes thought she might have made Deacon up too.

They had lived in the same halls of residence. Deacon, in his third and final year, was as cool and dark as Tarn Hows, not part of the knicker-twanging Boys' Brigade chalking up their conquests with collected earrings.

They seemed always to meet in the kitchen at midnight, Grace, working late, waiting for toast, Deacon wandering in, barefoot, to snack and flick through a leftover newspaper. She would walk past his room, the desk light lending a glow to the bare cell of the place. A chair. The books. Shoes under the bed. A waft of supermarket aftershave and used socks.

One midnight she was late in, draped and pinned into a sheet from a stupid toga party. She passed by Deacon's room to see him sitting on his desk, his feet on the chair, a pencil tapping. He had crossed the room as if to close the door, instead opened it wider. Looked at her. No words. Just kisses.

After that they had been the inseparable weirdos.

During her second year at university she lived in a Victorian terrace in Leamington Spa. Deacon, now studying for his MSc, lived in a much grander white-iced cake of a house on the other side of town. He was sharing with Wazz and Geoffrey who thought themselves the post-grad nuclear physicists of their age. They had been in the back kitchen, on the first floor, a morass of pots and pans and beer cans. Outside, the overgrown garden sloped away towards the river and Jephson Gardens. They had been talking, shouting, laughing, Geoffrey and Wazz peeling cans of beer from a cardboard supermarket slab. It was a bright white January day and the window was open wide to let out the twin smokes of Wazz's burnt curry and Geoffrey's cigarettes.

'Course Jesus was gay. For fuck's sake he hung around with twelve blokes. It's a no-brainer.'

'Yeah. But twelve blokes and a prostitute. You can't take the prostitute out of the equation, Wazz.' Geoff grabbed the gas bill from the worktop and a pencil from the pot. 'Look, let's start with X being Jesus—'

'No. J for Jesus. X equals the prostitute . . .' They began to joke and argue, Wazz scribbling his equation, Deacon watching the pencil make the marks, Geoffrey lighting up a fresh cigarette.

'I just have to make a departure,' said Deacon Massey and in a fluid diving movement he flipped himself out of the window. Time stalled for a moment, the curry billowed more smoke and suddenly they were all cramming at the window, watching Deacon pick himself up from the overgrown shrubbery and stride away. Grace had said nothing as he hoiked himself over the rotting back fence, to be swallowed by the ivy and Russian vine. Her last view of him was the grubby grey-white underside of his left trainer.

Seven weeks later they still hadn't heard from him and Grace quit her course, headed home.

Grace had come back to number 11 Springfield Court and shoved all her suitcases and carrier bags into her old room. 'Get your glad rags on and fuck someone,' was Nan's advice. 'That's what you need.' It seemed that now Grace was nineteen she couldn't keep her trap shut with coke floats and Genoese fancies, but she could be got out of the way with carnal pursuits. *Long as she's out of my sight.*

Nan had gone out with Ken later and Grace had picked up all her baggage and gone to a bed and breakfast. Ken had telephoned and called her ungrateful. Nan had not phoned her at all. Within a week she had found the horrible yellow flat. She had never gone back to Springfield Court. Not until the funeral.

The dream was brick-red and blue-striped. She was in the meat locker, Nan standing behind her puffing on a cigarette. 'Get fucked,' she said and Mr Roberts's pinny flapped over Grace's head, his penis, in heart-attack purple, a thrusting bratwurst before her. 'Hands,' Nan demanded. Grace gave up her hands and Nan smacked her face.

She woke up with a yelp in her throat, soaked with sweat. Out of the darkness, Fraser moved to the bed, Grace grabbing for him.

'Fraser? Fraser?'

'Hey.' His voice, safe and quiet, exactly how she wanted him to sound. His arms folded around her, there was a scent of new wood and dust on his shirt.

'Don't go.'

And he didn't.

20

LIVING THE LIE

Alec marked the days, just as he had in prison, but instead of measuring the distance from his past he marked the moments until Grace. She left in the mornings and he set about the work on the house. He was carpentering a new set of balusters for the attic stairs, a sawhorse set up in the garden in spite of the pre-Christmas cold. Although no longer confined to the attic and having the full freedom of the Inside, Alec liked Outside. He had been too long without it.

It felt like a fairy tale, as if their real lives took place at night. As dusk fell he would begin to prepare the meal. Grace had been half-starved, neglectful of herself. Alec found he enjoyed the safety of their once-a-week round trip to the supermarket. With Grace, no one could point a finger. Without her he wasn't so sure.

Each night he set the table, lit the candles. He would hear her key in the door and wait as she moved through the dark to the kitchen. More than anything he cherished the look on her face each evening as she appeared in the the doorway and saw him. Still here. When the time came, and he knew it must, the memories of that expression on Grace's face would keep him alive.

At night they would lie together like spoons and he would fall asleep, his face against her hair, the scent of her shampoo and the captured aromas of Archie's Market in his nostrils. Usually he slept deeply and woke refreshed and relieved to find she was still there beside him, snoring slightly as she lay on her back. It struck him one morning that she did sleep with him. Deeply. Dreamlessly. Falling into him.

This night they had eaten very late and talked later. 'If I give them to you, will you keep them safe?' she asked as they finished the meal. Her voice was as quiet as church, her eyes wide and dark. He sat at the table with her until the candles burnt away and then they sat some more. She told him her Mum Memories. Few. Far between. Small pebbles she had saved that she gave to him.

They moved through the house using the torch, finding their way into bed at last, Grace almost too tired to take off her clothes.

'Then don't. Sleep in them. Take them off in the morning,' he said and she lay down beside him.

'You never tell me about you, Fraser.'

Alec felt adrenalin rip through him. Grace yawned, pulled his arms tighter around her, turned her head slightly into his shoulder. 'It's because I didn't give you a history, not in my mind. I've made you mythical, springing straight from my forehead.' He felt her kisses, the way she relaxed into him. Alec did not relax. 'I should think up a past for you, Fraser . . .' She was sleepy now. Alec lay in the dark for a time but the scents of Grace did not work their spell tonight. She was asleep, he knew, before he spoke.

'My life is a lie.'

On his fortieth birthday they were in Jack's shed, sampling the latest vintage of his home brew. Not that anyone knew it was Alec's birthday. He had not even told Grace.

Jack was, it appeared, trying for some world land-speed brewing record. This latest vat left a sickly aftertaste.

'Overdone the yeast?' Graeme Denton swilled the brown cloudy concoction around the jam jars they were drinking from. Jack quaffed more, slooshed it around his mouth and, finding nowhere to spit it, sucked it down.

'Too much honey, I think. I was after the mead angle.'

'Bit of an acute angle.' Alec winced through zinging teeth which felt fizzy, as if they were dissolving. This was not how he had pictured his fortieth birthday. He had pictured himself chained to a cliff face, the eagles pecking at his eyes. He felt compelled suddenly to chink Graeme's jam jar, take another death-defying sip.

'What do you think, Fraser? Should I leave it to brew some more?'

The brew heated through him with a slow torchlike golden burn. 'I don't know. I think it might already be approaching critical mass . . .'

'You should patent it, flog it to NATO.' Graeme belched.

They emerged into the grey December day just as a mist of icy rain began to fizzle around them. Alec bundled the sawhorse and his tools in through the French doors. He liked the damp weather and the iciness refreshed him, the earth an invigorating brew of smells, of earthworms and blackbirds' footprints. He saw the rooks then, bedraggled into the treetop. They could oversee the vegetable patch he would dig out.

He did not get very far. As he stepped into the garage to retrieve the spade and fork he saw Mrs Hadfield's door open and Ged exit. They exchanged a few short words on the doorstep. Alec, edgy, stepped inside the garage. His heart was wedging itself tightly into his gullet so he felt he wanted to gasp and be sick and was prevented from doing either.

The moments seemed elastic, stretching ridiculously taut. He would look as if he was hiding. The policeman must have gone by now, sated with cake or whatever else Mrs Hadfield gave him. Had she lured him in with a mouse too? Alec reached for the fork and spade and stepped outside. He was aware he flinched as he spotted Ged, still somehow loitering at Mrs Hadfield's gate. He tried not to glance across, tried not to see the challenging look that Ged threw his way.

He was in too much of a sweat now and the soggy weather didn't help. His hands, workworn as they were, blistered in new raw places. He moved inside, the grey light making the day seem further on. He tried to chop onions for the meal and sliced into his thumb.

It was a deep gash and for an hour he cursed himself, afraid that he might have to go and have it sewn up, but he held on to the thought that Grace might do the job and he could avoid the hospital. Then she might ask why and he might tell her.

At last, it stopped bleeding and became a flabby white trapdoor of skin, sharp with pain. He'd reddened a couple of tea towels in his fight with it and now, injured hand immobile with bandage, he chucked them into the bottom of the washing basket.

Grace had fared no better during her day at Archie's Market. A tribe of schoolgirls had scoured through the market that afternoon filching and stealing. They had landed on Grace's stall, two of them distracting Grace as a third girl, greasy and rodent-like, had made off with a basket filled with cheap brooches. They were cheap, they were not selling but it was the loss, the frustration and fear of the thief girls and their sudden vanishing that threw her. They had been there, solid, chemically scented, loud, and then . . . gone.

As she had sipped at tepid tea and realized she couldn't even face a consolation bun from the bakery stall, the day dipped further with the arrival of Maisie. She was not consoling; this time she needed consolation.

'It isn't that Hugo had a go at me, Grace. I don't care about that. But, you know, you made me . . . look . . . I don't know what . . . Beyond stupid, like a . . . like a liar.'

Grace was silent, swallowing down the liquorice that leeched onto her tongue. She should not lie her way out of this.

'I don't know what happened, Maisie. Truly, I—' But Maisie's face scorned the word 'truly' and she, too, was gone.

Grace packed up early, fobbing off a last-minute customer who had already been around three times and now wanted to haggle the price.

'I'm sorry. I'm closing,' Grace said, giving the shutters a determined tug.

'But it's only just gone four. Your sign says you're here till six.' Grace clipped the padlock in place. 'So much for customer service.' The woman was snide.

Grace turned on her. 'You aren't a customer. You didn't buy anything. You haggle so much you almost qualify as a thief.'

Grace watched as a tiny snowflake of her spit launched itself at the woman, tumbled downwards to land on her shoes. Grace saw the expensive leather. 'Bet you didn't haggle in Russell Wantage.' She growled and walked away.

As usual the house was in darkness when she arrived back. She let herself in quietly, wanted to hear Fraser making kitchen noises, unaware that she was back.

There was silence. Grace stood delaying the moment she would step into the living room. Wanting to see the moment when her lie switched on, when she looked through the kitchen doorway and Fraser was there. What if tonight the kitchen were empty? She thought she couldn't bear that.

'It was my fault, Fraser.' Grace held his damaged hand as if it were as fagile as a shell. 'It's my fault because I lied to Maisie . . . that's what twisted things.'

'It was my stupid fault. Chopping onions.'

Fraser half-turned away but Grace fussed, doing and redoing the bandage. She caught the way he was looking at her as she worked, as if he was afraid.

'It doesn't matter . . . forget it.' He tugged his hand away.

Grace knew that somehow her frustration with the thief girls, Maisie's distress and her own anger at the customer had burnt into the true lie, had hurt him. A physical manifestation of what she'd felt. It frightened her, this proof, this damage.

Later, she came out of the bathroom and he had vanished. She knew. She had changed something, had broken the spell.

In the attic, Alec, on his haunches under the skylight, felt fear shock through him. When she had held his hand, tended the wound, when she had turned her head, he had seen Debbie Winstanley in her stead. That faerie face looking up at him so long ago, wanting to be helped. That was all he could see, the tumble and riffle of the images he had kept for so long in his head. Gold. Blonde. Sour. Dark. Smoky. Tears.

'No. Don't switch the light on.' He stood by the bedroom door.

Grace shifted upright in bed, moved to make room for him. 'Come to bed.'

Grace listened but there was silence. She thought she could just make out his shape in the darkness, then his voice reached out to her.

'Grace, my name is Alec Holm. My name isn't Fraser.'

Grace was silent. Alec hoped she was listening and not simply terrified. He thought he could still trace her shape in the bed. A car passed by, the sweep of light illuminating her, the curved shape of her shoulder then darkness again.

'The worst part,' Grace said, her voice steady. 'Tell me that part first.'

Alec took a shallow breath, about to speak, but Grace continued, 'Then it will be my turn.'

21

COMMUNITY POLICING

It was a courtesy call more than anything. Gloria Hadfield needed the company and the drama and, as the sergeant said, it was all part of the community policing brief. They just weren't doing their job if people, ordinary people like Gloria Hadfield, didn't feel safe in their homes, didn't feel they could call on them twenty-four hours a day.

Last year, the big drama for Gloria had been the dognapper. A couple of border terriers had been snatched from Cornerstone House round Easter time. And it was true that there had been a run on border terriers and that a couple of miniature schnauzers had gone west. The schnauzers turned out to be victims of a divorce custody battle, abducted by their pining 'daddy'. Ged and his community policing partner, Ella, had taken statements from Mrs Walters at Cornerstone House and she had been sanguine about her chances of getting Sanderson and Digby back. Ged and Ella had also been called into the park, into the hinterland beyond where the lawns gave way to the snarl of trees and undergrowth that the council insisted on calling Coverts Wood. There one of the council foresters had shown them the dismembered body of what could have been a border terrier. There were just three paws and a fractured splinter of jawbone sitting in a sticky black toffee of blood.

'Big cat,' the forester assured them. 'I know. I used to work at the zoo.'

They had kept schtum about it. After all, as the sergeant said, it was their brief to make people feel safe in their homes not create a panic.

Bernadette at the Cats' Cradle Rescue Home was going out of business due to a lack of feral cats. Ged and Ella asked for Bernadette's help plus her van and traps. She was on permanent secondment to them now and had successfully trapped a juvenile puma in Coverts Wood. She'd not been successful in trapping the parents. 'Yet,' said Bernadette.

But as they maintained radio silence about the big-cat crisis ('They're pushing their territory off the moors just into the cover of the wood. That's all. It's a lockdown situation,' Bernadette had assured a meeting of the community policing department), so Gloria Hadfield made a new crisis all on her own.

'Evidence? How about the evidence of my own eyes?' she'd argued, unable to substantiate a claim she was making that Graeme Denton across the road was trading in illegally obtained border terriers.

'Fair play.' Ged had given up arguing. 'What did you see?'

She'd seen Graeme Denton covering up a dog in the boot of his car. He'd carried it out of the garden hidden under a blanket. It looked drugged, she finished. Ged doodled as if making a note.

'You are aware that Graeme's dog Max died that week? He took him to the vet only it was too late.' Ged watched Gloria's face, felt Ella wince beside him as Gloria's expression ignited.

'What's that prove?'

In the end, as a goodwill gesture, they had offered to visit Graeme.

'Don't mention Gloria,' Ged warned Ella.

Graeme was babysitting a pair of King Charles spaniels for a friend.

'Tenerife, eh?' said Ged as Ella fussed over the dogs.

'Yeah. Back Friday. I thought I might get a new dog, but I don't know . . . not sure who could fill Max's paws, gentleman duffer that he was.'

It was Ella who suggested volunteer dog-walking at the rescue centre.

Two weeks later Gloria presented them with a list of dogs and accompanying photos of Graeme with said dogs, which had subsequently vanished. 'Every couple of days he shows up with another dog.'

Graeme had dug up Max in the middle of the night and Jack and Hazel Spring had telephoned for help at 3 a.m. Graeme was drunk, the decomposing Max melting and flaking in his arms as he bellowed up at Gloria's bedroom window, 'Happy now? Happy now? You callous harpy!'

Now it seemed she had it in for Grace Storey.

'But I'm telling you, he doesn't go anywhere.'

Ella mentioned Fraser's travels, how, if you'd spent six months or more away in the Arctic you might fancy staying at home by your own fireside, cosy, with your fiancée. 'There is something odd going on over there. You watch them. He never answers the door to her. Not once. '

Ged couldn't remember seeing that listed as a major crime but he dredged a contemplative nod.

'When they go to the supermarket SHE drives. It's like she's afraid he might escape or something. I'm warning you, I want it going on record, every word I've said . . .' She tried to steal a glance at the doodles Ged had made. 'I want it noted, for when it all goes tits up.'

Ged remembered he hadn't had a cup of tea since breakfast. They were never offered tea at Gloria's. He pulled his face into his bobby-on-the-beat smile, took out a bigger notebook.

'Why don't you make us all a cup of tea and we can sit down and take some proper chronological notes . . .'

But he didn't get the tea and Gloria had already made substantial time-coded notes. It was an observer's record of one couple's tedious everydayness. She had logged how often he entered and left the garage at the side of the house. How the lights were hardly ever on even when the couple were in. How Fraser only had one set of clothing. Finally Ged grew weary. Ella had checked out Gloria's obsessive-compulsive notes and was sneaking looks to Ged.

Finally, they found themselves walking up Grace Storey's path to mollify Gloria Hadfield.

'What're you going to say?' asked Ella.

Ged rapped on the door, 'Hello?'

Now he spotted the bell. As he rang it, it gave out a weary

asthmatic sound. They got no reply. Gloria's notes had mentioned the inordinate amount of time Fraser spent in the garden so the police officers made their way to the side gate, past the roses, under the apple tree. Ged was envious suddenly, thought of his concrete yard and knew that if he owned this garden he'd spend an inordinate amount of time in it too.

There was no one in the garden, no one, it appeared, in the house, although Ella insisted that the mug of tea on the kitchen table was steaming. Which gave Ged the idea that the day was cold and the coffee shop would still be open for lunch.

Ged watched the froth make a soft white moustache on Ella's animated face. He was struck by the desire to kiss it off. She jolted forward, stifling a laugh, swiped at the froth with her sleeve.

'Listen, listen, Ged: "Wednesday a.m.: Fraser took bin to kerbside. Wednesday p.m.: Fraser took bin in." Every Wednesday the same note, Ged. Christ . . . Oh, 'cept for this one: "Thursday a.m: Fraser put bin out."' She looked at Ged, puzzled.

'Recycling day. Collection's a day later,' suggested Ged.

'Hold up, hold up . . . juicy bit . . .'

'Let me guess. Jiffy bag parcel? Jehovah's Witness?'

'Nope. Much better. "Unidentified Fancy Man seen to barrack Grace Storey through front door. Door opened by F but UFM not admitted to premises. After short fracas UFM seen to leave, seen off premises by F." She's got the reg of his car, everything.'

Ged watched as she slurped more cappuccino and another soft white froth moustache graced her top lip. He lurched across the table at her, knocking over his own mocha, dipping his sleeve in hers and, at last, kissing her with one long lingering tender kiss, his coffee-soaked sleeve dripping as he raised his hand to cradle that square edge of her jawline, to twist her hair into his fingers and keep kissing. Eventually he remembered they had to breathe.

'D'you want a fancy man, Ella, or will I do?'

At Ruskin Road Alec had looked through the skylight towards Gloria's house. He couldn't see her but he knew she was watching. He had no idea how long he had, whether Ged and Ella had radioed in and were even now waiting for back-up at the junction with Elgin Avenue.

He just knew the moment he had dreaded was here. It was time to leave.

22

THE NEIGHBOURHOOD WATCHES

She had not switched on the light. She had waited for the moment
when he would meld out of the darkness and take shape. All he
had told her had been the history she had made, the murder a
mirror to her own circumstance, the mysterious gold-ringed man
in a brown leather coat her very own Davey. The sense of being
imprisoned, wasn't that how she felt, had felt since that moment,
the silvered steel of the blade, of Nan's hand around it, the gold
ring on her left hand? The sour smell of her, her breath pure
smoke, the blonded highlights in her mother's hair. No tears. No
tears.

All her guilt, her fear, her loss, all of it had funnelled into this
man. His eyes, she saw, contained her sadness. He was not a
golem fashioned from mud, he was the sum of all her grief.

And now he was gone. She sat at the kitchen table hoping that
at any moment he would light up the gas on the hob, heat up
some soup he'd prepared. Or her favourite, chicken paprikash.
She imagined him at the worktop. Pictured clearly, the angle of his

chin, the soft curve of his ear. He would be smashing garlic with the side of his knife. But however hard she willed it, he did not appear. She needed him. Why had he gone?

Later, she moved into the sanctuary of the workroom and began to search out the colours with which to keep him. A background of blue, inky and saturated because of the night. Their time. The green of his eyes that needed to be knitted in like supernovaed stars.

Later still she took the spade and began to dig. If she dug out the vegetable patch he would have to come back to plant it. She sprinkled the seeds they had bought.

'You have to come back. You have to come back now. You have to.' She said it over and over, dug it into the earth she turned. He would be summoned back. 'Comecomecomecomecome,' she called as once the rooks had called her to safety. The rain came instead, soaked her, so she took off her clothes, tearing at them, burying them, jabbing and hacking at the soil, her hands raw, the skin white and puffed with blisters. On her knees she begged the dirt, 'Come back to me.'

She was at the market before six, wired and awake, more awake than she'd ever felt. She was imagining Fraser. No. Call him Alec. Perhaps that was last night's mistake. She thought of him as Fraser still.

He was gone. The vegetable patch was not a patch, it was a rent, a gash. It lay bare. She spent the night in the workroom, knitting until her fingers were speared and sore. The blisters from her digging split open and wept into the wool. She had chosen wrongly. She needed a circular needle, no endings, no edges. She unravelled all she had done, took out the circular needle and began again. Did it seem that her stitching was stronger?

But the kitchen remained blank and empty.

The next morning Elke called Maisie from the phone box by the bakery.

'I think you should come down here, Maisie. Now, if you can.' Elke's voice was calm. She was watching Grace, seated at the back of the stall, the black blanket knitting before her, her fingers an intricacy of bone and yarn and needle points, indistinguishable.

'I'll be there at lunchtime,' Maisie hedged, busy office noises in her background.

'Now, Maisie.'

And Maisie knew why when she saw Grace.

'He didn't. No. When I told you that, he didn't. But then. He did. He just came down the stairs and... And now, I don't know why he's gone. I don't understand how I can get him back.' What Maisie saw was how the house had been transformed since she'd last visited. It was clear how much work Grace had put in over the last few months.

'Look. See? All this, all of this is Fraser ... except he wasn't Fraser. He told me. His name was—' But she halted, uncertain, afraid of breaking whatever new magic she might be weaving. She should not tell Maisie. Maisie was a weak point.

Maisie watched and listened and thought that Grace had simply reached the vanishing point of her grief. This, she decided, was the result of all that pent-up sorrow and guilt about the whole 'Nan' situation. Grace had never talked it through, never mourned. She had skimmed past it and it was plain to see she should have taken stock. This was the backlash to avoiding feelings; suddenly they just piled in on you. Maisie saw that Grace, as well as putting in long hours at the market, had clearly been putting in a lot of time at the house. Everything was repaired, fixed, painted, refurbished. Except for Grace, who was exhausted. Maisie thought she had better have a cup of tea to stave off a breakdown.

Grace calmed. She settled into the workroom chair, wrapping herself in the almost-finished night blanket. If Maisie had looked properly she would have seen the glassy blackness of that calm, would have noted the night blanket, but Maisie was high on being a best friend. It seemed obvious to her that the whole Fraser encounter as described by Hugo was a big face-saving device. Grace had told him where to go at last and he just hadn't been able to stomach it, had clung instead to Fraser's imagined existence. And this loss, this imaginary man leaving, that was a good thing too, symbolic of Grace leaving her past behind. It was all about the future now.

Grace woke to the sound of the radio and the kettle, and a vast desert of disappointment unrolled before her as the workroom door opened and with a 'Ta-dah!' Maisie entered with a breakfast tray.

'You look better. Rested and new.' Maisie was cheery, picking up a croissant from the tray. 'I found these in the freezer. They're gorgeous, where on earth did you buy them? In that little baker's on the high street?' She slathered a bloodbath of raspberry jam all over the curl of golden pastry. Grace said nothing as she watched Maisie scoff the last of Fraser's home-baked croissants.

She did not feel like driving so Maisie insisted on giving her a lift, dropping her at the market.

'I'll pick you up later. We could go for a chinese?' Maisie suggested. Grace shook her head.

'No. I can't tonight. It's the Neighbourhood Watch meeting. Thanks, though. And I'll be fine.' Grace could taste the liquorice as she fobbed off her friend. There was no meeting. She was not thankful. She would not be fine until she stepped into that kitchen and Fraser was there.

She opened the shutters, rearranged the stall, trying to think back to how it had been, to set it straight. But there were things missing, the cheap bits the thief girls had taken, the coats she had sold.

She couldn't knit there. He had not been to the stall so she would be knitting in the wrong elements. If she was going to get her golem man back she had to make him according to a ritual and a recipe. She considered the ingredients she'd worked with before: fear, guilt, shame, grief, desperation. She still had them in abundance. That afternoon she formed them into skeins in her head. On the outside she seemed to be putting her stall in order, moving on.

At the house, during the nights of emptied kitchen, she fell back far too easily into a routine of mouldy bread and hard cheese. On her way back from the stall that first night she had bought baked beans and fish fingers, the staples of her childhood. She didn't attempt to sleep in the bed, their bed. Instead she knitted furiously, fell asleep in the chair, wrapped in the blanket, letting her dreams tangle in the weft.

Jack Spring watched her leave one morning a few weeks later. He saw Gloria Hadfield's venetian blinds shudder slightly and tilt open like the last eyes of Argos waking. For once, he wanted to cross the road and ask Gloria what was going on.

They had not seen Fraser for nearly three weeks and while it wasn't unusual, after all, he didn't live in Jack Spring's pockets, there was something different about Fraser's absence. His absence felt like Gwen Mellor's absence. They hadn't seen Gwen for a few weeks and Bill had looked, well, he had looked not dissimilar to the way Grace looked now: thinner, a loss of sparkle. Hazel had mentioned it, had seen her in the supermarket yesterday with a basket and only a mean offcut of plastic cheese and a lone loaf of industrial bread. 'Didn't seem right. Fraser's always cooking. What do you think?'

'I don't know. What do you think?' But he knew what Hazel was going to say.

'I'm thinking about Bill Mellor that time and his tiny tin of beans and sausages.'

Although they were both worried they didn't want to interfere. It wasn't their business.

'I think that house is cursed,' Hazel declared over a cup of tea by the compost heap. They glanced up at the windows next door. It did seem sombre and brooding and the frill of rooks picking bugs from the gutter didn't help. Hazel had given a shudder and gone inside.

Graeme Denton stood in his back bedroom and looked out over Grace and Fraser's garden. The lawn she had dug up that night was weeding over now, frosted hard with January rime. Everyone thought that they had gone away over Christmas. Other people had come and gone. Hazel and Jack had been away for a week or so to stay with their eldest daughter in Scotland. Barbara and Jeff had taken the deerhounds down to her sister's farm in Devon. But Graeme hadn't gone anywhere, had no one and nowhere else to go to. He'd watched her from the windows and he knew she was alone.

They had seemed so happy together, he thought, and then one afternoon when he was cleaning the moss off his path he thought of Fraser and he realized he had never actually seen them together.

Ged wished he had come earlier. He'd been ignoring Gloria Hadfield's calls since New Year's Eve and now they were almost at Valentine's Day. The second she opened the door he regretted his actions.

He had made an assumption. New Year. Auld Lang Syne. Gloria just wanted a drama to fill her empty evenings, a bit of company, and he had been in no mood to oblige her. Since then she'd been a nagging toothache. Now she glared at him, ushered him quickly and officiously into a hallway stacked with mail and looking dusty. Gloria Hadfield had never looked dusty before.

'This way.' She hurried up the stairs. As he followed her he noticed she was thinner, and not in a good way. They passed a washing basket filled with dank-smelling towels and clothes. She pushed into the front bedroom.

There was no bed in here. Instead there was a camera rigged up, a spotting scope and what he finally recognized as night-vision binoculars. He looked at Gloria.

'My brother got them for me. Army surplus.' She was checking a small black and white television monitor. Rewinding a street scene on some video or other. It didn't look like a soap and yet it

was familiar. Then he realized that the screen was CCTV record-
ing the street outside. He watched as Jeff walked backwards past
the house with the deerhounds.

'You're too late, you know. You've left it way, way, way too
late.' Ged did not like the harsh tone of *'way, way, way'*. 'God
knows what she's done with him. I tell you, New Year you
might, just might –' again the tight dry sound in her voice –
'have stood a chance but no, you've given it to her. Played it her
way. Again.'

Gloria reached to her ponytail, her fingers spiderish, uncoiling
the scrunchie from it. She pulled at her hair, dragging and twisting it, snapping the scrunchie back in place. Ged watched. He
saw her hair was a long dark ponytail of grease. Gloria Hadfield
had always been the most 'done' woman he'd ever met. Nails.
Hair. Clothes. She was in the dictionary beside the word 'immac-
ulate'. He saw her nails now, the fake ones broken off unevenly,
no polish. He regretted what he had not done.

'I don't know how to go about this, Ged. But I'm telling you
she's not getting away with it this time. You have to point me the
right way. There're protocols and all that, I imagine.'

'Protocols?'

'Do I report him missing first?' Gloria was energized and then
the word popped into his head. 'Manic'.

'Report who missing?'

'Fraser. Over the road.'

Ged looked through the slats of the blind at the house opposite.
'Don't you think Grace Storey would report that?'

'Oh for Christ's sake,' Gloria spat the words. 'She's going to
report bugger all. I didn't see the murder. The murder is just my

theory . . .' She started plucking papers and videotapes from the desks standing side by side behind the door.

'Whoa, whoa, just a minute, Gloria. Slow down.' Gloria looked at him, her eyes bright and clear and determined. She licked her finger and tugged another sheet from an organized array. He was to blame. He'd let it get this far. If he'd only responded earlier. What a mess. Gloria thrust the paperwork at him. He glanced down at time-coded typed pages as she rammed a video into the player and gestured past him for the remote. 'What are you on about, Gloria? Start from the beginning.'

'I'll play you the tapes. He's gone. Vanished. He goes in. Never comes back out. I warned you. She's killed him.'

23

IT COMES OUT IN THE WASH

'You smell.' It was something only her best friend could tell her and clearly it pained Maisie to be her best friend at this moment. Grace was cobbling together some tea in the back storeroom. Her stock, she noted, was running quite low but all her time at home now was spent knitting the night into her blanket.

'I've been busy. I did run a wash on Wednesday . . .' She'd taken off the clothes she was now wearing, had been wearing since Fraser had vanished, she'd put them into the washer, waited naked at the kitchen table for them to be washed and dried so she could, according to her ritual, put them back on. But she was thinking that the Wednesday wash had been last week, not this week, or maybe even the week before that.

However long she sat in the kitchen, naked, clothed, hungry, fed, he did not come back.

'I think you've got a point Maisie,' Grace said, suddenly aware of the sour savoury smell of herself.

'Why don't you just shut up shop?' Maisie glanced around at

the few scraps that remained on the shelves and hangers. 'I'll run you home, you can have a wash and brush up, change your clothes –' Maisie was certain Grace had been wearing the same jumper, T-shirt and jeans every time she'd seen her since the New Year – 'and you can come out to the pizzeria with me and Lisa, Chloe and Netta from pottery.' Grace was shaking her head. Maisie did not back down. 'Grace, I will bind and gag you if I have to but you are coming to the pizzeria.' No need to tell Grace that Lisa was a community psychiatric nurse. They would just talk, Lisa might be able to help. It wasn't as if she was going to have her straitjacketed and carted off to the Roundhouse Mental Health Unit.

At Ruskin Road Maisie found the fridge not just empty but smelling of emptiness. There wasn't even milk for tea, just a whitish substance in a plastic bottle that had transformed into yoghurt and now had ambitions to be cheese. Maisie could hear the shower upstairs and was filled with a sudden panic that Grace was up there trying to slash her wrists, lying, incarnadine, in the shower cubicle.

Maisie tapped at the bathroom door. 'Grace?' There was no reply. Maisie tried the door; it opened but as she pushed it there was movement at the edge of her vision. She turned, startled. It was Grace standing at the bottom of the attic steps, the door open behind her.

'He isn't there. I thought . . . I just . . .' She moved across the landing, looked at Maisie. 'I need to change.' And peeling off her jumper she handed it to Maisie. 'I've been wearing this since he left. It isn't right. I need to wear something else.' Grace pulled down the jeans and handed them to Maisie. 'Just dump them by the washer, Maze. I'll sort it out later. I need to do something.'

Beside the washer Maisie considered. This shedding of clothes was a step forward too, a positive against all Grace's recent negatives. Maisie sniffed at the sweater, the dampish smell it gave off. She opened the washer. It was musty inside, gave off a fungal mouldy smell from having had the door closed too long. Maisie saw the washing basket was already full and thought she might as well make up the load. She pulled out another damp-smelling sweater, a shirt and some bedding, tucked them into the drum, and lastly a bath towel. She filled the powder compartment and clicked the washer on. A slooshing and humming began that soothed Maisie, felt homely and busy.

The remaining washing gave off an odd rank smell. Maisie looked through the items; they had obviously been in the basket since before Fraser left. As she sorted whites from colours ready for a second load, she saw the tea towels. They were deep brown now but it was a rusted thick organic brown like the smell they gave off.

The machine clicked through its cycle, its noise increasing, sounding tense and panicked as if it, like Maisie, couldn't decide exactly what stained the tea towels.

It was gravy. It was coffee. It was not blood.

She turned to make the tea and as she stirred the pot she glanced into the garden, saw at once the dug-over patch, and now what was that poking up among the clods and weeds? It was dead leaves. It was the brown twigs of a dead perennial. It was not a sleeve.

Grace entered, towelling her hair. She had changed her clothes.

'You need a trip to the supermarket,' Maisie commented. 'Want me to come along? We could go in my car.'

Grace shook her head. 'No. Thanks. I'll go later.' And in her head Grace knew that today she would because it was a Fraser place. She could roll into the car park and he'd be there, waiting at the door, with the trolley and a list.

But the doorbell rang.

'It's just a courtesy call, Miss Storey, to let you know that your neighbour across the way there – Mrs Hadfield – has some concerns about you and your fiancé. Fraser? Is that right?' Ged thought he would probably end up in trouble over all this and he wasn't sure how he was going to voice his concerns. He was relying on something polite and simple popping into his head.

Grace, watching him, could taste liquorice. The old lie was damaged because it had moved beyond her. She needed to finish that and begin again. Here, it seemed, she was being given that opportunity.

'Yes. That's right. Fraser.'

But the friend standing by the sink, chipped in with, 'What are Mrs Hadfield's concerns?'

'You are?' Ged flipped open the safety line of his notebook. When in doubt, look official.

'Maisie Partington.'

He wrote the name and as he did so he took in the state of the kitchen, the smelly washing on the floor. He thought of the notebooks full of Gloria Hadfield's obsessive-compulsive observations, the set-to with the rival lover at the doorstep. 'Okay. Right.' Ella seemed to be deserting him, she had moved to the French doors, looking out. 'Mrs Hadfield, erm, let's say she takes her Neighbourhood Watch duties very seriously. Okay? Now, last year we had some missing dogs and Mrs Hadfield . . .' He really shouldn't be saying this, even to give Grace Storey the background. He'd have to sidestep, backtrack . . . Oh, bollocks to it. 'Well, forget that. Let's just establish that she takes it very seriously and she has some concerns regarding the whereabouts of your fiancé. In order to keep some sort of peace and stop all this getting out of hand, I'd like to ask you and Fraser a few questions. It's a courtesy call really, just to reassure you . . . and Mrs Hadfield.'

He looked at Grace Storey's face and saw an emptied landscape; he was reminded of a beach he'd been to in Norfolk last Easter. Grace nodded assent. Beside him Ella seemed to tense but he could not look away from Grace's face. 'Is your fiancé around at all?' Ged asked, keeping his voice soft and calm, ready to be shot down because this was none of his business.

'No.'

'Is he away . . . or . . .'

'He's at the supermarket.' Ged was struck by the tiny gasp the friend gave, the way her eyes swivelled out to the garden and back, the way all the colour drained from her skin.

Grace, with her true lie eye, saw Fraser very clearly, growing a bit impatient – no, not Fraser, it was not in him. Worried. He'd be worried by now: where was she? 'In fact –' Grace reached for her bag, her keys – 'I'm late already. I'm supposed to pick him up.'

Ged looked away from her and the fact of her tiny bird hands clutching the keys, towards the expression on the friend's face. Mavis or Maisie was wild-eyed and beside him Ella was opening the French doors, despite the fact that it was beginning to rain, and now he saw the friend step back and kick at the pile of washing and he saw the tea towels, thick and brown, and as he did so

Grace Storey collided with him in her total desperation to leave the room.

'If I could just delay you for one more moment.'

He could see Ella through the kitchen window, saw her squatting on haunches to examine a patch of dug-over lawn, and the friend, too, looking out at the lawn and at Ella, becoming more wild-eyed, taking in a hyperventilated breath.

'Just a couple of questions, Miss Storey. Clear this all up.'

Grace jumped up and over the table, like a bird in flight. Ged lunged and fell and did not stop her but Ella had come through the side gate and was already at the front door, scrapping with Grace, the cuffs glinting silver in the afternoon daylight. Ged looked at the friend then asked, 'Is he at the supermarket?' and as she shook her head it felt as if someone had just filled his stomach with stones.

Purplegreen. Blueblack. Grace had not been swift enough and now she sat in the windowless room and waited for the police officer to offer her sweets. They had left her for a moment now, one woman officer standing sentinel by the door, and Grace had time to look out of herself. She thought it might be the same room she had sat in all those years ago. She saw Mum, that last moment, a red gargled 'Grace' on her lips, and then it wasn't Mum any more. It was Fraser and she would never see him again.

They had spoken with Maisie, she knew, although what would Maisie tell them except the truth? But what was the truth? She'd made up a man who came to life and they had all lived like dolls within her lie. Only she'd damaged it, broken it, hadn't she? If they had let her go to the supermarket alone, he would have been there. She wished the door would open and Fraser would stand there holding out his hand for her to take and they would just walk away, not even back to Ruskin Road, just away. Elsewhere. But the door did not open and she had no wishes, only lies.

'Naked?' Detective Sergeant Wilson wanted to make certain he'd heard correctly. Graeme Denton nodded.

'I'd got heartburn. Spag bol does it every time; don't know why I bother but there you go. I was getting up to find the Rennies and I happened to look out because I heard a noise. Her digging probably. You know what the back's like, it's burglar heaven the way the bridleway snicks along.'

Detective Sergeant Wilson nodded. He knew the houses well, played golf with Graeme.

'Grace was in the garden. In some distress. I thought she was in pale clothes at first but she was, you know, without her cloak, so to speak.'

'Okay, okay, what then?'

'She was sobbing in the dirt. After a while she went into the house.' Graeme looked perturbed. 'I should have done something. Gone round or something. They're a good couple. He's a top bloke, that Fraser, done wonders on that house.'

'Never heard them fighting. Not a raised voice ever,' Jack confirmed. He was angry as he sat there, angry at the way a police station and a loaded question could make him feel guilty. Plus, he didn't like this Wilson chap. He'd bumped into him a few times at the golf club when he'd tagged along with Graeme. You only had to see how he spoke to this female detective constable to see he was a chauvinist. Jack felt more guilty still when he thought about Gloria Hadfield and how furious he was at this new mess she'd caused. In fact, now it came to him: 'You know that Gloria Hadfield is a troublemaker, I hope? Remember that dognapping nonsense last summer when she had the knives out for Graeme after Max died?'

Detective Sergeant Wilson flicked inefficiently through his thought files.

'Ged mentioned it in his report, sir.' The female detective leaned forward with a relevant page.

'Oh. Yes. Rings a bell,' the sergeant lied and Jack bristled.

'It's none of her business. It's a shame, that's all.'

'What's a shame?' Wilson pounced.

'Them breaking up. That's all this is. And he's the travelling type. He was in the Arctic until a couple of months ago.' Jack wasn't certain but he felt some frisson of knowledge pass between the detectives.

'I wonder, Mr Spring . . .' The woman smiled at him with intelligence and concern; Wilson should watch this one, she was going to get answers by being human, Jack was attentive. 'Mr Spring, have you ever seen Fraser and Grace together?'

'What sort of ruddy half-arsed question was that?' Detective Sergeant Wilson was crabby with Detective Constable Prior. He had only drunk three pints of coffee today but it seemed to him that the 'fancy man' gave them a motive. The tea towels were a solid bit of evidence already in DNA analysis. The Arctic job had proved a fake. Plus, Grace Storey had been here before, only now there was no grandma sobbing in the background to save her. It was all very clear. Textbook possibly. A serial killer? Not on his watch.

'It was just a thought. Only Gloria Hadfield seems to have seen them together. They didn't go out much. I don't know. I was trying to connect into Gloria's observation that he was sleeping in the attic. Get another angle on their relationship. It was just a detail really.'

'I was her boss. We had the usual joking-around situations.' Hugo occupied a lot of space at the other side of the table.

'You were harassing Grace Storey at work,' Detective Constable Prior put in. Wilson let her run with this one, after all this was a woman's angle; she had already unsettled the bastard, who knew what might turn up? Perhaps if they stripped this bloke's car they might find Fraser the Fiancé where the spare wheel should be.

'We had a working relationship. Nothing serious. As I've said, I discussed it at the house with Fraser and—'

'You had gone to the house to harass her further, after you'd harassed her at the market?' Prior pushed slightly.

Hugo raised his eyebrows to the ceiling and gave a weary huff. 'You know, harass is a very strong word.'

'All right, Mr Barton. Our witness says you were "barracking" Grace Storey through her letter box.'

'She wouldn't open the door. You can't have a civilized conversation through a letter box. And just for the record, you know *he* set upon *me*. Also Grace Storey has punched me. In many ways I'm the injured party.' Hugo looked at Caitlin Prior with what he imagined were golden Labrador eyes. She stared back at him like a pointer. 'Anyway. He and I . . . I agreed to leave. Simple as that. I haven't been back. Don't want to go back. Grace is a prickt— troublemaker. And that's the politest word I can think of. D'you think I can go now?'

*

Caitlin Prior was stunned when Hugo Barton, with a casual smile, approached her outside in the corridor and said, 'I couldn't have your home phone number, could I? Just in case I need to contact you in an emergency?' He winked.

Caitlin knew she was standing there open-mouthed, and a few seconds blinked by before finally she was able to work her jaw.

'Mr Barton, there is no emergency for which you will require my services,' she said, politely.

Hugo grinned, the tip of his tongue tasting his lower lip as his eyes swivelled down to assess her cup size. 'I'm sure I can think of something.'

'She wouldn't piss on you if you were on fire.' Detective Sergeant Wilson barged from behind, shuffling Hugo along the corridor.

Later in the canteen, quaffing more coffee, Wilson expounded his opinion that Grace Storey had killed the wrong man although he realized that Hugo Barton buried under the vegetable patch might taint your cabbages. But it worried Caitlin that he had decided Grace Storey had killed someone. Caitlin Prior was not so sure.

Prior and Wilson interviewed Grace again, in the presence of her Yellow Pages solicitor, who was, to Grace, another threatening stranger. This time Wilson and Prior showed her the clothes that had been dug from the garden.

'Mine. I took them off. I wanted to bring him back.'

'From the dead.' Wilson didn't even couch it as a question. Grace did not want to think of that possibility. Her solicitor gave Wilson an expression of disapproval that Wilson ignored.

'Bring him back from where, Miss Storey?' Caitlin Prior asked more gently but Grace's mind wouldn't show her a picture, only his face, his eyes, that night. When he had told her the worst part. And, as she remembered, Caitlin Prior and Wilson took out two evidence bags containing tea towels. Dirty. Brown. And they told her the worst part.

The world was heated metal around her, the dark walls, the light above, the whirring tape in the interview-room deck, the harsh table, the stiff chairs, which she saw with sudden horror had legs splayed just enough to trip you. What she saw in her mind was the dark red lake and the silver dart of a steel fish and she spoke and it wasn't lies or truth, it was everything. And at last, inside her, the deep cool tarn of tears began to break its banks. She felt grey inside, she couldn't stop. She sobbed on and on, her words drowning and hiccuping as her face grew hot and her skin was parched with the salt of herself.

'She's a basket case. I want our shrink, Smedley-Wyatt, down here sharpish so we can have her assessed and charge her. And chase up that woman who dealt with her in '75.'

'Rachel Windrush?' Caitlin prompted. Wilson nodded, striding forward checking his watch. 'But, guv, we don't have a body. They've taken up all the lawn and Fraser isn't under it.'

Wilson thought that DC Prior had a lot to learn and he did not want to spend his time teaching her. He was too old and too cantankerous to be arsed with her and her 'details'. She never listened to him either, that was the real stick in his craw.

'Details, Prior. Do as you're told. Read the records.'

Caitlin took a deep breath and tried not to speak but her mouth would not obey her. 'But there isn't a body.'

Wilson looked utterly infuriated and faced her off, arms

akimbo. 'She did her mother when she was nine and now she's done this bloke too. Only now she doesn't have her nan here to cover the tracks.'

Once again Caitlin's mouth ran away without her. 'The inquest returned a verdict of accidental death on her mother.'

Wilson took in a deep breath ready to shout at her and then couldn't be bothered. 'Instincts, Prior. You've got to have instincts. It isn't always what it seems.'

'I agree. With everything. But there isn't a body.'

'One word for you, Prior, and then no more.'

Caitlin waited, wondering what the word would be and how many letters it might contain. Her guess was four.

'One word for you: Yet.'

He let the word jab into her face and she saw his eyes widen slightly that she didn't flinch. There was a moment of impasse between them, then he took a deep breath.

'Strip the house, strip the car, and for Christ's sake check the freezer – she could have ragu-ed him into a selection of Tupperware boxes by now and wiped her bloody hands on the tea towels . . .'

Caitlin Prior did as she was told. She bit her tongue and could not tell him why it was all wrong.

A few hours later Caitlin Prior lied that Dr Smedley-Wyatt was at a psychiatry conference in Bournemouth and couldn't be reached for twenty-four hours and she lied even more about not being able to find a current contact number for Dr Rachel Windrush. Now she was aware, as she pushed open her own front door, that it was late. But it wouldn't matter, she knew. She had the number and there was only one phone call she needed to make.

24

IF

Alec hoisted himself up, tearing and ripping himself through the hedge at Ruskin Road. It was as if it tried to stop him. He fought it and crashed through at last to drop into the disused bridleway. He could just make out, through the thick hedge of brambles and ivy, the old boundary wall of the derelict towelling factory behind. It was like Sleeping Beauty's castle, a tangle and torment of vines and tendrils that seemed to bar his way. Going to the right would bring him out at the end of the little alleyway beside the video rental store, so he turned left.

He followed the bridleway until it gave way to towpath and then he followed the towpath to what he hoped was north. He had learned last time that he could not live rough in the urban areas, could not settle in a pee-stinking doorway. The built-up noises bothered him. He felt a different, more dangerous form of invisibility as he moved through shoppers and officer workers as if he could be disregarded only because they chose not to see him. Once he was in the woodland or beside a waterway he felt he was in control.

His diet of muddy fish was meagre due to the season and the weather. He needed to look elsewhere to find food. He spent one day snaring rabbits on a brambled canal embankment, roasting the meat once darkness fell and he thought it was late enough for everyone else to be asleep.

Roadkill. He had walked far enough to be hungry enough. He'd never owned a car and a life sentence had curbed the usual jaunts in the countryside. One afternoon he crossed a B road to pick up the public footpath that would take him across country. As he reached the opposite side he was aware of a small body, grey, furry, where the hedgerow met the tarmacked road surface. The first word that came into his head was 'fresh'. He examined it, the head newly crushed.

He ate the squirrel. It tasted like lamb as he squatted on his haunches by the fire. A steady cold drizzle had begun to fizzle into the fire and he would have to find shelter. He would have liked to use a phone, to call Grace and ask her to come and find him, trundle towards him on the little B roads in her runabout car. But he had no phone. No money. No number. In the weeks he had stayed there it had never occurred to him to find out the number. He saw himself in a call box asking directory enquiries, messengers to take him to Grace. She would be sitting in the back room, her workroom, in the leather chair, knitting him a huge and baggy jumper to keep him warm upon his travels.

He found the hollow of a tree to curl into, pulled dry leaves into a semblance of covering and crouched there, still, as darkness fell.

And with darkness, came Grace. Every night, no matter how fitful his sleep, she would come to him. 'Come to bed.' And she would spread the blanket of dried leaves wide to welcome him.

The leaves fluttered and frittered and she was not Grace, she was the winter wind blowing cold on his back.

He needed a hostel. Felt he could stand that for a few weeks until March and the better weather. That's all it would take. Breathing space.

He had been in town for a week and despite the cold weather he felt four-walled, wanted to move on. He took time in the stark bathroom to clean and trim his beard, to scrub and clip his nails. He was making ready. He had noticed in the week he'd been walking around town that bags were left outside the charity shops in the main street.

'What's the use of the sign?' the woman at the Heart Foundation grumbled as she picked over the remains of a torn dumped bag. 'What do cats want with jigsaws, eh?' Her colleague smiled benignly. But each evening the townsfolk came in their cars and unloaded their junk.

Teenagers were hanging around the slatted benches built into a chunky brick-raised flower bed. Alec dared not approach the charity shop bags yet. He did not want to draw attention. He had calculated how many beers the group had brought along, and now as they crushed cans and chucked them at each other he thought they might be thirsty and restless. There were no fresh cans being shaken and opened; they might think about how much beer they'd wasted on each other, soaking into the seams of their jackets. Alec felt the cold seeping through him. If he died in this doorway the street cleaners could come past in the morning, spear him on their end of their pick-up stick and hurl him into the shopfitters' skip outside the optician's. By the time he'd laughed sourly to himself at this tidy scenario the teenagers were drifting towards the park. A noisy car zoomed towards the group, music as deep as a heart-beat banging against the shiny metallicized windows. Doors opened. Boys scarpered. Girls climbed in as music barged out. Then silence. They were gone.

He crossed quickly to the charity shop. Toys. Clothes – women's. Curtains and old bedding. More clothes. Here – men's clothes. He pulled out a sheepskin jacket, unable to believe his luck. The suede outer was greased with age around the button-holes but the lining, thick, soft, seemed to give off warmth even before he'd pulled it on. Trousers. Trousers. And more trousers. They all seemed to be tartan golf slacks. Beggars could not be choosers so he pulled on the darkest pair. A ginger-orange win-dowpane check on a chocolate-brown ground. They were just slightly too long, which was much better than slightly too short. Shoes. The shoes had been zipped into a giant crackling plastic bag in red, white and blue. Three pairs were high-heeled and strappy although he considered that the shiny brown pair would match the ginger and brown golfing slacks. He laughed, imagin-ing himself teetering along the canal path. Then his breath choked as he imagined Grace, naked in the leather workroom chair, her legs dangling, these strappy somethings buckled to her dainty feet.

Here. Yes. Boots. Good quality and hardly worn. Two sizes too big but there would be socks somewhere or newspaper. Solid. Leather. Yes. These would take him north and then some. He should head over to the recycling banks by the supermarket and see if he could salvage some newspaper.

At the paper bank there was a vast overspill. Papers lay about bagged into overstretched carriers. Alec decided he would take a bag with him. The newspaper would be a good insulation and he could leave town tonight. If he chose he could make a newspaper nest in the country park in that vast stone Temple of Apollo built on the hill. The Temple of Apollo, what five-star luxury that was! He wanted to be on his way. He felt itched at. He sat on some of the other bags, took off his worn-out boots and peeled off some newspaper from a nearby stack. He folded out a few pages and placed his foot ready, like a fish to wrap. As he stooped over in the darkness he saw it. The words illuminated by the cool white supermarket security lighting.

Woman held in missing fiancé mystery

*

The taxi driver regarded Alec's face with suspicion. One of the drivers behind, there were four at the rank, flashed his lights in warning, the first driver catching them in the rear-view mirror.

'It's hell of a way, mate, that's going to cost you.'

Alec had no money, nothing but a few coins and the clothes he stood up in. 'It's a long story,' he said to the driver, aware that it was an immense tale and might yet have a bad ending. Then Grace seemed to stand beside him, her thin fingers curling them-selves into his. 'I've been away. To the Arctic and the airline have buggered up my baggage and the flights and I can't—'

But the second cab driver was getting out of his vehicle in a rush, leaving the door standing open as he approached his col-league and Alec. His arm was waving, aggressive. 'Hoi. You.

That's my bloody coat. How the fuck did you get that?' Alec did not know what to say. Everything failed him. He could be naked in the street in the next five minutes. If he could just explain. But he was tired of explaining to people who didn't listen. 'What sort of sorry fuck nicks from the charity shop!' The cab driver's voice had risen in a steady crescendo of outrage. 'And my fucking slacks!'

Alec heard him even as he strode away, rounded the corner, began heading off down the street. He was thinking of that fairy tale his mum had told him, wishing that a pair of seven league boots had been at the bottom of the charity bag and in three strides he could be with Grace. He didn't even look where he was going, just felt the concrete resonance of pavement under him, the places at ankle and little toe where the nearly new boots would rub him.

As he tried to cross the road another cab kerb-crawled beside him. The driver was an Asian man of about thirty.

'Where you off to, did you say?' There was no anger or threat in his tone.

Alec told him, but kept striding because only striding was going to get him there in time to break Grace free.

The cab pulled around the corner ahead of him, the driver leaning over, the door clicking open.

'You'll take me?' The man nodded. 'But I don't have any money.'

The driver shrugged, gave a wry smile. 'No. But you don't look like you're going to puke all over my seats and I'm bored out of my tree sitting here every night of the week. So. Do you want the ride?'

Alec had it all ready in his head, how he had been to the Arctic and how he was a mining engineer, and his imaginary luggage and fantasy flights. It was neat and tidy and just how Grace might have told it.

But as they drove up the motorway the driver was relaxed, one finger guiding the wheel, and Alec found himself talking only of Grace and getting back to her.

Going home.

25

DETECTIVE INSPECTOR
FRY IN A MACHINE

'No idea,' Carla said as Derek Fry approached the phone. 'Someone called Caitlin Prior. Ring any bells?' Derek took the phone from his wife, the former WPC Smethurst. She moved towards the kitchen to make a start on tomorrow's trademark breakfast bread for their B & B guests. It was their nightly ritual, the dough given a slow overnight rise and then baked in flower-pots at six the next morning.

'Hello. Derek Fry speaking.'

'Oh hello, Detective Inspector.' The young woman's voice startled him. No one had called him Detective Inspector in fifteen years. These days he was Derek from Beckmere B & B. 'My name is Caitlin Prior. You worked with my dad, Bernard Prior.' Fry's heart went cold, he hoped he wasn't going to be told Bernard was dead – they'd just been invited to his wedding. 'I was talking over a case I'm involved with, with Dad.' No. Bernard wasn't dead, so now his heart raced in anticipation instead of dread. 'And he gave me your number. I hope you don't mind. I really need your advice.'

'Go ahead. I'm listening.'

Something to do with running a Lake District B & B? How to fry the perfect egg? Something about wedding presents for her dad?

'I'm a detective constable here. The case involves a missing man and his fiancée. It looks as if she's killed him. She even tried to do a runner when the community police officer approached her . . .'

Derek Fry was waiting for the 'but'. There was a silence on the other end of the phone. He tried to prompt. 'He's missing. Have you found a body?'

'No.' Caitlin paused again. Fry could almost hear the cogs turning in her brain, was itching now, his instinct rousing from a long slumber. 'Not yet.'

'So how can I help?' There was more hesitation. A pause for thought. Derek Fry held his breath.

'There's no scent of almonds.' As she said it he heard her exhale all her pent-up frustrations.

Fry's heart and mind seemed to operate in a vacuum of space. He took a calming breath. Bernard's girl had the Scent. He spoke.

'Where else can you look? Is there anyone else involved? Other leads? Anywhere the fiancé might have run off to?'

'No. I've interviewed everyone. There doesn't seem to be any other option. But no one's come up smelling of almonds. Not one whiff anywhere from anyone.'

'What's your guv say about this?'

There was another pause. 'Well, I didn't mention the almonds . . .'

'No. Obviously. But his general feeling about it?'

'He's convinced she's guilty. I can't try to persuade him because I've nothing concrete to bring to the table. Plus, there's a complication.'

Caitlin paused again. Fry thought he heard a tiny gasp of frustration.

'Go on.'

'There was an accident. When she was nine. She stabbed her mother.'

Fry was silent for a very long time.

'Hello? You still there Detective Inspector?'

'Yes.' Fry was waiting. Obviously there were still a few seconds to go before the planets aligned.

'Detective Inspector, the oddest thing happens . . .'

Tick.Tock.Tick.Tock.Tick. Jupiter slid a degree north. 'She smells of liquorice.'

The helicopter landed in a playing field. Caitlin Prior was by the goalposts, her car parked at the edge of the field by the ramshackle pavilion. She had not expected DI Fry to arrive like this, she'd checked out a train timetable and suggested a motorway route, but he'd said he'd call back with arrangements. It was his wife Carla who called back half an hour later, by which time DI Fry was already airborne, and gave Caitlin an ETA and the rendezvous.

They got into her car, the helicopter peeling off into the air again.

'You must have one hell of a pension,' Caitlin joked.

'Friend of mine. Owns half of California but he lives in Troutbeck.'

'And he happened to be popping out for some milk?' She grinned as she started the car.

'Yes. He's got a farm in Cullompton.'

'Do you want to drop your—' Caitlin noticed he did not have any baggage with him. She looked up into his face.

'No bags. Take me to her. Let's see her before your guv comes back on shift.'

He saw that Grace remembered him. He was shocked to see how dark the circles beneath her eyes were, how thin and fragile she looked.

'Hello, Grace.'

As he took up his seat he saw Beverley's face that day in her kitchen: 'you can live with the lie', and his rejoinder, 'But can they?'

He wanted to test his liquorice theory and had explained to Caitlin how they would do it.

'I'm here to ask you some questions about when your mum died, Grace, all right?' He felt uneasy as the dark eyes seemed to deepen as if he was at one end of a train tunnel and Grace was disappearing into the dangerous train-filled blankness. 'Could you tell us about your mum? You'd been on holiday, hadn't you? To the Lakes?'

'Why? What's that got to do with this?' Grace couldn't tell a true lie, she knew it was everything to do with Nan and Mum and that day in the old kitchen. This was all the consequence of her lie. She was caught out at last. 'But . . . I didn't stab him. He's just gone. It isn't the same . . .'

Caitlin's pencil hovered over her notebook, she did not look at Fry.

'You were nine, if I remember. That right?'

Grace felt nine now, felt as if she'd never got out of this room in all the past years. 'It was an accident,' she began. Her mouth watered, a sudden liquorice rush for the old, old lie. Caitlin Prior made a tally mark in her notebook and did not look at Fry. 'The knife. From the drawer. I had the knife. I picked up the knife. Made me think of a fish.' More liquorice, another mark and another and another on the notebook's lined page. Grace saw the marks. Like Mr Pownall ticking sums. No. Like birds. Perched on a telephone wire.

And the rooks came, as surely as guardians. Sitting on the wires of the page as she spoke.

'I heard your nan died a few months ago.' Fry kept his voice even and gentle.

'Nine months.' Grace was surprised she had kept count. And then was not surprised. Detective Inspector Fry saw the darkness deepen, was almost afraid he had come too far. Then he knew that they had not yet gone far enough.

'Grace, you know, you can tell me now.'

Grace looked at him, unblinking. She seemed to have stopped breathing, then, with a gasp, she began.

Ella had seen the blanket strewn across the leather chair. Now they were going through the house with a fine-tooth comb she made a point of being the person who searched the workroom. The thick dark of the wool drew her and as she opened up drawers and didn't find any evidence she thought she could smell the night, as if someone had opened a bedroom window at 3 a.m. and let the cold dark inside. Only this cold dark was enchanted. The moment her hand touched the night blanket, the room seemed to expand outwards for her, the sky a cathedral dome above her.

Ella did something she had never done. She folded the blanket, a hard task since every time she made contact with it it took her breath away in a chilled midnight cloud. She folded it and put it into the back of the panda car.

Later, she called Ged. Later still, they vanished into the night blanket.

'Who the FUCK, are you? And what the FUCK are you playing at, Prior, getting your GRANDAD in on my case?'

Fry objected to the 'GRANDAD' comment. He remembered Wilson as a rookie, working in traffic, the only officer he had ever encountered who was capable of absorbing all the carnage of an RTA and then shitting it back out with yesterday's curry. He was a marvel. They all said it. They all wanted him with them, their very own human shield.

'I couldn't contact Rachel Windrush –' Caitlin Prior lied and Fry noted that she too had missed out the correct 'Doctor'. '– so I contacted DI Fry, as was, because it was his case. We've been going over the details, guv.'

'More details? What about joining up some dots?'

'We're getting there.'

'Right, well while you get there I'm getting some coffee to gee up before we formally charge her. You've got fifteen minutes. Tops.'

And he headed off as if it was all done and dusted.

*

'True lies?' Fry could see how she'd formulated the theory and that she believed she had conjured this Fraser bloke from thin air. She had said it herself, she was desperate. She believed he was real but only because he was made from her. She talked rationally, although he didn't doubt Rachel Windrush would tick other boxes on that one. Fry pondered it all, felt there was some detail he had missed.

'I can't bring him back.'

Fry was touched by the grief in her. The same grief he had seen fifteen years ago when she had sat in this exact room sipping Carla's tea. Had she lived a life or a sentence in between?

'Maybe it's all finished now,' she whispered.

'He was real to your neighbours, Grace.' Fry watched her. She nodded, thoughtful. ' We just have to keep looking.'

'No one can look for Alec if he isn't there to be found.' Her voice tiny, her skin paling, made it seem as if some higher authority were rubbing her out.

'She called him Alec,' Caitlin said just as Fry opened his own mouth to speak. They looked at each other.

'How do we keep your guv busy, then?' asked Fry. Caitlin had packed a herbal laxative for this very emergency. DI Fry considered that this wise and intelligent young woman should go far.

Caitlin called Graeme Denton back in to help with their enquiries. She reasoned, from all she had put together, that Graeme Denton had spent the most time with the missing man. In a side room they put together a photofit.

The word 'shit' did not figure largely in Caitlin Prior's vocabulary. She had never been much of a curser. Her partner, Jakey, liked her to say 'fuck' so he could laugh at how like a naughty schoolgirl she was. But *'SHIT!!!'* was the word, capitalized and accompanied by exclamation marks, that rammed against her head when Alec Holm finally revealed himself from the dimmest and darkest corner of her computer search. He looked a model prisoner if you overlooked the initial murder. A model prisoner until he'd absconded. *Shit.* Followed by a siren. *Shit.* A red-alert light blinking on behind her eyes. *Shit. Shit. Shit.*

Outside, the taxi idled. Alec sat for a moment, watched an officer walk down the short flight of steps at the front of the building and cross the neat vehicle-crammed car park. Tall security gates sealed the side entrance of the building. All the information posters looked accusing.

The driver, Anil, would take no payment. Alec promised, if he would just wait, if he could just go inside, but Anil handed a card to Alec. 'I wanted the drive. Here. Recommend me.'

Fry looked over the information on Alec Holm and thought God was a prankster.

'Who knows what's gone on?' Caitlin assessed the options. 'He could have been hiding there with her under duress. Maybe this is like that Patty Hearst thing, where you fall for your captor. There's a name for it, isn't there? Stockholm Syndrome? Or she might have kidnapped him. Found him on a bench in the park. He's living rough, she latches on. God knows.'

But Fry was pondering. This man had no other record of violence, did not appear to have treated Grace with violence unless you could count the way Cupid had shot her full of arrows. Yes, he was a convicted murderer, but his prison record was a guide to hard work and rehabilitation. And what had he done since absconding? Had he robbed and attacked anyone? No. He'd refurbished a house. Made a home and friends.

'I don't know, Caitlin. I just don't know.'

They were moving back along the corridor to speak to Grace. Wilson had barked at them that he was going to charge Grace Storey with murder as soon as his bowels had settled. He sent one of the women officers off on a mission to the chemist.

'I just have a couple of loose ends first, guv,' Caitlin pleaded.

Wilson growled, 'I suppose you think that's funny.'

Now as they turned into the corridor Fry felt something scratch at his instincts, a warning, a call. He turned. Dawn from the front desk was puffing up the stairs accompanied by the crackly sweep of her tights rubbing together at the top of her rounded thighs.

'Caitlin . . . man downstairs . . . says he's come about Grace Storey. Says his name is Fraser.'

'Your name isn't Fraser.' Caitlin laid it out plain.

Alec shook his head. 'No. It's Alec Holm.'

Caitlin's pencil hovered over the lines of her notebook. She took in a deep sniffing breath.

'Let Grace go now,' was all Alec said.

Neither Fry nor Prior moved for a moment, then Caitlin Prior looked at Fry and said, 'New wood?'

Fry nodded agreement.

Then, when they asked him, Alec, at last, gave them his list.

Fry took the look on Grace Storey's face as the gold clock of his retirement. Later, back home in Coniston, he would hold Carla just the way that Alec Holm held Grace Storey, until Carla wriggled free to breathe and stare at him and, laughing like a drain, kiss his face.

Grace and Alec did not let go of one another. Caitlin took them out to the desk just as Inspector Wilson, his face looking quite as pinched as his bottom, vacated the staff toilet.

'Hold up . . .' He was still tucking in his shirt. 'What's going on here?'

Fry saw their hands fuse, you could not have prised them apart.

'Who the hell . . .?' Wilson began to bluster.

Fry saw Alec Holm tense with fifteen years of injustice.

Caitlin Prior spoke up. 'This is Fraser, sir.'

And Alec Holm held out his free hand.

26

CONISTON WATER
AUGUST 1991

The boat idled on the glassy black water. Alec had watched the skies all morning, saw them bulge and swell with the bluegrey purple of rain. He thought he could never tire of looking at that sky, the way it loomed over the fells, always full of meteorological surprises. As the passengers boarded Alec took deep breaths, scenting the rain. There would be plenty of it.

He turned to see how many takers they'd got for the two-thirty jaunt. Grace was taking fares, her hair pinned up haphazardly, her slim figure hidden under the big burnt-orange cagoule she favoured, her small birdish hands dipping in and out of her leather money belt. As Alec turned, a group of four boys came hurtling down the jetty and bounced into the boat. They lurched from side to side, Grace restraining one who was leaning too far over towards the water. They had grown but Alec knew them at once and he did not dare look back at the jetty.

'MU-UU-UUM, HURRY UUU-UU-UUUP!' It was the bright-haired blond lad, Jerome, second eldest and buzzing with energy.

His older brother, Joseph, bumped him into the seating. The two set upon the third brother, Job, pummelling him into the seat beside them while the youngest, Jonah, still leaned slightly too far over the side. Joseph grabbed at his brother's waterproofs. 'Watch it.'

Ruth Standforth, a blond infant a year or more old slung onto her hip, took three confident steps down onto the deck. The Reverend Standforth was not with them. Alec looked away. Started the engine. Began the trip. Became invisible again.

An hour or so later and Grace tied them up back at Water Head Pier, and the passengers began filing off. The hairs on the back of Alec's neck were prickling and he was unsure whether it was fear. He heard Jerome, eager to get off, 'But Muu-uu-uum,' and Ruth's quiet tones: 'In a minute, pud. Let everyone else get off first.'

'Hello,' she said to Alec. 'It is you, isn't it?' Her eyes glanced over his beard and then anxiously at Grace as if she might have overstepped a mark.

But Alec nodded, looked into her face. No dark circles now. She had put on enough weight.

Ruth looked tearful, her smile deepening as she hitched the child higher onto her hip. 'Well, here you are, this is him.'

Alec looked at the child nestling his head into his mother's shoulder.

'He made it. By the skin of his teeth.' Ruth nuzzled at the little face. 'We both did.' Then she reached to Alec, kissed his cheek. She turned to Grace then. 'Did he ever tell you he saved our lives?'

Grace looked from Ruth to Alec, saw how his eyes watched the baby.

'I got to choose a name this time. No more lives of the saints or books of the bible.'

'What did you call him? Alexander?' Grace asked with a smile to Alec. Ruth kissed her son's tiny face again.

'No. This is Fraser.'

Later, they were alone and out on the water. Alec switched off the engine. The boat swayed slightly on the chopping surface and the thermal rushed in under the scalloped canopy. Grace stepped up beside him at the wheel and unscrewed their flask, put out their enamel mugs. She poured the tea and they drank as the first of the raindrops fell making neat diver splashes on the surface of the water. Faster they fell, drumming on the canopy. Alec folded himself around her, inhaling the wet-pebble scent of her hair. She wrapped her arms over his arms, slotting her fingers between his.

Grace did not need her binoculars to see the trio of rooks as they shied upwards from the jetty at Water Head Pier to nestle in the treetops across Coniston Water.

Epilogue

NOW YOU SEE HIM
1975

Davey had no idea who the do-gooding bastard was. He wasn't shaken. Nah. He was pissed off. That was it. He could have had it all over and done with. If he got in the car now he could be home in a couple of hours.

He lit up a smoke and knew he should have stayed away. Debs was not one of his better ideas, he knew that. A long drag later, he decided. Give them an hour's grace and he'd go there, see her. He had to clear the decks here, otherwise he couldn't go back to Loll. He needed better plans than the ones he'd been making lately. Loll looked like a future. He thought about her.

Thought he would buy the kid a pressie. Those white mice, from the cash and carry.